back rubs

....

back rubs

transitional tales by women

edited by
Alison Campbell, Caroline Hallett,
Jenny Palmer and Joanna Rosenthall

Library of Congress Catalog Card Number: 96–67911

A catalogue record for this book is available from the
British Library on request

These stories are works of fiction. Any resemblance to
persons living or dead is purely coincidental

The right of the individual contributors to be acknowledged
as authors of their work has been asserted by them in accordance
with the Copyright, Designs and Patents Act 1988

Copyright © 1996 of the individual contributions
remains with the authors
Compilation copyright © 1996 by the Editors

First published in 1996 by
Serpent's Tail, 4 Blackstock Mews, London N4,
and 180 Varrick Street, 10th floor, New York, NY 10014

Phototypeset in 10pt Plantin by Intype London Ltd.
Printed in Great Britain by Cox & Wyman Ltd., Reading, Berks.

contents

....

Foreword   vii

Breaking Sugar   *A.L. Kennedy*   1

The Ocean of Brisbane   *Janette Turner Hospital*   16

Halloran's Child   *Susan Hill*   36

Climacteric   *Idious Buguise*   55

Inuuk   *Margaret Elphinstone*   62

Mysteries of the Ancients   *Erica Wagner*   69

My Beautiful Wife   *Kathy Page*   98

A Man Needs Many Wives   *Buchi Emecheta*   108

On the Wall   *Melissa Murray*   126

Leaving Home   *Sylvia Brownrigg*   143

Mrs Benton's Dildo   *Carla Toney*   156

Taking Flight   *Joanna Rosenthall*   162

Making Hay   *Deborah Moggach*   177

The Real Thing   *Glyn Brown*   189

Back Rubs   *Joanna Torrey*   204

About the Authors   214

foreword

This book is concerned with change, longed for and feared, coming as it does with an increased awareness of an unknown future. The stories in *Back Rubs* are about celebrating change, marking change and separating out a "still point" where we can savour and mourn what has just passed and is lost and celebrate what is about to become.

In choosing this theme we were interested in how important rites of passage are experienced and received by others and how they have been incorporated into public life. The anthropological view defines the rite of passage as a public ceremony which marks a significant individual change which has a social and cultural meaning. In our search for material we found surprisingly few stories which described the more obvious transitions such as birth, naming ceremonies, marriage and death. What came in plenty were stories about internal transformations and changes of identity, reflecting, we imagine, a late-twentieth century Western pre-occupation with change, which tends to be more inward-looking and individualistic. Many of the stories are about emancipation of the self.

These stories are written by women, but are not exclusively about women. The common thread is a feeling of heightened experience, and of being on the threshold of something unknown.

a.l. kennedy

breaking sugar

"This bread tastes sweet."

"Mn?"

"This bread, it tastes sweet."

"No, I don't think so. Do you think so?"

"Of course I think so. I wouldn't mention it if I didn't."

Nick bit again, chewed warily. She watched him, also wary, but differently so.

"Sweet?"

"Sweet."

"Probably brushed against something at the bakers – you know."

"It was the same last time."

"No, it was brown last time."

"But it was still sweet."

"Really? No, not sweet, surely."

"Yes. The bottom edge. Definitely. Sweet."

"I'll look into it."

"Look into it?"

"With the baker."

She couldn't tell him. He wouldn't understand.

He would fail to see her point. Nick was a clever man and she couldn't doubt that he was good, but they did have to keep their differences, here and there. She no longer saw any purpose in openly rehearsing these odd little shades of thinking and ideas because she would end up having to differ about them and differing was no fun.

What was more, differing simply involved you in saying out loud what you already knew you believed in and then possibly ended up feeling even more when your opposite party most likely did much the same but in a differing direction.

Being experienced with Nick's mind, she could see it was a nice one but also that it clearly wasn't hers – not even close.

Except, of course, on the point of Mr Haskard; there they had been perfectly agreed. He was the right man for them. They were both very lucky in Mr Haskard, very fortunate and blessed.

In the matter of Mr Haskard's skin which was pale and dry like a powdered bandage or perhaps more like an expensive tablecloth, they were fortunate. Nick's mother had a similar complexion which made her greatly sought after, quite apart from her many other charms. In comparison, for example, to her dusty chin, her glistening lips and the plush interior of her mouth – casually glimpsed – seemed hypnotically moist and intriguing. In comparison to her arid cheeks and forehead, her eyes were a pure liquefaction of lapping thought, brimming at every available hour of the night and day.

So Nick liked Mr Haskard.

In the matter of Mr Haskard's pipe, which was small and fragrant and illuminated solely in areas set aside for smoking use, they were blessed. She would watch the corner of his mouth peaceably loosing rounded spouts of smoke and remember all her catalogue of relatives who had not ever smoked. She had always wanted to be on amicable terms with a domesticated pipe – to reap the benefits of its occasional, contented vapour without unsightly bowl scraping or spit. Now Mr Haskard and his friendly briar contributed to her atmosphere most beneficially.

His moustache, she and Nick both agreed, was glorious. Thick and plump and succulent, waggish and probably ticklish in a soft, fine, animal way. It was strokable. Although they didn't dream of stroking it, naturally. They only watched and grew used to the modesty of his half-concealed smiles; the sudden, red laughter; the possibilities of hidden bite.

They loved to know that Mr Haskard lived above them, slightly like a quiet household god, slim and undemanding, up in the two connecting rooms they were happy he should rent. He patronized the launderette, rather than disturb their washing machine, left the kitchen truly cleaner than he'd found it and she had never once feared that in the bathroom he might let his urine drip astray.

And if she liked Mr Haskard better than Nick could, this was purely because she saw much more of him. Nick's life was increasingly full of lectures and night classes and intensive seminar weekends, while she stayed largely at home, not giving lectures or night classes or even considering seminars. The possibility had always existed, in a theoretical way, that they might both work. They might even have been capable of both holding posts at the same university, but their approaches had been too differing, as had their results. She had slowly found herself unable to relish her teaching or its success. Her life was now the house and its lodger and her research. When her private studies were complete, she intended to write a book. A good, exhaustive, independent book. Nick did not know of these private intentions because they would cause him to differ with her again.

Mr Haskard was in no way cowed by the intellectual atmosphere of his new home. She became oddly used to sitting with him by the window and sharing conversations during which he would offer up the proofs of his own learning.

"Your dress fastens at the back."

"Uh, yes it does. Nick bought it for me."

His left forefinger cradled his moustache and concentration winked behind his eyes. He swallowed, then held his own hands, soft and still.

"Now I might well advise against that."

"I beg your pardon."

"Against backward fastening. There are three reasons."

"Really."

"Yes. In the first place all popular means of restraint for lunatics tend to fasten and buckle at the back. This is a bad association. In the second place, most clothing designed specifically for the dead is opened, for post-mortem convenience of dressing, at the back. This is a bad association. In the third place, backward fastening disempowers the wearer. Like an invalid or a child, one may not always be able to dress oneself unaided. One becomes dependent."

"I can see you've given this some thought."

"Some thought, yes. But I intend no offence. The dress is extremely flattering, offering, as it does, little or no distraction between the motion of your form and any observing eye. I do hope it is also comfortable."

"Quite. Thank you."

He studied her kindly, as if she were a well-phrased headline or a foreign stamp.

Nick had conceded that all Mr Haskard's rent money should be hers, to spend as she wished. This was not as good as earning her own money in the course of pursuing a satisfactory career, but it wasn't entirely without its rewards. Mr Haskard always settled promptly in advance with a fold of notes he passed from his hand to hers as if he were returning a happy loan. She never felt like his landlord – or landlady – more like a rediscovered friend.

"Another calendar month, then. Thank you."

"Thank you, Mr Haskard. And, ah, Mr Haskard?"

"Yes."

"Do you like it here?"

"Of course."

"You could pay quarterly, if you wanted to. You have been so reliable."

"Oh, no. No, thank you."

"To pay every month has something temporary about it, even untrusting. And frankly, I'm surprised you don't consider a mortgage – your job ... I mean to say, are we going to lose you, Mr Haskard?"

"Well. I don't think so, not for a while. To explain myself, I am something of a freelance. Systems analysts of my calibre – if I might be permitted to say so – are in constant demand. Mobility is an asset. And I also disapprove of mortgages and the blights of private ownership."

"I see. Thank you for answering so comprehensively."

Curiously, the demands Mr Haskard mentioned meant that she saw a good deal of him during the day. Often, while she was sleeping beside Nick, Mr Haskard's cellular telephone would quietly call him away to pad invisibly down the stairs and out across the city, its tall, dark streets and narrow lights. Tight up under her dreams he would search and correct the programs that ran for ever and nowhere in their silicon labyrinths. He understood and tasted their atoms' electric shake, admonished the ignorance of their languages, loved and scolded like a father, noted each trace of disease.

Perhaps as she stirred her mid-morning tea, she would hear the open and shut of his door, the bath starting to fill, the toilet flush. Perhaps she was glad to be aware of his company and to wait for his stepping into the kitchen, his face still slightly softened and coloured with washing and sleep.

"Furniture should be taken outside as often as possible."

That morning Mr Haskard had unveiled an especially alarming lack of health within a banking company's patterns of thought and he was in fine spirits. There was almost a purr in his voice, a small wicked note that could make her wonder if he lifted out all the diseases he found or simply changed them, left them behind to switch and oscillate as signs of himself.

"You have extremely suitable chairs here, they should be in the sun."

A young summer was blazing, its sunlight pleasantly bitter against the skin and Mr Haskard pattered along the hallway at her side with a surprising lack of physical reserve.

Within minutes, at his suggestion, she caught herself lifting her kitchen chairs and table out onto the grass at the back of the house. She and Nick had bought the house for its garden – the kind of lazy, unruly expanse that made her imagine English country lunch parties and more money and security than one generation would ever be likely to amass. In fact, their garden wasn't so terribly big as all that, but had enough size to encourage imagination and to accommodate – she now discovered – a considerable range of furnishing.

Mr Haskard jogged over the grass, positioning wastepaper baskets, table lamps, a random selection of ornaments. Her belongings looked tired and silly in the sun, too formal and too dull.

"Now you understand." She discovered he had been reading her face, the disappointment. "All of these things, they are really no protection, not in the face of nature. In this country, our surroundings are, currently, gentle; we can imagine they are tamed and patient. But when we take our indoors out of doors we see how dead and insubstantial our achievements and defences are."

"Yes, Mr Haskard, I suppose we do." She sat down on one of her transplanted chairs and felt it sink into the grass.

"Would you like some pear?"

Mr Haskard had picked out a likely fruit from the bowl near his feet and was cutting it with a little pocket-knife.

"Thank you."

In her mouth, the soft wedge of pear was sweet with a tiny shiver of salt where his thumb must have rested against its skin.

The sun dipped late and slowly for them, burning along the chair backs and sparking out from the group of cream jugs Mr Haskard had set on the table. Before dark and before Nick returned, they knew without telling each other that everything should be back where it used to be – warmer and scented with grass and the open air, but back where it used to be.

She walked behind Mr Haskard as he picked up the breadbin from close by the hedge. Their shadows darted ahead of them, narrow and the colour of wet earth rather than of darkness.

"Look." Her voice stopped him, held him absolutely, until he could execute a turn to face back at her. Startled by his complete attention, she repeated herself, "Look."

"Oh, yes. Our shadows."

"But look at them."

He did so, quietly, neatly. "Tell me."

"Well." She wanted to be clear for him, to match his patterns of expression and then join him inside them. Generally, she had noticed his sentences felt as comfortable as her own within her mind. "Well, I see myself there, pulled along in time to something I can't know. I see how strange and flexible I can be. A little bit of sun can tip me out in the grass like paint." He had, she noted, tilted his head to listen. "This makes very clear how small I am and how tiny any risk I take could ever be."

He nodded, appreciating her point, and considered the parallel progression of the two shapes they cast on the lawn. "I see time." He began walking towards the house, stopped and without looking back said, "I always do see time. And I think, yes, that I would rather walk this way and see time laid down at my feet. This way I see what I mean. I have myself in perspective. I like that. Thank you."

★

Having given them courteous notice, Mr Haskard would leave them alone for a matter of days every two or three months. In their different ways, they felt his absence, but were surprised at how great an influence he could be even when he was gone.

At these times, she and Nick talked together a little more than they might have done and perhaps, in addition, they listened to what each one said for the other. Nick would come home sharp, rather than spinning out the time around night classes and ultimately returning sodden with the smell of cigarettes, gin and sweat. He had occasionally given her cause to doubt him. But not now.

"Come on."

"Not here."

"Why not. He's away, come on. We used to do it out of the bedroom all the time."

This was a lie, but an attractive one. She still shook her head, smiling, shivering out of his arms.

"Why not?"

She backed through the doorway and into the hall, keeping her focus on his eyes, imagining the tilt of his emotions, his likely response. "Not here, upstairs."

"Ach."

"No, right upstairs."

She watched Nick thinking, beginning to smile.

Mr Haskard's rooms were easily opened – she had the spare key. They crept through his dustless, orderly study, vaguely aware of the books he'd added, the small coloured pictures he'd hung on his walls. She forced on, pushed back the door to his bedroom, plain and peaceful.

For no reason she could imagine, she sat up on Mr Haskard's naked dressing table and waited for Nick to look at her.

The table was built at an oddly convenient height. Her

dress, Nick discovered, fastened and unfastened completely with a number of tiny buttons, at the front.

They easily accomplished the necessary act and allowed a degree of unusual passion to overcome them both. She welcomed Nick into her arms and self, closing her eyes and inhaling the brusque, warm scent of Mr Haskard which was, quite naturally, all that filled his rooms.

For some considerable time, she continued her intimate life in much this way. Whenever Mr Haskard left, she found she would take advantage of his living space, would cautiously enjoy his unwitting accommodation.

Nick always remembered to open a window and thoroughly dissipate tell-tale scents and she checked they removed any items they might have brought with them and then left to lie.

Whenever Mr Haskard was at home, she continued to enjoy the pleasure of his company and to think – now and then – of her uncovered skin against his doorframe, his wallpaper, his carpet, his dressing table, his wardrobe and his desk.

"Might I ask you something, Mr Haskard?"

"Yes."

"Where do you go to? When you go."

"I'm afraid I don't understand."

"When you leave us; your trips away. If you don't mind my asking. It's really no concern of mine, naturally."

"Ah. Where do I go – that's easy, I go to apologize."

"I'm sorry?"

"No. I am sorry. That's why I go. Will I show you? Yes. I think I will."

He motioned her further along the hallway, smiled and ascended the stairs at a trot. She followed. His door was unlocked, needed only a turn of his wrist and it was wide.

"Come in. I was a little fast for you there, I think."

"No, no."

"But you're out of breath."

"Then maybe you were faster than I thought."

"You should exercise."

"I've been taking more lately."

"Good, good. We all have to, don't we. Please, come in."

She moved inside with him, noting the unfamiliar signs of his occupancy.

"I don't mean to disturb you."

His lamp was set to shine at a soft angle and his cardigan draped easily over a chair. His desk was studiously cluttered with papers and a partly folded map. She felt a stranger here, breathing in the strong new atmosphere of fresh laundry and shaving lotion and warm, unfamiliar skin.

"You're working – I don't want to take up your time."

"You don't. Any more than I want you to. And no one can work all the time. Come here now."

His hand extended smoothly, heavily towards her and she stepped to meet it, to feel the calm pressure of his fingers, the tug in. When she was standing beside him, he released her again and spoke.

"This is where I go."

Because she was looking at his face, she did not at first understand him.

"Here. This is where I go."

He nodded to the pictures on his wall, made a neat smile.

Photographs. Regular, rectangular, commonplace photographs of uneven fields and hillsides, strangely insubstantial buildings. Each of his images had an emptiness about it, as if he had arrived too late to catch the heart of it.

"This is only a selection. I travel extensively."

"But there's nothing here."

"I suppose not – not any more. That's why I go. There, the tower you're looking at, is in York. Built to replace the wooden one, burnt around the city's Jews. Here – torture and execution of Welsh resistors to English rule. Next is the site of a mining disaster – the owners succeeded in drawing out blood from stones. I drove between those two in one day. And that's where some of the men were killed at the Bloody Assizes. People remember these things, the names and the places can be found out."

"Why?"

"This one is near the place where I was born – said to be the pool where witch-finder General Matthew Hopkins was thrown, bound hand and foot. He floated, so they burned him as a witch, like the hundreds he'd condemned. A lovely place. I do go back there, but not as often as I'd like. No time."

"Why are you doing this?"

"Because I know it happened. I can't be sure how I began to, but now I do know. And I disagree. As deeply as I can remember, I disagree. I drive where I have to and I speak to what people I can and listen to them and then tell them what I know. We all do know. Something. I take my photographs. I pray."

"Do you do any good?"

"Yes. I make myself content. I hope I may go on to Africa, India, North and South America. There are so many places and so many times, naturally increasing, and no one has ever regretted them formally. I can see I may well be busy until I die. I cannot live in an evil present with any comfort, feeling the harm rack up around me. Perhaps I shall never leave this island. There is so much here to take into account. And perhaps we should go downstairs now. It's such a lovely day, I would hate to miss all of the sun."

She watched him take a chair out into the garden and sit, gently rolling his shirtsleeves up on his arms, and she thought how strange it was that all the harm and death he must have in his head didn't show. He was only ever peaceful.

The next time she embraced Nick up in Mr Haskard's rooms, she found her eyes ticking aside to the photographs lined near the bed. She considered for a moment the drive he was making that morning, away from her house – the city square, where authority once fired on peaceful demonstrators – Glencoe's taste and shadow of political massacre – two forts of armed occupation – then Inverness and Culloden and more of the ache and the darkness of old blood. Mr Haskard had outlined his route. He had also talked of the beauty he hoped to encounter in the available countryside.

"What's wrong?"

Nick could be remarkably alert, even as he held her, even as he seemed to lose himself in the thought and the reality of her moving reflection in another man's looking glass.

"Oh, I was thinking of Mr Haskard, how long he would be away."

"Really."

Although her answer had been almost true it seemed to displease Nick. He seemed to have misinterpreted her sense, to have given her a different meaning.

"We don't have to bother with him now."

"No. Of course."

"This is our house."

"His room."

"Oh yes, and his bed."

"No. Nick."

"We gave him a double bed – the poor old bugger doesn't need it. Why not?"

"It's . . . It would cause problems."

"We can deal with them."

She washed and dried Mr Haskard's sheets, remade his bed, replaced his folded pyjamas under the pillow where they would be safe. He must have another set for when he travelled. Unless he slept naked while he was away from them.

When she held her hands up to her face they smelt of cotton and of night and of her certainty that she would never say what she had done, even though Mr Haskard might be able to guess.

Nick left to teach his evening class and stayed out late – lost in a discussion too interesting to curtail.

She only realised she had not been waiting for Nick's return when he had settled himself coolly to her left and her restlessness remained.

Three hours later the front door snapped and sighed open. Mr Haskard was home. She lifted herself full awake and listened for the fast, light movement on the stairs below and then above her, the gentle setting down of a travelling bag. Mr Haskard creaked softly across her ceiling, became silence and almost allowed her to sleep before his descent began again. She could only think he had noticed their intrusion and abandoned his rooms.

The kitchen door was closed when she reached it, a big, numb dark swung out to meet her as she moved inside. She must, after all, have miscalculated, misheard. Mr Haskard must really be sleeping upstairs as usual – only her guilt could have made her think otherwise.

"Do close the door."

She span left and felt her hand bark suddenly against wood.

"I am sorry. I imagined you knew I was here."

"Mr Haskard?"

"Certainly not an intruder. You didn't think I was?"

"No."

"Good." He didn't whisper, his words made one low, even tone. In the absolute blackness, his sound was almost solid. "If you step forward and very slightly right, you'll come to a chair. When you sit I will be beside you. Mind the table."

"It's so dark."

"Yes, I've drawn the blinds and the curtains. It has to be dark."

"For your photographs."

"Oh, no. I haven't the slightest idea how they're made. This is something else. Watch."

She listened as Mr Haskard's hands made a gentle disturbance near her. Then she heard a soft, sudden impact, saw a splash of violet light. Another stroke fell, more light.

"What are you doing?"

"Breaking sugar."

"No, what are you doing?"

"Breaking sugar, I said. Here – that's it, that's the hammer. Now – " Something slid towards her. "This is your bread board, feel it?"

"Oh."

"Yes, that's the sugar and there's a cube I haven't crushed."

"But – "

"Ssh. Check where it is and then move your hand. Hit it."

She released a line of purple sparks where the hammer struck some scattered fragments.

"No, remember where it is. Now."

The tiny explosion flared for a moment and then stained the dark against her eye.

"I've always loved to do this, since I was a boy. I would look at people stirring their tea and think I knew a secret – that sugar was more than sweet."

"It's not the sugar, it's the crystal. The structure, you know. If you crush a crystal, you get light."

"Really? That's even better. A law – under the most extreme pressures, there will be unexpected light. And no one can ignore the laws of nature. Yes, that's very good."

"Mr Haskard, I think you should know – "

"I know." She felt his fingers find her hand. "I do know

and I quite understand. I happen to have some more sugar here; would you like to go on?"

She and Mr Haskard could not break their sugar without making sugar dust to coat the floor, the table top, their clothing, their hands. This was only a small inconvenience, water soluble and easily removed. A morning after sugar need never differ from a morning after undiluted sleep. They were both well able to scrub their bread board, to wash any possible imprint of sweetness away. She could only suppose they did not wish to, that she and Mr Haskard liked sweet bread.

janette turner hospital

the ocean of brisbane

His voice came out of the black space between the two projectors. When a slide slipped off the wall, dropping into nowhere, the tiered funnel of the lecture theatre was so dark that the darkness seemed to rub itself against her, furry, like the legs of spiders. She shivered. Then a bubble of light would come, a coloured diagram or a photograph would appear on the screen straight ahead but below her, and words would unfold themselves on the other screen, the one that was angled across a corner of the room, high up, and therefore eye-level with the tier where she sat. She would see him then for a moment, shadowy, a juggler of ideas, images, impenetrable words, remote control buttons, a magician waving his arms in the twilight cast by the screens.

I watched her watching him.

She was trying to explain him to herself.

I watched how she held onto her own body, arms hugged tightly, and how she kept shivering (it *looked* like shivering) in the sweltering airless room.

Don't worry, I wanted to whisper to her. I wanted to put my hand on her arm, soothing, but it would have alarmed her. Don't worry, I wanted to whisper. He's just as much a mystery to himself.

He spoke, and his words settled lightly onto the cantilevered screen in black block capitals, crowding, jostling like branches full of crows, she had always been frightened of crows, the way they swooped at you, dive-bombed, that time on the farm at Camp Mountain, long before Brisbane, she was still a child at Camp Mountain, the beaks slashing at her head (or maybe magpies, was it? had they been magpies?), they go for the eyes, *Always wear a hat*, teachers warned, *and if attacked, cover the eyes.*

ELECTRON MICROSCOPY, the screen said.

OF CRYSTALS.

And then in a fluttering rush: OF AN ALPHA-HELICAL COILED-COIL PROTEIN EXTRACTED FROM THE OOTHECA OF THE PRAYING MANTIS.

The black letters swooped at her and instinctively she covered her eyes. I watched the way her hands shook slightly (how would she speak to him? how had they *ever* really? and yet after all these years she had been hoping ... but what language could they possibly use?) and all the time, through her fingers, she was watching for crevices of hope, for something to grab onto, and *there* was something, *crystals*, yes, she recognized that, he used to have a set, those heavy headphones, telling them he could hear Indonesia, England, the cricket scores, winding the world into his room, swallowing it, he had this terrible hunger, this unnatural ... this kind of greed, she could never predict what ... and it was never big enough for him even then, his room, their house, their lives, Brisbane, the country, the world, he was like one of those alien children on the late late movies, growing into strangeness, his mind butting against the ceiling, webbed toes, a third eye, foreign to her from the beginning. She pressed a hand against her stomach and stared at it. Where had he come from?

"Coiled-coil," he was saying, from the dark space between the projectors. On the lower screen were intricate diagrams that looked like tangled chain-necklaces, or twisted ropes of sausages perhaps. "Solving the structures," he said. "Electron diffraction . . . especially certain membrane-embedded protein strings resistant to X-ray imaging." A ghostly pointer picked out the braided strings, and she turned to look at me suddenly, so specifically, that I heard her thought, heard the click of association, or saw it, and felt for my plaits against my shoulders. It was like groping for an amputated limb, the coiled coils of childhood.

It seems only yesterday . . ., her look said.

The coiled coils of language, I thought, and knotted myself into the puzzle. I saw diagrams of shared and divergent lives braiding and unbraiding themselves. Alpha-helical, alphabetical, we both rode in an Alfa Romeo once, it belonged to someone his older brother knew, I think, someone from Sydney, the wind whipping through the coiled coils of our hair and we two thinking we were Christmas, swimming through Brisbane like fish. There was nothing to it in those days. We could walk on water. We thought we were the beginning and the end, the ant's pants, the ootheca of the praying mantis, no less.

O-ith-*ee*-ka.

   oh I *thee* thir,

      thaid the blind man

         though he couldn't thee at all.

What the hell did *ootheca* mean?

Bet you don't know, bet I do, don't, do, don't too, do so, don't, do. Those two, our mothers used to say, will argue till the cows come home. Fish out of water, other kids' mothers said, but we weren't, we were in our own element, we porpoised through books, we dived into argument, we rode our bikes into endless discussion and rainforest trails where we disappeared and swam in private time, no time, timeless rainforest rock-pool debate time. We cavorted in the ocean of Brisbane, our own little pond.

I computed the odds against solving the structure of memory which dissolves and devolves and solves nothing.

*

Afterwards, waiting for him under the jacarandas, we fanned ourselves with the lecture handouts. From time to time, she smoothed hers out against her skirt and studied it with intense concentration, as though memorization of the print might yield up a meaning. When she saw me looking, a kind of rash flared across her cheeks and she scrunched the handout into a fan again and whipped it back and forth. She said nervously, apologetically: "Me and his dad ..." Then she panicked about her grammar and bit her lip and began again. "His father and me ... *I*, I should say, I and his dad ... the Depression and the war and everything ... You know Philippa, I'm sure Brian's told you, we only got to Grade 6."

"Oh heck," I said, "Brian's stuff is Double Dutch to me too. To nearly everyone. To 99.9% of the people in the world, I would say."

"Is it?"

"Oh God, yes. Brian lives in the stratosphere. He's really – oh, please don't, Mrs Leckie."

"I thought ..." She was fumbling in her handbag, sniffling. "He's not very ... I thought it was just me. I don't want to embarrass him."

"You won't, you *won't*! How could you even think such a – " There were people jostling us, and we had to step back, step aside, adjust ourselves. We eased our way to the outside edge of the crowd, beyond the cloisters, away from the hot blanket of bodies. "He's proud as punch that you're here. Look, he's just coming out now, he's looking around for you, see?" I waved madly and Brian made a sign of acknowledgment with his hand and went on talking to some colleague.

"You can't blame him," she said meekly. "It's just, sometimes we wished ... his dad wished ..." She mopped at her face with the Kleenex she had fished from her bag.

"It's dreadfully sticky, isn't it?" I could feel runnels of sweat making a slow tickling descent across my ribcage.

"I wished for his dad's sake." She studied her much creased fan again, its print smudging from sweat and oil. *Electron microscopy of crystals of an alpha-helical* . . . "Me, actually, to tell you the truth, Philippa, I got to Grade 8 but I never let on. Not while his dad was alive." A little smile passed between us, woman to woman – *Well, that's what we do, isn't it?* – and then she said wistfully, "His dad used to talk to him about the crystal set, he understood all that, they used them in the war, I think."

Delicately, with the thumb and index finger of both hands – handbag slung at crook of left elbow, lecture handout pressed under upper right arm – she took hold of the front of her bodice, just below the shoulders on each side, and lifted the polyester away from her body, raising it gently, lowering, raising, a quick light motion, ventilating herself. "*Your* dad, Philippa. That was a nasty bit of a turn. Is he all right?"

"Yes," I said, startled. "He's fine." I fanned myself vigorously, guiltily, because I had forgotten, completely forgotten, *like a fist squeezing his heart, he says,* an item in letters, *just a warning, the doctor says, Doctor Williams it was, you remember him, he says at our age you've got to expect* . . . "How did you – ?"

"Your mum, I think it was, told me . . . yes, I saw her on the bus one day. Going into the city. We had a chat about you and Brian."

"Oh dear!"

"She had pictures of all the grandchildren in her purse, I couldn't get over it, little Philippa Townsend with those big teenagers. And all that snow, I just can't imagine. It's funny, isn't it, how we . . . ? To me, you're still that little girl swinging on the front gate talking to Brian after school. You don't look a day older, Philippa."

"Oh, don't I wish!" I was swamped by the smell of frangipani beside their front gate. It was so intense, I felt dizzy. Lightly, indifferently, I asked, "The frangipani still beside your gate?"

"Fancy you remembering! His dad planted that. His dad was very good with his hands."

"Yes, I remember. Your roses especially – "

"He was a quiet man, Ed, a very shy man, but he was a *good* man, no one realizes how ... such a *good* ..." She began pleating her skirt in her fingers. "I suppose Brian told you about the nights, but it wasn't his fault, those awful nights, those terrible ..." She turned away. "I feel ..." she said, putting out a hand, casting about for some sort of support. "I don't feel too ..." Her hand drifted aimlessly through the wet air. "I think I have to sit down," she said.

"There's a bench, look." I led her towards it. "We don't have to go to the reception if you're not feeling well. I can drive you home."

"I don't know," she said uncertainly. She pulled at the damp frizz on her forehead, trying to cover a little more of the space above her eyebrows. The space seemed vast now. Her fingers explored it nervously, scuttling across what felt like an acreage of blotched skin. I shouldn't have had it permed so soon before, she thought wretchedly. This dress is wrong. I should have worn the green suit. I shouldn't have worn a hat. She said plaintively, "You were so clever, you and Brian. Such clever children." Her voice came from a long way back, from our high school years or even earlier, from the times of swinging on the gate. "*He'll go far*, teachers used to say," and her eyes stared into nothing, following the radiant but bewildering trajectory of Brian's life. She spoke as sleepwalkers speak: "*He'll go far*. They always told us that, I remember." She looked vaguely about. "I mustn't miss the tram, Philippa."

As though the action were somehow related to the catching of trams, she stretched her hands out in front of her and studied them, turning them over slowly, examining the palms, the backs, the palms again. Her hands must have offered up a message, because she gave a sudden sad little yelp of a laugh. "I'm being silly, aren't I? There's no trams anymore."

"Oh, I do that too," I said. "The trams still run in *my* Brisbane," I tapped my forehead with an index finger.

"You know who I ran into in the Commonwealth Bank one day? Last year it was, the big one, you know, in the city, on the corner of Adelaide Street? Mrs *Matthews*!"

"Mrs Matthews?"

"Richard's mum, you remember?"

"Oh, Richard," I said, dizzy with loss. It was so unsettling, this vertigo, hitting sudden pockets of freefall into the past.

"Richard went away too, she said. They never see him. It just seems like yesterday when Brian and Richard and you and the others ... and Julie ... and Elaine. It was terrible what happened to Elaine. I cried when I read it in the papers. It's not fair, it isn't fair." She picked up a leaf and began shredding it nervously and then dropped it. She ventilated herself again, holding the dress away from her skin, shaking it lightly. "Everyone's children went away."

"God, it's hot," I said. "The staff club will be air-conditioned though. For the reception. I wish they'd hurry it up."

"But you come back a lot, Philippa. I saw in the paper – "

"Oh yeah. Every year. Brisbane's got its hooks in me, I reckon. Look, he's coming at last, he's seen us. Oh damn."

We watched the student who had intercepted him: jeans and T-shirt, sandals.

"They all look scruffy," she said. It was an affront to her. Even the adults, the university people, the ones who would be at the reception, even they looked scruffy. Well, not scruffy exactly. But more or less as though they were dressed for an evening barbecue at the neighbours'. I shouldn't have worn the hat, she saw. I shouldn't have worn the corsage.

But how could she have known? She had thought it would be like going to a wedding.

And he could have been a bridegroom coming towards us, easing away, trailing worshipful students like membrane-embedded alpha-helical streamers. He had the kind of bridegroomly self-consciousness and forced gaiety that goes with weddings.

"Dorrie!" he said loudly, full of energetic joviality, hugging her.

He had always called her that, from before he even started primary school. At five years of age: Dorrie and Ed. Never Mother, Father; certainly not Mum and Dad. It was as though even then he knew something they didn't. And they had been too apprehensive, too apologetic, to protest. They had never even asked why.

"Philippa."

"Good on ya, mate." We hugged, old puzzle parts locking together. "You were bloody amazing. I'm speechless, I'm dazzled. What the hell's an ootheca?"

"What's a *what*?"

"An oo-ith-*ee*-ka." I pronounced all four syllables carefully, the way he had, the stress on the third, treating each sound like glass. "The ootheca of the praying mantis."

"Jesus, Philippa!" Brian laughed. "Typical. Absolutely peripheral to the lecture. Trust you to focus on a fucking *word*."

"What does it mean?"

"It's the ovum sac," he said.

"The *ovum* sac. Hmm. So the breakthrough was dependent on female biology."

"Oh, fuck off." He made a fist and shadow-boxed, stopping an eighth of an inch from my nose. "Listen, *Dorrie* . . ." – turning toward her. He had a message of great urgency and import.

"Brian," she rushed in eagerly, tripping over her nerves.

"I remember about the crystal set, you and your dad, how you used to hear foreign languages."

Brian frowned, at sea. He just stared at her, disoriented, and then looked around nervously. ("You actually *blushed*, for God's sake," I told him later. "As though anyone would give a damn, even if they'd heard.")

"Now, Dorrie," he said gently. "There's this ghastly reception that Philippa and I have to go to, it's a stupid boring thing, and there's no sense in the world making you put up with . . . So listen, I'm going to call a cab for you, all right? And we'll come on later for dinner, just like you wanted. All right?"

"All right," she said, parrot-like, meekly, looking somewhere else. *And then afterwards there's a reception*, she'd told the saleswoman, seeing white linen and cake and champagne, and *I think this little one*, the saleswoman had said, adjusting a wisp of feather at her brow, *this little number will be perfect. Just the thing for mother of the famous man. Just the thing for the scientist's mum.*

It's because I wore a hat, she thought.

"Look," Brian said, raising his arm, waving. "Here's a Black and White." He hugged her again. "Take care of yourself now, Dorrie. Go and put your feet up on the verandah for a while. We'll see you later."

He said something to the driver, gave him money and then waved. We kept on waving till the taxi disappeared.

"Don't look at me like that, Philippa."

"Like what?"

"Just cut it out, okay?"

"Don't try and dump your guilt onto *me*."

"She would have hated it. She's terrified of social stuff, always has been. They never went anywhere. I was being kind, if it's any of your business."

"Jesus, Brian. That was brutal. And so totally unnecessary. I would have kept her under my wing."

"She would have hated it," he insisted. "Anyway, I'm not even going myself. I'm off to the Regatta. Let's go."

"What? But it's in your *honour*!"

"I don't give a stuff and nor do they. No one'll even notice I'm not there. It's the free booze and free food they're after, that's all. C'mon, let's go. You got your car here?"

"You think it's because I'm ashamed of her," Brian said moodily on the verandah at the Regatta. "But you're wrong. It's not that."

I sipped my beer and stared across Coronation Drive at the river. Two small pleasure craft, motorboats with bright anodized hulls, were whizzing upstream, and a great ugly industrial barge from Darra Cement was gliding down, shuddering a bit, moving its hips in a slow, slatternly wallow. The sight of it filled me with happiness. *Good on you, you game old duck*, I thought fondly, and raised my glass to it. "Probably the same rusty tub we used to see when we were riding the buses out to uni," I said.

"Probably," Brian said lugubriously, slumped over his beer. "Everything's stuck in a bloody time warp, it's like a *swamp*" – he waved his arms about to take in the verandah, the Regatta, the river, the whole city – "it's like a swamp that sucks everything under, swallows it, stifles it, and gives back noxious . . ." His energy petered out and he slumped again. "There was this funny little man in the front row who used to sit in on lectures when I was in first year. Flat-earth freak, or something, he used to buttonhole people in the cloisters. We all used to duck when we saw him coming. Must be ninety now, if he's a day, and there he was in the very same seat. It gave me the shivers."

I squinted, and lined up the top of my glass with the white stripe on the broad backside of Darra Cement. "I saw in the paper that home-owners in Fig Tree Pocket and Jindalee and those newer suburbs are trying to get the dredging stopped. One of these days we'll come back and the river won't be brown anymore, it'll be crystal clear. I suppose that'll be a good thing, but it's funny how I get pissed off when anyone tampers with Brisbane behind my back. God, I love being back, don't you?"

"I hate it," Brian said. He'd thrown his jacket across a spare chair. Now he undid a couple of buttons on his shirt and rolled up his sleeves. "Look," he said with disgust, raising his arms one by one, inspecting the moons of stain at the armpits. "A bloody steam bath."

"That's what I love. This languid feeling of life underwater."

Between us and the river, the traffic rushed by in beetling lines but the noise was muffled, a droning damped-down buzz. Everything was fluid at the edges. Cars seemed to float slightly above the road and to move the way they do in old silent movies. Even the surface of Coronation Drive was unfixed, a band of shimmer. A drunk man was shambling along the tow path giving off mirages; I could see three of him. I could see the gigantic bamboo canes at the water's edge doubling, tripling, tippling themselves into the haze. I could see wavy curtains of air flapping lazily, easily, settling on us with sleep in their folds. "The only reason I don't come back to stay," I said drowsily, "is that if I did, I would never do another blessed thing for the rest of my life. I'd turn into a blissed-out vegetable."

"It makes me panic, being back," Brian said. "I feel as though I'm suffocating, *drowning*. I can't breathe. I can't get away fast enough. I get terrified I'll never get out again."

"Go back to Bleak City then," I said. "Stop whingeing. You sound like a prissy Melburnian."

"I am a Melburnian."

"Bullshit. You'll be buried here."

"Over my dead body. I can never quite believe I got out," he said. "I've forgotten the trick. How did I manage it?"

I shrugged, giving up on him, and let my eyes swim in

Coronation Drive with the cars. An amazing old dorsal-finned shark of a Thunderbird, early sixties vintage, hove into view and I followed it with wonder. "Who was that friend of your brother's? The one with the Alfa Romeo. Remember that time we came burning out here and the cops – "

"You've got a mind like the bottom of a birdcage, Philippa," Brian said irritably. "All over the shop."

"Polyphasic," I offered primly. "Highly valued by some people in your field. I read an essay on it by Stephen Jay Gould. Or maybe it was Lewis Thomas. Multi-track minds, all tracks playing simultaneously. Whatever happened to him, I wonder?"

"To Stephen Jay Gould or Lewis Thomas?"

"Neither, dummy. To that friend of your brother's. How's your brother, by the way?"

"He's fine."

"Still in Adelaide?"

"Mnn."

"Did *he* stay married?"

"Knock it off, Philippa."

"You stay in touch with her?"

"No."

"I'm sorry, Brian. I'm really sorry about all that. Are you, you know, *okay*?"

"Yeah, well." Brian shrugged. "It's easier this way. No high drama, no interruptions. I practically live at the lab."

"I read a glowing article about you in *Scientific American*. It was an old one, I picked it up in the waiting room at my dentist's."

Brian laughed. "There's achievement for you."

We lapsed into silence and drank another round of beer and stared at the river.

"Your mother said she ran into Richard's mum."

"Don't get started, Philippa," Brian warned.

"I miss them, I *miss* them. I miss our old gang. Don't you?"

"No."

"Liar."

"I never miss *anyone*," he said vehemently.

"Your mother said – "

"Okay, get it over with."

"Get what over with?"

"The lecture on how I treat Dorrie."

"I wasn't going to say a word," I protested. "But since you mention it, I don't understand why you feel embarrassed. You were actually *blushing*, for God's sake. As though anyone minds."

"You think I'm ashamed of her."

"Well?"

"It's not that. I'm not. I'm *protecting* her. I can't bear it when other kids smirk at her. At them. I can't *bear* it."

"Other *kids*?"

"There's a lot you don't know, Philippa."

"I don't know why you think they were any different from anyone else's parents."

He signalled for another jug, and we waited until it came, and then Brian filled both our glasses.

"They were," he said. "That's all."

"They weren't. I spent enough time at your place, for God's sake."

"God, I'm depressed," Brian said.

"I spent time at Richard's and Julie's and Elaine's. They weren't any different from anyone else's mum and dad." Brian said nothing. With his index finger, he played in a spill of beer. We were both, I knew, thinking of Elaine.

"Sorry," I said, "I shouldn't have ... That's something that happens when I come back. Every so often, you know, maybe once or twice a year, I still have nightmares about Elaine. But not when I'm back here. When I'm here, we all still seem to be around. In the air or something. I can feel us." I stared into my glass, down the long amber stretch of the past. "How long is it since you've been back, anyway?"

"Five years."

"That's your average? Once every five years?"

"It's not that I want to come that often," he said. "Necessity."

I laughed. Brian did not. "You're not usually this negative about Brisbane," I protested. "When was the last time I saw you? Two years ago, wasn't it? in Melbourne. No, wait. I forgot. London. June before last in London when you were there for that conference – Yes, and we got all nostalgic and tried to phone Julie, tried to track her down . . . that was hilarious, remember? We got onto that party line somewhere south of Mount Isa."

"It's different when I'm somewhere else," Brian said. "I get depressed as hell when I'm back."

"Boy, you can say that again."

"Last time ever, that's a promise to me," he said. "Except for Dorrie's funeral."

"*God*, Brian." I had to fortify myself with Cooper's comfort. "You're getting *me* depressed. Anyway, speaking of your mother, we'd better get going. What time's she expecting us?"

"Oh shit." Brian folded his arms tightly across his stomach and pleated himself over them.

"What's the matter?"

"I can't go."

"What?"

"I can't go, Philippa. I can't go. I just can't. Can you call her for me? Make up some excuse?"

I stared at him.

"Look," he said, "I *meant* to. I thought I could manage it. But I can't. Tell her I'm tied up. You'll do it better than I could."

"What the hell is the matter with you?"

"Look, tell her – " He seemed to cast about wildly for possible bribes. "Tell her we'll take her out for lunch tomorrow, before my afternoon flight. I'm staying at the Hilton, we'll take her there."

"I won't do it. I'm not going to do your dirty work for you. This is *crazy*, Brian. It's cruel. You'll break her heart."

Brian stood abruptly, knocking over his chair, and blundered inside to the pay phone near the bar. I watched him dial. "Listen, *Dorrie*," I heard him say, in his warm, charming, famous-public-person voice. "Look, something's come up, it's a terrible nuisance."

"You bloody fake!" I yelled. There were notes of rush and pressure in his voice, with an undertone of concern. It wasn't Brian at all. It was someone else speaking, someone I'd never even met, someone who couldn't hear a thing I was saying, someone who didn't even know I was there.

"They've got something arranged at uni," he said smoothly, unctuously. "I didn't know about it, and the thing is, I can't get out of it. I'll tell you what though. Philippa and I will take you out to lunch tomorrow. She'll pick you up at twelve o'clock, okay? and we'll all have lunch at the Hilton. Look, I've got to rush, I'm terribly sorry. Look after yourself, Dorrie. See you tomorrow, all right? Bye now."

"I'm going," I said as he lurched back. "I'm taking a cab right now to your mother's. I won't be part of this."

"Philippa, stay with me."

"I won't. It's just plain goddamn rude and boorish when she's got a meal prepared. At least *one* of us . . . I'm just bloody not going to – *What*? What is it? What the hell *is* it?"

He looked so stricken that there was nothing to be said.

"All right," I conceded, resigned. "Where do you want to go?"

"Come back to the Hilton with me. I don't want to be alone. I have to get blind stinking drunk."

In the cab I said: "How come I feel more wracked with guilt than you do?"

He laughed. "You actually think I'm not wracked with guilt?"

"Oh, I know why I am," I said. "It's because I'm a mother too." If my son did this to me, I thought, I'd bleed grief. My whole life would turn into a bruise.

"There's a lot you don't know," Brian said. "I can't talk about it unless I'm blind stinking drunk."

We didn't go to his room. It wasn't like that. We have never been lovers, never will be, never could be, and not because it isn't there, that volatile aura, the fizz and spit of sexual possibility. I vaguely remember that as we got drunker we held each other. I seem to remember us both sobbing at some stage of the night. It wasn't brother/sister either, not an incest taboo. No. We were once part of a multiform being, a many-celled organism that played in the childhood sea, that swam in the ocean of Brisbane, an alpha-helical membrane-embedded coiled-coil of an *us*-thing. We were not Other to each other or them, we were already Significantly *Us*, and we wept for our missing parts. We drank to our damaged, our lost, our dead.

When drink got us down to the ocean floor, I think Brian said: "It's the *house*. I really believe that if I went there again, I wouldn't be able to breathe. I'd never get out of it alive."

And I think I asked: "What did your mother mean about the nights? *Those awful nights*, she said."

And the second I said it, a memory I didn't remember I had shifted itself and began to rise like a great slow black-finned sea-slug, an extinct creature, far earlier than ichthyosaurus, earlier than the earliest ancestor of the Manta Ray. It flapped the gigantic black sails of its fins and shock waves hit the cage of my skull and I was swimming back to Brian's front gate, I was waiting for him there, fragrant currents of frangipani were swirling round, and these monstrously eerie sounds, this guttural screaming and sobbing, came pouring out through the verandah louvres in a black rush that whirlpooled around me, that sucked, that pulled ... I clung to the gate, giddy with terror.

Then Brian came out of the house with his schoolbag slung over his shoulder and he pushed the gate open and pushed his way through and walked so fast that I had to run to catch up. "What is it?" I asked, my heart yammering at the back of my teeth.

"What's *what*?" Brian demanded.

"That noise." I stopped, but Brian kept walking. "That noise!" I yelled, and Brian stopped and turned round and I pointed, because you could almost see those awful sounds curdling around us. Brian walked back and stood in front of me and looked me levelly in the eyes and cocked his head to one side. He gave the impression of listening attentively, of politely straining his ears, but of hearing nothing.

"What noise?" he asked.

He was so convincing that the sound sank beneath the floor of my memory for forty years, even though, two blocks later, he said dismissively, "It's nothing. It's Ed. He does it all the time. It's from the war."

And forty years later, swimming up through a reef of stubbies and empty Scotch bottles, he said: "He never left New Guinea really. He never got away. And it was *catching*. After a while, Dorrie used to have Ed's nightmares, I think."

"Oh Brian."

"Sometimes the neighbours would call the police. The only place they felt safe was the house. They never went *anywhere*."

"I never had any inkling."

"Because I protected them. I was magic. I designed a sort of ozone layer of insulation in my mind, you couldn't see through it, or hear, and I used to wrap them up in it, the house, and my dad, and my mum."

My dad and my mum. It would be something I could give her the next day, something to put with the corsage.

It was a long time after I rang the doorbell before anyone came. And when she came, she didn't open the door. She just stood there on the verandah peering out between the old wooden louvres. She looked like a rabbit stunned by headlights.

"It's me, Mrs Leckie. Philippa."

"Philippa?" she said vaguely, searching back through her memory for a clue. She opened the door and looked out uncertainly, like a sleepwalker. She was still in her housecoat and slippers. She squinted and studied me. "*Philippa!*" she said. "Good gracious. Are these for me? Oh, they're lovely. Lovely. Just a tick, and I'll put them in water. Come on in, Philippa, and make yourself at home."

It was eerie all right, one little step across a threshold, one giant freefall to the past. There was the old HMV radio, big as a small refrigerator, with its blistered wood front. There were two framed photographs on it, items from the nearer past, tiny deviations on the room as I knew it. One was of Brian's wedding, the other of his brother's. I picked up the frame of Brian's and studied it. I hadn't been at his wedding. We'd all got married in the cell-dividing years of the us-thing. I'd been overseas, though my mother had sent a newspaper clipping. I was trying to tell from the photograph if Brian had been happy. Was he thinking: *Now I've escaped?*

"I don't understand about marriages these days," she said, coming up behind me with the vase. She set the flowers on top of the radio. "I always thought Brian would marry you, Philippa."

"That would have been some scrap," I said. "We were always arguing, remember?"

"You would argue till the cows came home," she smiled. "I always thought you'd get married."

I set the frame down again, and she picked it up. "They didn't have any children," she said sadly. "Barry either. I don't have any grandchildren at all." She returned Brian and his bride to the top of the radio. "I wish they'd known him before the war, that's all. Before it happened. I just wish ... But if wishes could be roses, Ed used to say, or maybe it was the other way round. Would you like to see them, Philippa?"

I scrambled along the trail of her thought. "Oh," I said. "Yes, I would. I noticed them from the gate. And your frangipani's enormous, it's going to swallow up the house."

"Ed planted them," she said. "He was always good with his hands, he had a green thumb. I have to get the boy down the road to mow the lawn for me now. Watch out for that bit of mud, Philippa, there were some cats got in. These ones," she said, "Ed planted when the boys were born, one for each. This one was for Brian."

It was a tea rose, a rich ivory. Champagne-coloured, perhaps. Off white, I would probably say to him in some future joust. His mother hovered over it like a quick bird, darting, plucking off dead petals, curled leaves, a tiny beetle, a grasshopper, an ant.

"You've kept them up beautifully," I said.

"And I call this one Ed, I've planted a cutting on his grave."

There was something about the way she bent over it, something about her gaunt crooked arms and the frail air of entreaty, that made me think of a praying mantis. Maybe she heard my thought, or maybe the grasshopper she pinched between finger and thumb reminded her. "He said something about a praying mantis," she said. "You asked him about it, Philippa. What was that thing?"

"The ootheca."

"Funny word, isn't it?" She pulled her housecoat around

her and tightened the sash. "He won't be there for lunch, will he?"

I bit my lip. "He had to take an early flight," I said. It was and it wasn't a lie. We both knew it. "He had to be back in Melbourne."

She concentrated on the roses, bending her stick limbs over them, a slight geometric arrangement of supplication. "Anyway," she said, "I don't like going out. We never did, Ed and me." She straightened up and turned away from me, walking toward the gate. "I hope you won't mind, Philippa, if I don't . . ." At the gate, she reached up and picked a frangipani and gave it to me. "Could you tell him," she said, "that I've still got his crystal set? It's in his room. I thought he might, you know . . . I thought one day he might . . ."

I held the creamy flower against my cheek. It's excessive, I thought angrily, the smell of frangipani, the smell of Brisbane. I had to hold onto the gate. There was surf around my ears, I was caught in an undertow. When I could get my voice to come swimming back, I'd tell her about the safety layer that Brian kept around his mum and his dad.

susan hill

halloran's child

He was eating the rabbit he had shot himself on the previous day, separating the small bones carefully from the flesh before soaking lumps of bread in the dark salt gravy. When they were boys, he and his brother, Nelson Twomey, used to trap rabbits and other animals too, weasels and stoats – it was sport, they thought nothing of it, it was only what Farley the gamekeeper did.

Then, Nate had gone by himself into the wood and found a young fallow deer caught by the leg, and when he had eventually got it free the animal had stumbled away, its foot mangled and dropping a trail of fresh blood through the undergrowth. Nate had gone for his brother, brought him back there and shown him.

"Well, it'll die, that's what," Nelson had said, and shrugged his thin shoulders. It was the first glimpse Nate had had of his brother's true nature, his meanness.

"Die of gangrene. That's poison."

He had wept that night, one of the few occasions in his life, and got up at dawn and gone out to search for the wounded animal, remembering the trembling hind quarters and the sweat which had matted its pale coat, the eyes, where sticky rheum had begun to gather in the corners. He found only the blood, dried dark on the bracken. It led him towards where the bank of the stream fell away at his feet, and he could not follow further.

After that he abandoned the traps, though there was nothing he could do to stop his brother from setting them, even if he had been able to talk to him. He was very tall, with long, pale, hairless arms and legs, and beaky features, and he spoke little. He kept his violence well hidden. When he left school he went as apprentice to Layce, the rat-catcher, and took over the job himself three years afterwards when Layce died. Then, for forty-eight years, he had left the village at seven each morning, the rat bag over his shoulder, and the two small dogs at his heels. He always wore the same long, beige raincoat and cap, and when one of the ratting dogs died, it was replaced by another identical dog, so that to everyone in the village the two seemed to have lived forever. He had always given his dogs the same names – Griff and Nip.

Over the years, Nelson Twomey began to stoop at the shoulders until a few years before his death he was bent almost double. His face was sallow and expressionless.

Once, Nate had gone with him to watch the rat-catching in a grain barn over at Salt, and been half-excited, half-sickened at the sight of the dogs, inching forwards, bellies to the ground, snuffling, waiting for the command, and then darting forward like arrows, teeth bared, down onto the hidden rats. He could still remember the look on his brother's face as he stood half in the shadows, thin and pale and grave as a ghost, unmoving; he could still smell the musty smell of the grain. He sensed that Nelson enjoyed it, that his job satisfied some appalling need with him. But he was highly thought of, because of his skills, and well-paid too, for rats were a menace and greatly feared. Nate himself went in terror of them until he was a grown man. But he never ceased to be afraid, also, of his brother, so that it was almost a relief when he died and the cottage was empty of him.

But Nate Twomey continued to shoot rabbits, that he did not mind, for he had a keen eye and a sure hand, the animals never lingered, half-alive, and besides, they were pests, there had to be some way of putting them down. Nor did he mind wringing the necks of the hens his sister kept. It was only the traps that he regretted, the traps reminded him that he had been linked by blood to his brother.

The flesh of the rabbit fell away moistly from the bones. But in the middle of eating he had to raise his handkerchief to his left eye again and again, where the chip of wood had flown into it that morning, leaving it watery and sore. So that when Bertha spoke to him, he could not see her face and so missed what she was saying. He read her lips more easily than those of anyone else, she had only to mumble and he knew, for it was she who had first taught him, and shown him how to write, too. She had been more patient with his deafness and dumbness than either of their parents, who were uneasy, never knowing what he might be thinking, and frightened of being judged and blamed by the rest of the village. There had been one other child, also a boy, who had died, but he had been quite sound, they felt bitter that it was Nate who grew up in place of him.

Bertha Twomey waited. She always ate her own meal alone, after her brother had gone back to the workshop, and now, she stood beside the wooden kitchen table until he had finished wiping his eyes.

"You damaged yourself then, haven't you?"

He pointed to his eye.

"Splinters. You want to be more careful – putting your head too close to that bench, that's what. I told you before about that."

He shook his head but his eye was watering freely, he had to wipe it again, and then she insisted on looking at it more closely. It was bloodshot and swimming with tears. In the end, she got the splinter out with the twisted corner of a clean handkerchief. "You be more careful what you're doing in future, Nate Twomey." He grinned, nodding at her. They had always been like this together, she treating him like a child, while still knowing that he was not a fool, just because he was deaf and dumb. She was two years older but she had been the first one to push him out, not so long after she had learned to walk herself, they were very close.

Bertha Twomey always wore black – long, full skirts and loose cardigans and heavy black shoes on her wide, painful feet, and so she had looked like an old woman for years. There were lines in her face, they had come there when she was still a young girl, but she had been pretty and her face still had distinction, though she wore her hair scraped back and knotted behind her head, making herself severe.

When she was nineteen, she had been married to Hale, the farrier's son, from Salt, there had been a supper on trestle tables set out in Mid New Common one hot June night, and dancing until sunset, and then Nate had gone to live with them, for his sister had said she would never leave him. Hale had not objected. Nate had an attic room and helped out with the horses, before being apprenticed to Rob Riddy, who was undertaker for all the villages around. Bertha's husband had taught Nate how to shoot. And then, only a year later, he was dead, killed by lightning up on the Top Field, and the very next day, Nate and Bertha had moved back to their own family.

He looked up at her now, at the wide, serious face with the lined forehead, the strong bones. He had never known what she felt about her husband's death, never seen her weeping and she had told him nothing. She had taken a domestic post at the Lodge, and done most of the housework for her mother too, as though she could not bear to be idle for a moment. Otherwise, she kept herself to herself and looked after Nate. But she had changed, age had come to her overnight, and she had never gone out of black.

His eye was easier, it no longer watered. He took up a spoonful of gooseberries, thick with syrup.

Bertha said, "The doctor was sent for to Halloran's."

He stopped eating. So she had been waiting to tell him this then.

"I haven't heard more."

The fruit had turned sickly in his mouth, he could not swallow it. His sister sat down and watched him. She knew. Nate shook his head.

"You'd best finish it." But she saw that he could not and, after a moment or two, got up slowly and took the dish away.

Nate went to the back door and opened it, and the sun shone full into his face, comforting him, he smelled the fruit bushes and the scarlet bean flowers. At the bottom of the garden the hens were russet coloured, like squirrels, scratching about. He went down to them. When he opened the gate in the wire they took no notice of him at all, only went on pecking at the soil for the last of the meal Bertha had thrown. The sun was very hot here, the air still and dry. Nate's ears rang with silence.

Halloran's child. He tried to believe that it was nothing, that she would certainly be well and coming to talk to him in the workshop, soon enough, that he would see her sitting up on the bench watching his hands move to and fro, planing a piece of oak. But nobody sent for the doctor until it was unavoidable and besides, she had been out of hospital for less than a month.

He stared down at the hens.

In the kitchen, Bertha Twomey cleared the dinner table and

took the blue and white checked cloth to shake outside the back door, at the same time looking down the garden at her brother, and then she felt all the old anxiety for him lying heavy as a stone in her chest, though he was sixty-eight years old and she was nearly seventy.

There had always been Twomeys here, but neither Nate nor Nelson the rat-catcher had married, and so they would be the last. She had not wanted to tell him about the Halloran child but he would take it better from her than from some stranger coming into the workshop, and in any case, there was no hope, it was certain that the child would die, though no one knew when.

The thing she was most afraid of was that he would want to go to the Halloran house. He could not do so, because they were Twomeys, because of the way people thought of him and the work he did, because of all the old suspicion.

He was still standing motionless in the hen run, his head bent under the hot sun. She thought, say something to him, tell him . . . But she would not. He knew for himself. He was deaf and dumb but a grown man. The midday air stirred a little, moving the long lines of tinfoil tops, set across the vegetable patches to scare the birds away. Say something to him.

But she turned and went back inside.

It was common knowledge that a Twomey had been taken for a witch and some said burned, some said drowned to death. So there were superstitions about the family which died hard and when Bertha Twomey's husband was struck by lightning, what people felt was somehow confirmed and they kept their distance. Now, to the children in the village, Bertha looked like a witch, they stared at her from a safe distance, awed by the black clothes, and had nightmares, too, in which she set evil upon them. All of it she knew and was accustomed to it, it only served to make her draw further inside herself. She spoke to no one, not even to her brothers, about how she was feeling. And to them both she had been a rock, taking the place of mother and father and wife, they could not imagine her capable of any weakness.

From Nate Twomey, too, people kept their distance but that was because of the work he did, for he himself was amiable enough, and harmless, nobody blamed him because he could not hear or speak. Nevertheless, the odd noises which he made, the grunts and choking sounds in his throat, which were how he tried to imitate what he saw of laughter, frightened the children. All except Halloran's child.

The Hallorans had come down in the world. Their grandfather had owned land, kept a few dairy cows and called himself a farmer. But when his son inherited, there were more debts than profits, and the land had to be sold. Arthur Halloran had lost heart very quickly, watching his father struggle, and when he was seventeen he left the village altogether and went for a sailor. He returned with a damaged leg, married Amy Criddick and now he was only a casual labourer, working on hedging or hay-making or picking potatoes and paid by the hour. He was a bad-tempered, disappointed man, suffered in the village rather than liked. They had one child, the daughter, Jenny. She had never been strong, never been truly well since the day she was born, and when she was a year old and began to walk her limbs seemed incapable of holding her up, she was unsteady and sickly. At the age of four she had rheumatic fever and almost died, and Halloran had said in public hearing that he wished for it, wished to have it over with, for who wanted an invalid for a child and how could he bear the anxiety? She had been forbidden to run or even walk far, though she went to school when she was five and there was treated like a fragile doll by the others, who had been put in awe of her. She played with no one, though sometimes, as she sat in the classroom or, in fine weather, on a little stool in a corner of the playground, one of them would take pity on her and bring pick-sticks or a jigsaw and do it with her for a little while. But she seemed to be separated from them, almost to be less than human, because of the transparency of her skin and her thin, delicate bones, because of the fine blueness tingeing her lips and the flesh below her nervous eyes. She was neither clever nor stupid, she said very little. In the end, they were bored by her.

Then, she began to visit Nate Twomey in the carpenter's shop at the back of Coker's Lane. He could say nothing to her, which seemed to put her at her ease, for she would talk to him more than to anyone else in her life, fascinated by the way he looked straight at her and watched the movements of her lips. She learned what the grunts meant which he uttered occasionally, whether they expressed his approval or not, though most often he would simply nod or shake his head and smile at her, before he went on with his sawing or planing or the hammering in of nails. If there was ever any question that needed a fuller reply, he stopped and wrote it down carefully on a page of his measurement book, with the thick, flat carpenter's pencil.

In the holidays she came almost every day. He gave her a drink of tea from the flask his sister put up for him, and grew used to her presence, it pleased him, made him feel somehow at ease, settled. She sat on the workbench – he had to lift her up there, and she weighed nothing, she was made of air, he was shocked at the frailness of her body between his huge hands.

For much of the time they were both of them silent. She liked the smell of the workshop and the rasping sound of the plane driving evenly over a plank of wood. Only the high-pitched scream of the electric saw terrified her, she would stuff her fingers into her ears and her head rang, though Nate only looked at her and grinned, bending his own head right down over the blade, hearing nothing. He could only try to imagine how the noise pained her by feeling the saw's vibration jar through his body.

Nate was the coffin-maker. Usually, at least once a week, there was a death in one of the villages, and he went there on his bicycle, removing his cap respectfully when he reached the front door, before going inside to measure up and receive the family requirements, written out for him on a slip of paper. The sight of death had never alarmed him, he had been used to it for so long and it quieted him, for he felt that if a man came only to this, this state of calmness and silence, there could be no harm, and nothing in the world could damage him.

And when he leaned over the bodies of the dead, when his hands touched them gently as he worked, he took into himself through them the certainty of resurrection, so that he returned to his workshop to make the coffin confidently, and with a sense of awe. He knew that he was a good craftsman and his work satisfied him when it was finished, it seemed altogether useful, altogether good.

But now, he could not conceive of death in relation to Jenny Halloran, he disbelieved in the possibility of it, though she was so frail. He had always loved her, they had accepted one another completely, and so he could not accept that she might die, or even worse, might suffer in her body. He was reminded again of the trapped deer.

A year ago, the child had been taken ill with some severe, unidentifiable pain and then, three times in the space of a couple of months, she had fallen over and broken bones which were now as brittle as the bones of birds and would not heal, only crumbled slowly apart within their encasing flesh. She was no longer able to walk or even to sit up in a chair unattended, for fear that she would fall out and, in the end, she was pushed about the village in a wheelchair by her mother – for Halloran himself was ashamed, he would have nothing to do with her. And they refused to let her visit the carpenter's workshop again.

Nate Twomey missed her. But if he thought about it while he was working alone, he knew that it was only what he should have expected, that it was surprising, indeed, that they had ever let her come here at all. For he was a Twomey and Twomeys were not trusted, though none of them had done harm to anyone. But a Twomey had been taken for a witch, and Bertha's husband had been struck down and Nate was born deaf and dumb. It was enough to make anyone wary, and glad that the Twomeys' cottage was a little way out of the village.

But Nate knew that what kept them most in dread of him was his job, for many people believed that if they came face to face with the coffin-maker, it meant death to follow and if you let him into your house, other than on his official business, you were surely tempting fate. Halloran was more suspicious than most men, he expected ill-luck because it was what his family had become accustomed to.

The child came out of hospital, looking even paler and thinner than before, and now people began to keep a little way from her, too, as she was pushed out on fine days in her chair, for she had the look of death about her. Once, Nate met her as he was walking home for dinner and he was shocked at the sight of her, at the small legs poking out like sticks and the neck bent like a stalk, the deadness within the child's eyes. Hers was the only suffering he could not accept. When he went home, he sat pulling at the edges of the tablecloth, rubbing his fingers together, or else standing at the back door, staring down into the garden. He seemed to Bertha to have lost heart for anything.

When she sent him to pick beans or strip the gooseberry and blackcurrant bushes of their fruit, he went heavily down the path and worked mechanically, without any enthusiasm, along the rows. In the old days he would not have to be told, the fruit would be there ready for her, glistening and ripe in great bowls on the kitchen table.

For the first time in his life, too, he began to resent his

own condition, to envy those who could hear and chat among themselves, to feel bitter. Why had he been born a Twomey? Why was the child ill and no longer permitted to visit him, what had he done to deserve any of it?

Now, on the day his sister told him the news about the doctor, he was reluctant to go back to his workshop, not wanting to be alone. But old Bart, the stockman from Faze Farm, was dead of a stroke, the funeral was on Wednesday and the coffin was not yet done. Nate envied Bart, who was a year his junior, for it seemed to him suddenly that death was an enviable condition, that Bart was well off and not many had any benefit in this world. He wanted to die himself. He felt exhausted.

While he worked on the coffin, the idea was growing within him, as his sister had feared it would, that he must go round to the Hallorans' cottage, must see the child, see her now, while she was alive and could still speak to him. He would watch her lips moving and be comforted and besides, he wanted reassurance that she was not in pain, that everything was being done for her. He worked on until his head was full to overflowing with pictures of her and he could not concentrate upon his job, was scarcely aware of the smooth wood beneath his fingers, the coldness of the nails. Bart was six and a half feet tall, it was a big coffin, taking shape upon the bench.

He kept the workshop door open so that a beam of sunlight fell onto the pale curled wood chips that strewed the floor, and warmed his back, too – it was a day he would normally have enjoyed, for the sun always soothed him. But in the end it was too much, in the end he had to go and see Jenny Halloran. At twenty minutes past three, he put his saw away, picked his cap off the hook and blew the dust off it, went out of the door.

The paving stones baked in the heat. There was no one else about as he walked slowly down through the village, a tall, shambling man, his head a little bent, and inside his head, the throbbing of silence.

He went up the front path, put his hand to the door-knocker and then drew it away again. No one saw him. The small front garden was overgrown, with stocks and petunias trying to struggle through thistles and bindweed. Halloran had lost heart.

Because he could not speak, he began to sweat with anxiety that they would not understand why he had come here, would not let him in. He looked up at the bedroom window of the cottage. There were net curtains. Nothing moved. A thin brown cat regarded him from the broken-down fence.

But he could not bear to go away, back to the workshop, without having seen her.

It was some minutes after his knocking ceased before Amy Halloran came to the door, opening it only an inch and peering out. When she saw Nate, her face twitched involuntarily and then closed up in fear, or dislike, he could not tell. She was not an old woman, she was not yet forty, but she looked old, her hair was streaked with grey and her rather square face had long, deep lines, from nose to mouth. Nate took off his cap and moved it nervously round and round in his hands.

"Nate Twomey."

He smiled. He was very hot and the air was dusty as he breathed it in, and thick with the scent of flowers.

"She's in her bed. She's ill. Doctor came."

He nodded and pointed into the house and then to himself. She hesitated still, her expression changing as she thought about it, he could see suspicion and tiredness and worry chasing one another like clouds across her face. More than ever before he felt the strain of his own disability.

People needed to speak, he needed to reassure her, for he was anxious that she should not be afraid of him.

But in the end she let him in, opening the door slowly and then leading him up the dark stairs. The carpet only reached as far as the bend, and then there were bare boards. The house smelled of old cooking and something else, some medicine or disinfectant. He knew that she was uncertain whether she had done right to let him in.

He was appalled at the sight of the child. She lay in an iron-framed bed, propped up on a single pillow, and she seemed to have shrunk, her flesh was thinner, scarcely covering her bones, and the skin was taut and shiny. Her eyes were very bright, and yet dead, too, there seemed to be no life in her at all. He looked down at her hand, resting on the sheet. It was like a small claw.

"Here's that friend of yours."

Nate stood uncertainly, cap still in his hand. He wanted to weep. Her lips moved and there was no blood in them, they were thin and dry and oddly transparent, like the skin of a chrysalis.

"I had the doctor come."

He nodded to encourage her, for while she could speak to him she was alive, there was hope for her. Amy Halloran stood by the door, not moving, only staring vacantly at her child. She seemed too tired, now, even to worry.

"I'm going to the sea. One day. I'm going on a holiday."

But it seemed to Nate that she did not believe what she told him, that she knew the truth. She turned her head slightly to look out of the window and for a long time she said nothing else, so that he began to be afraid that she was dead. His hands felt weak and sweaty. The room was very hot.

"Will you make me something? Will you make me a toy?"

For he had occasionally taken bits of surplus wood and carved out a rough doll's cradle or a model bird for her, though they were clumsy, he was not good at such delicate work. But she had always been pleased with them. Now he nodded and tried to shape his hands like a boat, looking at her intently, willing her to understand. She frowned. Then, abruptly, began to cough and her face went into a spasm of pain, the bones seemed to tighten, and her mother went to her and lifted her up, touched her hands again and again to the child's cheeks and forehead. He saw that her eyelids looked dusty and faintly mauve, beneath the skin.

"You've seen enough, Nate Twomey. Haven't you stayed here long enough?"

Nate turned at once and went out of the room, his face burning. But as he reached the foot of the stairs, the front door opened and Halloran stood there, with the bright sunlit garden behind him like the background of a picture.

Nate thought that the man was going to hit him. His face went dark and mottled with blood and he clenched his fist. But then, he knew what Halloran was thinking – that the child was dead, for why else would the coffin-maker be here, standing at the bottom of the stairs that led to her bedroom. He put out his hand, thinking to touch Halloran's shoulder, he pointed back up the staircase and smiled, shaking his head, he would have said, "I saw her, she was speaking to me. I saw her, she is not dead, she is not dead."

Halloran started forward. Stopped. Looked up, to see his wife there. The three of them stood, unable to move or speak, helpless. The air shimmered with heat in rings like haloes, over the flowerbeds.

Then, Halloran began to shout, though Nate could only see the anger, see his mouth opening and closing, the corners twisted, so that he could scarcely read what the man was saying.

"Get him out of this house. What did you want to let him in for, what right has he got to come here, what have I told you about him? He's not to see her. He can't be trusted. What are you doing letting a Twomey into this house?"

He swung round. Nate was half-way down the front path. The hollyhocks were full of bees, he watched their circling, though he could not imagine their noise. His heart thudded violently, though not because of Halloran's anger. He felt ashamed of himself, ashamed that he should be able to walk out, healthy and strong, while the child lay dying.

The door of the cottage slammed shut.

He could not go back to work, he was trembling and his head swam with the shock of seeing the child, he began to walk aimlessly out of the village in the direction of Salt, between the thick hawthorn hedges, which trailed convolvulus down onto the grass. The cows were all lying down, flies jazzing about their heavy heads under the trees. His own throat was sore and there was a pain in his chest which seemed to choke him. He knew that he had seen the child for the last time.

That evening he could not eat, he only drank two mugs of sweet tea and left the meat and potatoes and pie his sister had put out for him. What he had begun to feel was some sort of rage boiling up within him, he wanted to get up and beat his fists on something, to lash out in protest at his own dumbness, his own misery.

He rolled up his shirt sleeves and went off to the bottom of the garden and into the hen run, captured one of the birds and held it down in a flurry of feathers and clawing feet. From the kitchen doorway Bertha Twomey watched silently, as he wrung the animal's neck. She knew what had happened and could do nothing for him, she only recognised in him the violence that had also been in his brother. Nate was not the same, he was a gentle man, patient, and so he killed the bird swiftly and without pain. But there had been a rage in him, a viciousness she had never seen before. When he came back into the house carrying the dead bird by its feet, she drew back and told him to put it away in the scullery, she would pluck it the next day when the feathers and flesh were no longer warm.

"You'd best eat something."

He shook his head and his eyes were clouded with unhappiness. He went out again, carrying his gun, and shot crows and jays and pigeons in Faze's fields and over towards the woods, until dark, his aim was as sure as ever, though he had to grip his hands tightly around the gun barrel to quieten their trembling. He was sick with shame at himself, but he went on until he was exhausted, knowing that he had to work out his anger and frustration. When the gun went off, he only saw the puff of smoke and felt his finger jerk sharply back from the trigger. A bird fell somewhere but there was no sound, no sound.

In the west, over High Crop Wood, the sky went dark as damsons, spreading like a stain. The air smelled sweet.

When the gun was empty he went home, his arms and legs aching and his head numb. He was no longer angry. He felt nothing at all. In the kitchen, he tried to eat a slice of pie which his sister had left out for him under a cloth, but his throat contracted, he had to spit the mouthful out. His eyes were still dry and smarting and when he tried to soothe them by weeping, he could not do so, he only lay in his bed, staring up into the darkness remembering the child.

He woke, not abruptly but gradually out of sleep, and when he opened his eyes he saw that the room was filled with still, pale moonlight. Then he knew. He had been awakened by the death of the child. He lay filled with a sense of relief, as though he had recovered from a long fever.

If he put out his hand, he might touch her. If he could speak to her, she would reply. But he could only think inside his own head, and so she was there too. Above all, he was thankful that she had suffered no longer. That afternoon she had not seemed to be in pain, only weakened, tired.

Often in his life Nate had known about death. When his

brother Nelson Twomey died in the hospital at Garston, he had been selecting a piece of timber for a door panel in the Rectory, and he had known, his head had been filled with the awareness of his brother, whom he had both hated and loved, respected and feared, and when he had gone to the hospital the next day, they had told him the time of the death and it had been the same.

Now, he got up and went to the window. It was open and the scent of stocks drifted up into his face. The moon rode high over the wood. The night was quiet with the presence of this new death.

He had gone out to shoot and kill birds and to wring the neck of the hen and the reason he had done so was the violence boiling up inside him. It had not been necessary shooting. He was to blame. But he knew, sensing the presence of the child, that it was over, that he would do no such shooting again. He knew that some evil had been plucked out of him.

He slept.

They sent for him first thing the next morning and he was afraid to face them, and when he saw their figures standing at the door, he knew how much they hated and blamed him for the child's death. Halloran's face was flushed with anger and weeping, his eyes flickered like tongues over Nate Twomey, as he took off his cap.

"Get up there. Do what you have to. Get it over with."

For the second time he followed Amy Halloran up the stairs and at the top she turned to him, standing so close that her breath blew onto his face.

"He blamed me. He said I'd never to let you in and I did. He told me."

Nate stood still. He felt the bitterness and misery which were directed towards him and wanted to find some way of telling her that things were for the best, that it did not matter that the child had died. He could do nothing, say nothing.

He had expected to feel resentment and anger himself, on seeing the child's body, but it was nothing to him except a comfort. He had known more than this. There was nothing to her. The flesh was wasted and the brittle bones showed through, she measured very little. Her face was rather grave but it held no suffering, the brow was smooth and gleaming, like silk. He would not see her in the carpenter's shop again but that no longer mattered, because he had been with her at the time of her dying and he had all that he wanted or had a right to.

But he grieved for the parents, for Amy Halloran, who watched him, twisting her fingers together, standing at the foot of the bed, and for Halloran himself, who would not understand, would not accept. Should he himself not feel as they did? But he did not, for he knew the truth.

He finished his job and put the notebook and pencil away and looked down once more upon the child's body, before going heavily down the stairs.

Halloran was there, waiting for him in the path, his eyes looking swollen and bruised and his mouth working.

He said, "You came here. You brought it on us. Death. You came here and it killed her. You . . ."

Nate stood looking at him helplessly, unable even to shake his head. It was what he had expected. He was a Twomey, he was the coffin-maker. They could not love or trust him.

"You."

Amy Halloran was there, plucking at her husband's arm, trying to drag him off.

"It was you."

Then, suddenly, he lunged forward, his eyes wild with pain and rage, and swung his fist into Nate Twomey's face. The blow hit him like a stroke of lightning, he went down, his head spinning, the blood welling up behind his eyes. As he fell, it seemed to him that this was what he had waited for, because of his own anger of the previous day and the lives of the birds he had so ruthlessly and violently taken, so that it was almost a relief when he felt the impact of the ground and pain went like a blade through his body.

He lay for what seemed like hours and then, getting slowly to his feet again, wiping the blood off his face with the back of his hand, he realised that he was alone, that the Hallorans had gone inside the house, had left him. His skull felt as if it would break open. But he was calm. He knew that it was what had been due to him. Because he had loved the child and known of her dying, because he was a Twomey and maimed. He would not have expected anything else and Halloran was grieving, was beside himself with misery and despair. Halloran was not to blame.

The sun shone down on him and his shadow fell behind him, hard and dark against the brightness. He walked back to the carpenter's shop slowly, to begin work on the small coffin, bearing his own silence.

idious buguise

climacteric

I've been avoiding him for the past three months. Taking the tube at a different time. Waiting till nine-thirty when I know he's already left. Not buying the newspaper on the corner. Not taking the rubbish out. He might walk past. I can't bear the thought of running into him. I can't bear the thought of not running into him. Especially in the morning. That's the hardest time.

It worked. For three months I haven't thought of him. I went to the office. I made dinner. I slept with my husband – never pretending he was someone else. I coped. Well, sort of. And then yesterday I saw him again. Oh, God. I was coming out the door and he was standing on the pavement, talking to the postman. I walked toward them. It was difficult. I sucked my stomach muscles in. Stood up straight. Dropped my shoulders. Sucked my cheeks in. Held my chin up. Tried to make my double chin disappear. Tried to make myself not look fifty-five years old. It doesn't work. I feel so ugly. So ravaged by time. No one will notice me. No one wants me. My legs were wobbling and my face was trying to organize its friendly-muscles expression. Christ, I'm a walking timebomb. But I made it. The postman smiled and walked off. We were alone. I looked him in the eyes. I always do that. That's the hardest part. His eyes are really the only remarkable feature he has. The rest is just regular middle-aged, probably paunchy, middle-class man. Why does this happen?

He stares back. Very few men can do that. Most of them look away.

"Hi," I say, trying to look composed, feeling shattered. My mind is a pressure cooker.

"Where have you been?" he asks as he walks toward me, starting to come closer. Oh, God. Is he going to embrace me? Why? Does he really miss me when I'm not around? Is this all in my mind? He's looking at me. Not through me. But right at me. I pull back. I stiffen. He holds back. He senses my tension. He must. It's so obvious. He's nervous. No, it's not just my imagination. I'm not making this up. He must feel something. Why else would he notice I haven't been around? He must have missed me. That's clear. Is he scared of contact? Maybe just as scared as I am? Does he want contact? Just as much as I do? I can't talk. I know I have my vague, blank look on. I try not to slouch. I don't want my double chin to appear.

"Where have you been?" he asks again.

"Hiding out. Hiding and working. Working really hard. What's new with you?"

"Nothing. Same as ever."

Don't ask him where he's been. Pretend you haven't noticed the absence. Does he know I avoid him so that I can put some order in my life? Does he know I'm obsessed with him? I know I'm about to ramble. I know I'm about to start saying things that won't make sense. I better leave. That's it. That's all there is to it. Be casual. Be normal. Look him in the eye and say bye. Get out of here. Hurry.

"Bye. See you later." I go back inside, crawl into bed with my husband.

And now I have another conversation, another posture for my fantasies. I'll spend the next few weeks playing with these words, with his meaning behind these words, with his movements. I won't be able to concentrate on anything else.

I'll resent any intrusion into my thoughts. I'll be bitchy and mean to my husband, to the kids. My work will suffer. The people I work with will find me distracted and uncertain. No decisions will be made. Oh sure, decisions will be made but only insofar as they don't distract from my thoughts and his comings and goings. He'll be sitting on my head directing my every movement. I'll be out on the street all the time now. I'll be looking for him. I'll consider everything I say and do and hope he approves of my thoughts and actions. I can't stop thinking about him again. I sit in front of the telly. The news is on. I can't concentrate. Is he watching the nine o'clock or the ten o'clock news? I better watch both. I don't want to miss any of his experiences. Did he watch the program on ferrets? Did he read the article on Hemingway? Does he like Hemingway? Does he like the films better than the novels? Does he go to the movies? Did he see *Damage*? Did he think about me when he saw Jeremy Irons fucking his brains out? I couldn't stop thinking about him. My crotch was zooming off into clitoral fling land. Christ. I don't even know if he goes to the movies.

It's not as though my life is lacking in luster. It's even exciting most of the time. I have everything I want. Even more. Lots of travel. Great house. Great kids. Loving husband. I even have great sex. It's just that I want him. No. I don't. I want him to want me.

When I'm not working, I'm thinking about him. No. I'm thinking about him when I work. I think about him all the time. How I can meet him, what we will say, what our first kiss will be like, how we will get in bed, how we will get out of bed. I'm obsessed with what kind of sex he likes. Is he slow? Is he gentle? What does he smell like? Does he sweat? Is he selfish? Does he care about the woman he's with? Does he want to satisfy her? Oh, God. I don't mean her. I mean me. Does he want to satisfy me? Does he like to kiss? I mean, does he really enjoy it? Not just do it to get to another stage? What position does he favor? I don't care. I don't care. I just want him. I've got lots of scenarios in my mind. They often get tangled up so that the end product doesn't make much sense.

And then today we meet again on the street, this time near where we both work. Two days in a row. I can't stand it. Yeah. We even work near each other. I didn't do that on purpose. I had my job first. It's lunchtime.

I walk down Crumble Street. See him approaching. I pretend I don't see him. Either he's pretending he doesn't see me or he really doesn't see me. I've got to do something quickly or my chance will be lost. What can I say? Say something intelligent, slightly sarcastic. Sarcasm is the best. It will make me sound nonchalant yet knowing. I look up and say, "Hi. What are you doing here?" So much for brilliance. That was pretty trite.

"Joanna!" he exclaims. He seems pleased to see me. Is it just a pleased-nice-to-see-an-acquaintance face or is it a finally-we-meet-and-end-up-in-bed face? I don't know. I'm concentrating on staring into his eyes. I don't want anything to ruin this. Do I make the first move? Is that too forward? Can two people, male and female, meet on the street and have lunch? Is it allowed? Will he think ill of me? Does he want this as much as I do? Does he ever fantasize about me? Maybe he's shy and he can't make the first move. He's not shy. Don't be silly. I've got nothing to lose.

"What are you doing here?" he says. Do I read friend in his eyes? Is it maybe even lust? Is he nervous? God. I'm so nervous I can't think. Didn't I just ask him what he was doing here? Why is he asking me the same question and not answering mine? Is this a good sign? Is he just as nervous as I am? Or is he just being polite? Oh, God. Quick, answer him. Don't let him move. Don't let him get away.

Putting on a bored expression, I say, "Getting out of the office and getting something to eat. I'm famished." Maybe my expression was too bored. Now, do I ask him to eat with me? Oh, no, I can't put the words eat and me in the same sentence. I'd faint with pain and embarrassment. I can't say dine. That isn't me. I make fun of people who say dine. What do I say? I know. I know. I can say, "Do you want to have lunch?" No. What if he says no. I couldn't bear it. My hands are shaking. Can he see it? He isn't shaking. He's totally composed. He doesn't know what is going through my brain. I'm just fantasizing. He just thinks of me as an acquaintance. He has no idea. So there's no problem. I can ask him because he won't think it forward or rude. No, no, I'll wait for him to say something. Ask him. Control yourself and ask him. Get the words out. It's OK. He's only human. No, he isn't. That's the problem. I see him as superhuman. No, he isn't. There's nothing special about him. He eats, drinks, and sleeps like everyone else. I know. Imagine him snoring or worrying about prostate cancer. That will make it easier. He probably has hemorrhoids. That should help. Just visualize him sitting on the toilet and it will be easier. OK. Go.

"I like this street. There's this cheap Indian restaurant over there. I go there whenever I want to run away from work and relax," I reply. I know he likes Indian food. He told me that before. Oh, shit. I've told him I eat here before and he has never said, "Let's meet there. It's right by my office." So. He doesn't want to eat with me. Oh, God. There are those two words in the same sentence again. He doesn't want to spend time with me. He only thinks of me as a dumpy, slightly ditsy middle-aged crone. I don't know what to say now. He hasn't said anything. He hasn't put his hand on my shoulder and steered me toward the restaurant. He's going to go away. I know it. What can I say to make him stay longer? To make this accidental meeting something special? Something we will both remember. Don't say anything corny. Don't mess it up. Keep looking him in the eyes. It's getting harder. It's his eyes. I know. Pretend they aren't staring back. Pretend he has a stye. Oh, don't be stupid. He doesn't have a stye.

It isn't going to work. I'm sure he doesn't have hemorrhoids. And he probably doesn't snore. My legs are wobbling again. Not my legs, really. But my crotch. Oh, my God. I just felt his hand on my breast. I can't stand it. I've got to sit down. I've got to lie down. I've got to hold him. Those lips. Oh, no. I can't look at his lips. His lips are more sensual than his eyes. I never thought about that before. Now there're two things I have to focus on looking at and not looking at. Thinking about them, looking at them.

I lie down. He lies next to me. Suddenly we have no clothes on. We are drowning in a pool of feathers. His body is firm. Not flabby. Not the body of a middle-aged man. We are holding each other. Not tightly. Just gently. We are rocking. Touching each other. Softly. Everywhere. Our lips meet. They touch softly and then harder. We can't stop kissing. I can't open my eyes. I can't breathe. He rubs his leg against mine. I breathe in his smell. It is the smell of sex. Clean and newly born, fresh, scrubbed. I taste toothpaste. I feel muscles, strong and knowledgeable. I hear moans. I sit up. I climb on top of him. Put him inside me. Easily. He slips in easily. I sigh. I move up and down, over and over. I open my eyes. His are closed. Well, really half-closed. His tongue moves gently over his own teeth. I want that tongue in my mouth, not his. I want his taste in my mouth. I lean down and place my lips on his. Our mouths meet again. I don't want to let go. I want to feel this forever. I see apple orchards and sun and hear rushing streams from my youth. From the sex I used to know. From the past I want to relive. I am young and supple again. I have no ties. Total freedom. Lust and innocent pleasure. Moaning, he comes inside me. I can feel him spilling out of me. It is warm and clean. Again, there is the fresh, scrubbed scent of birth. I'm pleased and satisfied. But, I want more. I want to devour him. I want to be devoured. I don't want this to stop.

"Where's this restaurant?" I hear his words through a fog and a tunnel. Are they coming from him? I can't answer him. I don't know what he's talking about. What restaurant?

"Is it the one on the corner?" he asks, still looking into my eyes. His mouth is moving. I can't see his tongue. I don't feel his hand on my heart.

"Yeah. Yeah. The one over there on the other side of the street, next to the lighting shop. They have a lunch special. As much as you can eat for five pounds. Quite good." Well, is he coming or isn't he? Doesn't he understand this is my way of inviting him? Doesn't he realize we've just made love? Doesn't he know the colors and smells and sights are so much more vibrant now? Can't he feel the electric current running from my thoughts through his veins? How much longer can I live with this?

"We'll have to go there sometime," he says.

When, when? Now. Right now. Let's go now. We can make love under the table. On top of the table. Against the door. Anywhere. I don't care. I'll do anything. Just come inside me. I'll climb on top of you. You can slide in. No one will know. I don't care where. Let's just do it.

"Yeah. I need a good curry to get me through the day every once in a while," I say.

"Enjoy your meal," he says as he walks off in the other direction. I stand there alone. Does he know I'm not moving? He's not looking back. He's forgotten me. I no longer exist. I can't leave this spot. We made love here. He lay inside me. He came inside me. I was free. There was no pressure, no pain. How can he just walk off and leave me? Did he mean it when he said, "We must go there sometime"? Was he just being friendly? Did he mean just the two of us? Is he still thinking about me?

This story is part of an ongoing set of narratives.

margaret elphinstone

inuuk

Meanwhile, I'll talk to you. Inuuk will get me away from here, I know that. It can't end here.

It isn't what they think at all. He's not a devil. He came out of a much older world than God or Devil. They say not to speak of those times now, but it's different for my family.

We've always been at the edge, you see, looking the other way. Looking west. West is where the old world went when the priests first came. I've seen islands out there sometimes, Not so green as ours, not like earth, and there are no parishes out there. I never went against the church, you know that, I never had to do with evil things. We look west into the sea, and that doesn't change, and I can't change my dreams either.

So many bad harvests. I've done my best since my mother died. But it's all up to me now. My father is in pain all the time, and that takes all his attention. I'm not sure how much else he even understands. Years ago I stopped waiting for Tam to come home, and then the baby ... Sometimes it seemed too hard, but the minister said that was wrong. God gives us a cross to bear and we should rejoice to share his suffering. It was a hungry year, with so much snow. I never knew snow like that before.

The man – he is a man, I tell you – came ashore at Yule. I saw him in the voe, swimming low, his body hunched over his paddle that rested crosswise on the sealskin like unfledged wings. His head was huge, fur-covered; I was frightened. I stopped behind the black rock, watching warily. He beached on the sand. The tide was low, the marks left by the seals still not washed away. He stood up where the small waves curled over, and pulled the sealskin up behind.

Free of the waves he lost his strength at once. Poor soul, he was on his knees. His huge head fell back, and I saw a man's face. Seal hair, black and smooth, but not monstrous now. I crept down, treading carefully on whole stones that did not chink. I heard him breathe. Man breath, seal breath. At night on the beach the seals snort and snuffle and grunt like men, shuffling there in the dark. This one's breath was harsh and sore. His flippers came off, and he pressed a man's brown hands against his eyes.

Why do they say devil? Why not angel, tell me that? It was never luck to turn away the stranger. I put my hand on his shoulder. Fur. On the shore the seals mutter and sigh like men. At sea they sing. He muttered now, not human words. Then he reached up and touched me with his cold hand. The last hand I touched was cold with death, my baby's hand in mine. This hand was sea-cold, brown, and my hand over it was white.

I took him home. He was heavy, but not tall. I carried Tam, that last time, out to the waiting boat, so he'd be dry to go to sea. He'd never have gone, but it was a sour spring again, after a hungry winter. Gone to the whaling, and that was seven years ago. What did the sea ever give back?

I got the sealskins off him. Underneath he was just a man, I swear to that. Cold and brown. I wrapped him well and laid him in my own bed, and fed him milk and meal. You believe me, don't you? He was a man like Tam was, and I should know. Listen, you're one of my own people. That's why I'm trusting you. You think they'll let me out of here? You'll speak for me, at this trial? I'm telling you the whole story, because you're the first that said a kind word since they locked me in this place. The other man beat me: look. The night they both came, I thought they'd rape me, and so they would have done, but one said I had the devil in my belly, and it might bite. My other baby died: Tam's child. There's nothing left of Tam now, and on the island no harvest but frost and pain.

I meant to be wary of you, thinking it might be a trick, to make me suffer, and then to send someone to me with kind words, so I would speak. I would not speak before. If I can't trust you I think I shall go mad.

No harvest, I said, but this man made a harvest out of the worst of winter. When spring came he was afraid. He watched me dig the first furrow, and made signs against me, and would have stopped me. I took a handful of seed corn and showed him what we did. He watched, and in the end he laughed, and let me be. He would not touch the spade. But in winter he kept us when otherwise we would have died. He took his seal boat from the beach, east or west, depending on the wind, and brought back meat and fish. Oh yes, he killed seals, there was no question about that. He had a harpoon, but not metal; it had a hard white point like horn.

I thought we might starve before he came, and indeed I was starved, in my soul. The devil does not give the bread of life. It was a kind of hell before that, starvation and dying, and always cold. Three days he lay in the house, and I fed him what we had. The third night he came to where I lay, not with any question as to what he could get, but as if it were a matter of course, a thing already decided. Is that what you'd call sin? Tam was lost to the sea seven years ago. I remember the warmth of him. I've been cold ever since that day I carried him to the waiting boat. Although it was April I could see our breath like spun milk, two clouds meeting, and then blown away. I could smell snow away to the west.

A devil or a monster is cold as the sea it comes from. This man was warm like Tam. And now his child is warm in me. If it were not human I would feel it, cold as a fish. And I tell you it is not like that.

I am accused of sorcery, but I never knew of any such thing. How can I explain? When I come away from the island these days so few speak my language, and no one who matters. I only go to town once a year to sell my work. I listen to the jangled voices in the street, all Scots and Dutch. The old words are dying. But I am young still, and if I lived anywhere but on the island I would have learned the new ones. How could I learn? I speak to no one since Tam went. If father talks at all it is in the old tongue. And at this trial, you say, it will be different words again. Engelsk, Southron. Like the tower of Babel. I do not speak in tongues.

For a long time, Inuuk and I, we did not talk at all. Early on, I wished to know his name. I tried to make him understand. I pointed to myself – like this – and said, "Agnes. Agnes". He never tried to say what I had said. Then I pointed to him – like this – and made a question in my face. In the end he did speak. "Inuuk," he said. "Inuuk."

And that was all. No more words went between us. Only warmth, in the night, the touch of human skin for which I had been starved so long. It was not wrong for him, coming from out of the sea where the church could never make any lines between what you have done and what you ought not to have done. He was innocent as my baby that had no words, only my body which was everything to him, food and warmth and all the language in the world. Like Adam in Eden before God told him to give names to the animals. It would have been better if God had kept quiet, I think. There are more creatures in the sea than any man has a name for, and there is no sin there.

There were no words between us until after the spring came. When the snow thawed at last, he brought in the sealskin from his boat, and hung it in the byre to dry. He worked on it for many days. I could tell he was nervous, being helpless as a bird in moult. The boat had a frame – without its skin I could see it was just a boat. He tied it down by the hut where we had hung the seal meat to dry. No hungry spring this year. One day Tam's brother rowed across, and Inuuk ran and took his sealskin from the byre, and hid it inside our bed until the men were gone.

If I had taken it then ... It was my turn to be afraid when he lashed it on its frame again. He had his harpoon fixed, and put on all his sealskins, and one day, when the first green shoots were showing in the rigs, he went back down to the western shore where I had seen him first. I followed him until I reached the black rock. He turned then, and raised his hand in a way that said to come no further. I shook my head, and pulled my dress close round me, so he could see my round belly. It was just beginning to show. I had never said anything to him about it. We did not speak, you see. All those winter nights, we sat one each side of the fire, with my father on the bench at the end. I had wool to spin and stockings to knit. He used to carve driftwood with his knife. No, I can't show you what he carved. When Tam's brother warned me they were speaking of witchcraft I burned all the carvings, because I knew that other eyes would read them wrong. A man who goes looking for evil will find it in what he does not understand. I was sorry to give them to the fire, but he can make more, when we are safe again.

He looked at me, and I looked back. He had dark seal eyes, and I never knew if I could read his soul in them or if I were only looking at the reflection of myself. It was like looking in a pool and not knowing if it is deep or only the sky behind you. I used to look at him and wonder about that, and this time more than ever. But in the end he turned away and went down to the shore. I looked away, thinking that this I could not bear. I never heard him go. He was silent as a seal, and when I did hear the splash of oars, it was Tam's brother on his way home with a string of fish for us.

Then the blizzards came and the green shoots were burnt back to the roots and died. They say now I raised that wind. What sense is there in that? My father and I would be the first to starve if we have no spring. Our soil is salt and sour, although I brought up as much seaweed as I could and spread it after the harvest. I would not stay on the island without a man, only father will not leave. I have three shillings put by from the knitting I've sold. The first day I can, I'll shut the door for ever and come away. I have seen myself do that so many times: I lay salt across the threshold, and cold iron. I leave the Bible open on the table, and push the door to and wedge it with a stone. Then I go down to the boat and row away for the last time. A dying man is all that keeps me there, and that's God's truth. I starve out of compassion for him. Tam has gone and my baby died there. There's enough winter in this world without a weak soul like me trying to conjure more.

The cow died calving, but I pulled the calf out. It took all my strength. I fed it sheep's milk and that meant nothing for us but the seal meat he had left to dry. The sea was white right round the island, which meant no chance of a boat at all. I prayed all the time for Inuuk, out in that sea. I thought how he had been hunting all winter, which no ordinary man could do, and perhaps this weather suited him, in his element. But I guessed his journey would be cold and dangerous. I never knew a man so strong, and yet he was weak as a new baby that day he came out of the sea. Our land must have been very strange to him.

It was three weeks before he came back. I never saw him land. He opened the door and walked in, on a grey windswept day when we could do nothing but huddle over the fire. The door opened, and I gasped and made a sign against evil. No boat could have crossed the sound that day. I could see nothing through the reek. Then he crouched down by us, in his sealskins. His face was drawn, and his eyes looked hollow, as if the life were all drained out of them.

That night before we lay down, he took my arm, and began to speak. I listened, but could find no words in it. He grew urgent, and at last he said a word I knew. "Agnes." He pointed to me. "Agnes."

That might seem a foolish thing to make a woman cry, but I was tired. He waited until I could look at him again, and spoke more. I began to hear a pattern. It came again, and again. He was pointing to himself. I had thought Inuuk was his name, you see, but now I know he said that because he thought we were of another kind from him. He made me say it after him: "Kalasek, Kalasek."

For days after that it was all words. We were drunk on words. Fire. House. Boat. Fish. Earth. Sea. Seal. Bird. This. I. You. Here. Take. (Never ask why he wants to know. Never ask.)

Seed. Furrow. Paddle. Sea. Skin. Eyes. Hair. Today. Mine. Hold. Come.

They must have seen him from the cliffs of the main island. When the sea went down at last they rowed over. Kalasek ran to hide his boat. While he was gone they dragged me to the shore and brought me here. He would never have dreamed of them doing that. But he'll come. I do believe he'll come. And they can't find me guilty because I know that I am innocent. Do you think when they ask me questions this time it will be in my own language? Will you be there? Will you speak for me?

Maybe I should not have told you so much. But you spoke to me in Norn, and I found myself telling you everything. It's hard to belong to a place that is dying. Tam and I were first cousins, and our baby died. The place could bloom again, with new blood in it. Sometimes I feel this child move inside me already. If they let us live, I think it will be strong.

erica wagner

mysteries of the ancients

"I am thinking," my father says, his hands set like a little teepee under his chin, "that it would be nice to build one of those in America."

"One of what, Dad?" my brother asks. John is twelve. He doesn't have problems with questions like that. We are sitting in the living-room, the three boys, Mom used to say, watching the TV with the lights off. Now that my mother's gone, Dad doesn't bother to tell us it's bad for your eyes to do that. The TV is a big blue eye in the centre of the room, and we are shadows in the flickering corners.

"Like Stonehenge," and he nods towards the TV. We are watching a show that's on every week, *Mysteries of the Ancients*, and this week it's all about big stone things that no one seems to know much about.

"What?" my brother says. He rolls his eyes at me: I can see the whites turn in the light from the TV, like cat's eyes in the dark. My dad is not looking at either of us, but staring at the TV. He's turned the sound down so it's only pictures, pictures of stones.

"You couldn't use stones," he says, more to himself than to us. "Stones are kind of bulky and anyway, there aren't any around here." He stops, taps his fingers together, and then looks at me, smiling. "And stones aren't very American, are they?" Does he want me to answer? But then he goes on. "I'm sure," he says, "that there are other things you could use. All you'd have to do is give it a little careful thought."

He turns back to the TV, puts the sound up again. Now they're showing some place in Ireland, some big ugly tomb. The camera makes circles around it, and they play weird Irish music. My father points to the set.

"I've read about that one," he says. "There's a door to it, with a slit in it or something, and on just one day of the year, at just one time, the sun comes in and makes this bright light all inside the tomb."

John, who has been asking to watch some sitcom, shrugs. "So?"

My dad turns to him, really slowly, as if while he's moving he's thinking of important things, as if the way he's moving is making him think of important things.

"That's a good question, son." I can't remember him ever calling either of us *son*. It's like something out of a book. "That's a good question. I wonder that too. What's the big deal? But I'm looking at those pictures and I'm thinking that it is a big deal. It isn't about money. Anybody can have money. What it's about is energy." He says that last word slowly, en-er-gy, and stops just before he says it, like he didn't know what it was going to be until the second it actually came out of his mouth. "Energy. That's the important thing." He curls his hands into fists and presses the knuckles together. "That's what we need."

He's staring at the TV and I can see he's thinking hard. Since Mom left he thinks all the time. Mostly it doesn't bother me. My dad is a man who can do anything, in his way; not that he's ever done anything *important* in his life, not in the way anybody looking from the outside would see it. But when he says that word, energy, there is something new in his voice. My father's a practical man, he flicks past Oral Roberts on Sunday mornings and says, "You'd think Darwin would've taught them a lesson." But he says that word like it is religion, like whatever is, he's going to get us some.

My mother left us six months ago. I can't take this anymore, she said, I just can't take this. She was standing in the kitchen when she said it. I was sitting at the table at the time, trying to do my homework, and I looked up at her straight, thin back silhouetted against the window. Her hair was in a thick braid down her back, with little hairs standing out from it, wild, escaping the braid and the rubber band down by her waist. She turned towards me, and looked at me hard, as if I was someone she'd never seen before.

"I was your age when Matthew was born," she said. Matthew is my brother that died when he was two. My older brother. I think he still is my older brother, even though we were never in the world at the same time. "I was just like you, just the same." I didn't really know what she meant. Her hands were on her hips, leaving wet marks on her pants. She sighed, and dropped her shoulders down like she was tired. "I'm sorry, honey," she said. "I'm sorry." And she kissed me on the forehead and walked out of the room.

I went right on doing my homework. I'd heard her say funny things before; my dad said that's why he loved her, she was so unexpected about everything. I thought maybe she'd had a hard day at the plant where she worked, that she'd go out back and have a cigarette, come back and finish making supper. But she didn't.

At seven o'clock my dad came into the kitchen. "Hi, Champ," he said to me, and put his hand on my head. "Where's your mother?"

"I don't know," I said. "I thought she was out back. She seemed kind of fed up. She hasn't come back in here."

She wasn't anywhere. She'd packed a suitcase and gone. That was it. Like she said, I guess she couldn't take it anymore; maybe *it* was just us. After that, my father never really talked about her at all. It was like she was dead.

He takes out a little ad in the back of *The Phoenix Gazette*:

> WANTED!
> USED CARS
> ANY MAKE OR MODEL
> WILL PAY CASH!

And he puts our phone number at the bottom.

The ad went in on a Sunday, in the late edition, and on Monday morning I'm all set to walk out the door with John when Dad stops me.

"Hey, Champ," he says. "No school for you today. Come on back in."

John and I stare at Dad. John's mouth is hanging open so wide I can see his fillings, but mine is not. I have a feeling I know what is coming.

John says, "Da-a-ad . . ." the way he used to when he was little.

Dad glares at him. "You just stop that. Someone's got to stay here and answer the phone. I'll bet it rings off the hook."

"Why not me?" John throws his bag on the floor like nothing could make him pick it up again.

"Because I say. Because Greg is older. God knows what you'd say to those people. Now pick that up and get out of the house."

John mooches, kicks at his bag, twists his hands. Dad sighs. "It's no use," he says. "You're going to school. Come on, I'll give you a lift." John brightens, picks up his bag, and my dad puts his arm around his shoulder. "I'd better stop off at the school anyhow," he says, "and tell them how sick you are. Scarlet fever, right?" He winks at me. I'm still not sure what's going on.

"Scarlet fever, Dad," I say.

When they've gone I sit down by the phone. I don't know what to do with myself. It's not like I haven't bummed off school before, but this is different. I try to think what I'd do if I was just bumming off, no strings attached, and I think I'd probably walk out toward the sandy lots at the end of town – but then, I wouldn't be going there alone, there'd be a bunch of us and we'd do something. And anyway, I can't leave the house, I have to stay by the phone. I start to think, but what if one of my teachers calls? What if Mr Olsen decides he's got a used car to sell in his coffee break, and calls here? Should I answer the phone like I'm sick? Should I pretend to be someone else? This is what I'm trying to decide when the phone rings.

"Hello," I say. It comes out squeaky, like sick and not-me both at the same time. It isn't a good effect.

"... Hello? Is this 555–6759? Used cars?"

"Yes," I say. "Yeah, that's us."

"I got a Pontiac. '75. Want to get rid of it. Any offers?"

I have no idea. My dad said cash. I wonder what cash he meant.

"Look," I say. "It's not me that wants the car. It's my dad. Steve Snow. Can he call you when he gets home from work? That's about six o'clock."

The man at the other end of the phone breathes out heavily, which hisses loudly in my ear. "Yeah, I guess so," he says. "Your old man, huh? Opening a business?"

"Sort of."

"Well, good luck to him, I say." And the man laughs, not very nicely. But I take his number, writing it down, along with 'Pontiac – 1975' at the top of a piece of looseleaf I pulled from my school notebook. I take his name, too, Carl Felix. By the end of the day I have a whole long list of numbers, cars, years and names, which I hand to my dad when he gets home. He grins like he's really happy.

"Terrific, kiddo," he says. "A good day's work. How

about that." And he keeps on grinning, looking down at the sheet of paper. John comes in and peers around him to see what I've written, then stares at me. I shrug. Dad folds the paper carefully and slips it in the back pocket of his jeans. "Come on, buddies," he says, "let's go out for pizza."

"Pizza!" John gallops upstairs, thump thump thump, to get his jacket. He'll do anything for pizza, and it's the only thing guaranteed to cheer him up when the Firebirds lose a game or some other tragedy blights his life. We ate a lot of pizza right after Mom left, and for the first couple of months even that barely did it for him. But now pizza is back to being just a great thing for John, and when my dad takes us out, all three of us squeezed into the cab of the truck, it feels like a real boys' outing.

The funny thing is, these are the times I miss Mom most. Or not miss, exactly – I just wonder where she is and what she's doing, right at that very moment. We haven't heard anything from her, she could be in Alaska for all we know. So when Dad says we're going for pizza, I say it's great, and he gives me the keys so I can start up the truck, and then I hear John come running down the stairs, and the screen door slam. I'm glad that we fit so tight in the truck, because I feel pretty lonely and far away.

"Life," my father says as we work our way through a huge mottled wheel of pizza, "life is too mundane."

"What's mundane?" asks John.

My father chews thoughtfully for a minute. "Well," he says, "it's pretty much the same as boring. You get up. You go to work. You come home. You eat, several times a day. Then you go to bed and the whole thing starts again the next day. And that's the problem. That's what's driving people crazy. Everybody does the same stuff, shops at the same stores, everybody goes to Disneyland to have the same fun. What about that guy who killed all those folks at

McDonald's? What about Ted Bundy? What about Charles Manson? Those were people just bored out of their skulls, I'll bet. Boredom can do that to you."

John gives me another look, or tries to, but I put my face in my drink and won't meet his eyes.

"There's no greatness around here," my dad goes on. "Oh sure, there's the desert, and there's places like the Grand Canyon, but what do those do to people? Make them feel small. You stand at the edge of the Grand Canyon and think, well, just why *bother*, why bother with anything when there's this thing, millions and millions of years old and bigger than anything I'll ever be? People say it's uplifting, but I think it gets folks down."

He takes a swig of his beer and a big bite of pizza which he chews hard, his jaws moving from side to side like a goat. John begins to fidget, kicking his legs under the table, and occasionally kicking me. He stares at Dad.

"You have to give people something to admire," he says when he's swallowed. "Look at all those things they have in Europe. Not just those stone circles but huge cathedrals and castles that people can look at and say *we* built those, *we're* okay – even if they're just building highways now the same as us.

"But what have we got? Look around you. Restaurants shaped like giant hotdogs, like cowboy hats, all made out of shitty, mangy-looking plaster. And people *admire this*. They do. People write books about them. You can buy them in any bookstore, big glossy full-colour photographs of enormous disintegrating sausages. Makes me sick."

He sighs. I have to confess that at this point I'm staring too. I've never heard Dad talk this way. I've never heard anyone talk this way. It's like although I can hear all the words coming out, and I know what each one means, altogether they're a foreign language.

I look at John. John has red hair like Mom, and the same pale skin which means you can see everything he's feeling right there in his face. Right now the skin is red and blotchy, and his eyes have gone pink like a rabbit's eyes. I really don't want him to cry. So I kick him hard on the shin.

"Hey – !" He is surprised enough that his skin gets a little paler and his eyes stop popping out. I am relieved. Then he turns to Dad, like he's just woken up. "But so what, Dad?"

"So what? *So what?*" Dad shakes his head and looks at John. "My son, the So-Whatters of this world are the ones you have to watch out for. The So-Whatters of this world are the ones who *build* the huge plaster hotdogs and take pictures of them and go to Disneyland on their vacations."

We had never been to Disneyland. We wanted to go, but I thought that now was not the time to bring this up.

"Greatness. Greatness is what this world needs, what this country needs especially, and there just isn't enough of it to go around. And do you know why that is? It's because people don't understand that they have to make it themselves. I didn't understand that myself until – until a little while ago." I wonder if he means *until your mother left*, but if he did he would never say it. "So boys, we're not going to be So-Whatters anymore. Not this family. They're not going to watch us drive by and say, 'Wouldn't you know, there go the So-Whatters who couldn't give a damn.' Because we do. And we can make life better for everyone. Remember what I said? Energy? That's the ticket, boys, that's the trick."

My dad picks up his beer glass and drains it in one long gulp, his Adam's apple jumping up and down like a float with a twitchy fish at one end. When it's empty, he bangs it down on the table so hard I think it will break, and everybody else in the pizza joint turns to look at us.

"What do you say, kids," he says, and opens his arms wide. I notice the palms of his hands are cracked like they're not made out of skin but something harder. His eyes are nearly hidden by his smile. "Who's for an ice-cream sundae?"

We both shout yes, and my dad does too, and we pile out towards the truck to go to Grey's. It's like he hasn't said anything. It's like it's okay.

Dad spends almost all of next Saturday on the phone. I can see he's got my piece of looseleaf in front of him, the one with all the names and cars and numbers on, and as he's talking he holds the phone against his shoulder with his cheek and scribbles down the side of the page. When he's finished, about four o'clock, he shouts out that he'll be back in a while, and walks out the front door. When he comes back he's got some cans of soup with him, and another loaf of bread and some ham. This is what we have for dinner, sitting around the table and not saying much. Suddenly, John looks up from his soup and says, "How come we don't have cloth napkins anymore?"

We use paper towels now, which Dad folds carefully in two and places under our silverware. We used to have white napkins with lace edges that had E.B.F. embroidered on them, my grandmother's initials, Mom's mom.

"Too much trouble," Dad says. "You want to wash and iron them?" His voice is very even and logical.

"I guess not," John says. He looks down at his plate.

"Where are the napkins, anyway?" I ask.

Dad looks out the window, towards the desert. "I don't know," he says at last.

I guess she took them with her.

We are standing, all three of us, staring across a little piece of the Colorado River at the big stone arches of London Bridge, in Lake Havasu City. Dad's arms are wide out, and in between his hands is the bridge, all the length of it: if I squint it really does look like he's holding it.

"This is it, boys," he says. "*This* is the vision of a man who saw a lack of greatness around him. Game shows and beer are not what made this country, boys, not by a hell of a long shot. The Declaration of Independence. The Constitution. Four score and seven years. Manifest Destiny. I bet they don't even teach Manifest Destiny in the schools anymore." He peers at us as if we might be keeping something from him, but he doesn't let us answer.

"Once upon a time, boys, this country had the energy and the imagination to *do* things. Devise. Invent. The automobile. The airplane. Made men who could do things. And I'll tell you, sometimes those men are still out there. Robert McCulloch, he was one of those men; a man who believed anything was possible. And so he brought this bridge all the way over from London. Asked the Queen for it. 'Your Majesty,' he said, 'I'm afraid my people are in need of a little inspiration. A little of the loaves-and-fishes treatment. So if you don't mind I'll buy your bridge and I'll put it up in the desert and see what they make of that.' And she sold it to him. And here we are."

We stand in the morning sun, looking at the bridge.

"Come on," says Dad. "Let's take a walk."

We had left the house a little after seven in the morning. Sunday. Until about 6.45, John and I hadn't known we were going anywhere. For a long time he wouldn't say where we were heading.

WELCOME TO LAKE HAVASU CITY
HOME OF LONDON BRIDGE

You can't believe there'll be a bridge when you see the sign. Lake Havasu is one of those towns at the edge of the desert that make you wonder why anyone put it there, or at least that's what it must have been like before the bridge arrived. Now it's big, with a lot of stores and ice-cream parlours, everything open even on a Sunday. They brought the river into town just so it could go under the bridge. When we drove into town we could see it, reflecting the sunlight like it was made out of metal. The whole effect is pretty impressive. There were a lot of cars driving over the bridge, beneath the long tails of multi-coloured banners, and lots of people underneath, walking around with kids and strollers and staring at the little fake river and pointing at the big bridge.

Now Dad walks in between John and me, with his hands in the pockets of his jeans. Usually he looks straight ahead, so that he won't see you coming from the side unless you shout, but today his head is all over the place, turning this way and that with his eyes darting back and forth. It makes him look like a big bird, like a vulture or something, the way his neck is stuck out with his head twisting on the end of it. His neck is like a vulture's too, pink and wrinkly at the back. We get all the way to the end of the bridge and stop. Dad leans over the rail and looks down, resting his heavy forearms on the metal, his hands loose over the water below like they don't belong to him. I can see John bunching his fists inside his pants. I have a feeling he's beginning to think there aren't any explanations to anything anymore.

"So," Dad says at last.

"Yes?" I say. It sounds funny, but I think if I say "So?" too, he'll think I'm being smart.

"You didn't say anything about the bridge."

"Good bridge, Dad," I say.

"Yeah, Dad." John's eyes flicker between him and me.

"Well," Dad says. And then his eyes pop up from the river, and drill straight into mine. "You'll see,' he says. "You'll see."

*

It seems like every day I get home from school there is another car in the drive. Well, three actually fit in the drive: then they start to stack up, snaking out in a line down the block, across the street, double-parked. The neighbours come out on Saturdays and stand behind their lawnmowers, staring, the way neighbours do when there's something they don't like but they don't see what they can do about it. I don't think they'd mind if they were nice cars that my father is buying, but they aren't. They're shot through with rust and their seats are sprung; the tyre treads are worn bald. Dad is paying money for these things. And the more cars there are, the happier he is. He whistles all the time now, and slaps his hands on his thighs and rubs them together. In some ways, this is nothing new: I can recognize one of Dad's Projects a mile away. Usually they're pretty practical, or that's how they start out: building a garage, redesigning the kitchen – the refuse of these Projects litters the house and the garden outside. But nothing ever got finished; we were always tripping over the leavings of his work and once Mom got a really bad electric shock from some wires he'd left too near the sink. She screamed at him then, screamed and screamed. She'd never done that before.

So now I wonder about all this. I think a lot about the trip to Lake Havasu City, about Dad's long speeches, and tell myself he has a plan, which means at least he isn't crazy. John is not so sure. We begin to have the same conversation every night, when it's dark and safe and we can talk about things without having to see each other's faces.

"I'm telling you, he's crazy." John's voice drifts up to me. We have bunk beds.

"No he isn't."

There is silence. "Maybe you're crazy too."

"He's doing something. He's doing something important. He has a plan."

"So what's he doing?"

"It's something to do with what he said. With energy. Like those things we saw on TV. Like the bridge we went to."

"Those things were tombs." John's voice is sulky now.

"Not all of them. And the bridge isn't. He's not crazy."

"He wouldn't be doing this if Mom were around."

I know that, so I don't say anything.

Dad is standing outside in the drive, handing seventy-five dollars to a very fat man who drove up in a green Honda that looks like it's been run over by a truck. His very fat wife is standing next to him – she drove up in another car, a new one, the one I guess they'll drive off in. The phone rings.

"Hello?"

"Hi, Greg."

"Mom."

For a minute she doesn't say anything, but I know she's still there.

"How are you?"

"I'm okay."

"John?"

"Him, too."

I think I can hear her smiling. I am afraid she's making fun of me, calling from far away, a place that she knows but I don't.

"Where are you, Mom?"

"I'm – " I can hear cars going by in the background. She must be outside. "I'm pretty far away." Alaska, I think. But I know it could be anywhere. Down the street. Which would be worse. "I miss you."

"I miss you too, Mom." If I were John, I would ask, *so why don't you come home?*, and I try and think what she would say.

"How's your father?" she asks.

I can see him through the window, talking and laughing with the Fats. When the Fats laugh their legs and arms shake, and their cheeks are round moons. The woman has a beehive hairdo. Even her hair seems fat.

"He's fine." For a second I think that if I tell her about all the cars parked outside she'd come home, but it seems unfair. I like to think that all the rusting metal outside isn't her fault.

"Good."

I suddenly realize how awful this conversation is, and I want it to end though I don't know how to hang up and part of me still wants her to be there, on the other end of the line. I wish she would stay there, not saying anything, and I would put the receiver down and go cook dinner and do my homework and go to sleep – I'd sleep on the sofa, by the phone – just knowing that she was there, so I could talk if I wanted, though I probably wouldn't. But she's standing there, in some Alaskan phone booth, and she isn't going to stand there all night.

"I'd better go, Mom," I say. "I've got to get supper." Dad is waving to the Fats, now; they're wobbling off towards their shiny new car. Dad shoves the bills down into his back pocket and turns back towards the house, smiling.

"All right, darling," she says. Her voice is not sad, not happy.

"Should I say you called?" The screen door slams.

Then she sighs, and sounds afraid, and I wonder if she's sorry she called. "You do – you do what you think is best, Gregory," she says. I like it when she calls me Gregory. "You know I trust you. I love you."

"I love you too, Mom." I'm not crying. I'm surprised. She hangs up.

Dad pokes his head around the door. "Who was it?" he asks.

"Wrong number," I say, and go into the kitchen.

*

Then Dad sells the truck. I come home from school and he's sitting at the kitchen table with this amazing pile of money in front of him. There are hundred dollar bills. Benjamin Franklin is on the hundred dollar bill: I never knew that before. Dad has a yellow pad in front of him, which he is writing on with a pencil. Every so often he stops and leafs through the money, which is in several not very neat piles arranged around the pad.

"Wow, Dad."

Dad looks up, grins at me like we're sharing a secret. "Yeah," he says. "Something, isn't it?" He picks up a bunch of notes, flicks through them like a gangster in a movie.

"Uh . . . where did it come from?" I wonder if this is a bad way to phrase the question. Dad doesn't seem to notice.

"Truck," he says.

At first I don't get it. "Truck?"

"Sold it," he says. "Sold the truck." He is still grinning, like this is an obvious, wonderful thing to have done.

I know right away that this is part of the Plan. But there are a million questions I want to ask, starting with Why? and going on to How will we go shopping tomorrow? and How will we get to baseball games? I know that the answer isn't in all those wrecks because whatever is going on, Dad doesn't intend to drive any of them.

"Hey, kiddo, don't worry," Dad says. Sometimes it's like he knows what I'm thinking; but I guess it must have been pretty clear from my face. "Just you wait," he says.

The money from the truck goes to buy an empty lot at the edge of town. It's got a chain-link fence around it and it's covered with coarse, scrubby grass. And garbage – a layer of fading beer cans, plastic bags, old chairs – anything. People have just been tossing stuff over the fence for years.

I don't know what Dad paid, but I know he thinks he got a bargain.

He meets me after school one day. We all come out, and he's leaning against the fence, drinking a Coke. I go up to him with Billy and Mike, my two best friends.

"Hey, Dad," I say. Billy and Mike say hello to him, and they call him "Mr Snow" even though he's always telling them to call him Steve.

"Hiya, kiddo," he says to me. "Hiya, boys. I was wondering if you boys wanted to give me a hand this afternoon," he says. He rubs his hands together, like you see in cartoons. "If you don't have too much homework."

"What for?" Billy asks.

"I want to clear out my new lot. Get all the garbage up. I'll pay four dollars an hour to any garbage picker-upper who lends a willing hand."

"Sure, Mr Snow!" Mike swings his bag up onto his back, ready to go like a boy scout. Mike has been my best friend for a long time now, and I've spent even more time with him lately because his mom died when he was young and that makes me feel we have something in common. But right now I am annoyed at how eager he is, maybe because I want him to see that I am worried. But there's nothing I can say.

Billy and Mike say they'll go home first, and drop off their stuff. Dad tells them where the lot is, and we walk off in our separate directions. John has baseball practice; I can hear the balls popping against bats in the schoolyard. Dad and I walk home in silence.

We are already at the lot when Billy and Mike drive up with their dads. Billy's dad, Mr Melville, is an insurance salesman, and he looks like he spends a lot of time in his car, driving around with his elbow out the window. Mike's dad is a builder and smiles when he looks at Mr Melville. "Hi, Steve," he says to my dad. He comes to the store a lot to get wire and planks and things, and sometimes he and Dad have a beer.

"Hi there, Tom," says Dad. His voice seems really loud. "Hi there, Mr Melville."

"Snow," says Billy's dad, and the way he says it, it sounds like he's asking about the weather. "You bought this place?" he asks.

"Yep," says Dad, sounding pleased with himself. "Come on, boys, I've got a whole pile of plastic bags, just take one and grab whatever you see." Billy and Mike file in through the gate which Dad is holding open. "Every last damned can and butt and chewing-gum wrapper. I want this place *pristine*," he says. "I want virgin ground."

Mr Melville doesn't leave. Billy looks like he wishes he would. "Pretty scrappy piece of land," he says. "Can't imagine it'll be good for much. You planting? Or what?"

Dad looks up at him, one eyebrow cocked up nearly into his hair. "I guess you might say we're planting, Jack. Doing some planting, yes, of a kind." I try to look like I know what he's talking about. Billy keeps picking up garbage, faster and faster.

"Okay, Snow," Mr Melville says. "You know best." He scratches his neck. "You don't catch me calling you a crank."

Mr Melville gets back in his car and drives off in a cloud of dust and exhaust, and three of us wait for my dad to get mad. But he doesn't.

"A good thing too," Dad says to us, and bends down again, tossing junk into the swelling plastic bag on the ground.

Dad begins to refer to all of this as Operation Dynamo and he quits his job at the store. He doesn't tell us this for a while. When I hear it, half of me feels afraid, like when he sold the truck, but then I remember that we've managed without that, after all, and I realize that I still have a lot of faith in Dad. That night, we watch *Captains Courageous* on TV and Dad puts his arms around our shoulders.

The next morning the diggers arrive. They trundle by our house in a slow, dirty yellow parade, and Dad's voice booms out in the bright morning air. It's very early, and John and I are still in bed, but I lean down and shake his shoulder.

"... What?" John sleeps like he might have died. He never even messes up his covers at night.

"Come on, man." I jump down, thumping hard by his head, and begin to pull on my clothes. "Something's happening."

Outside, Dad is shouting and waving, giving directions, a thick bunch of papers held tight in his pointing hand. I can't hear what he's saying; he's talking to the guy who's driving the digger at the head of the line. They are huge things, bright yellow paint gone dark with dust and globs of oil, the windows so smeared with grime it's hard to believe the men can see out of them. I come up next to Dad and he turns to me like he knew I was there all along.

"This is it, kiddo," he says. "T minus zero. Lift off. It's happening. We'll show them."

"Are these all going to the lot?" I ask. I crane my neck because I'm trying to see the papers he has in his hand.

"Yessir," he says. "Yes indeedy!" He is excited like a little kid, like John is on his birthdays or at Christmas. But then suddenly he breathes in deeply, it's almost a sigh, and he turns to me.

"Greg," he says. I can see the broken blood-vessel in his eye that he got when I accidentally hit him with a baseball five years ago. "Let's go in the house. I want to show you something."

We go back in and sit down at the kitchen table, and Dad spreads the papers he was holding out in front of him. Maps and plans, xeroxed out of books, pages of yellowy newsprint with Dad's own plans in pencil. There are photographs too, very grainy but clear, of big stones standing up on grass, the spaces between them like big doors leading to nothing. When I look at Dad's face I can see that there's practically a light coming out of his eyes.

"Greg," he says again. "We're going to call up forces. That's the way I see it."

"What – forces, Dad?"

"The forces of the universe. This is where it's at. I tell you, I've been reading a lot – yes, that's right, me, sitting down every day at the library and reading like crazy. It's great, you should try it sometime." Then he winks, socks me on the shoulder, looks more like his old self. "Don't you worry, Champ, I know you're no dope. But I tell you, the thing I've found out from reading is this: the more of it you do, the less you really know. Every Mister and Doctor and his kid brother has a different opinion, a different solution to your problem, and maybe nobody even knows what the problem is in the first place. Everyone has a different theory for everything. Two guys look through a microscope, they see two different things in the same bug. Read history books – you find out nobody knows what *really* happened. Now look at Stonehenge. Some people say it's to worship the sun. There's other folks say it's to worship the moon, or it's a calendar, or a device to predict eclipses. Just about the only thing that all these professors agree on is that the stones – the huge ones – " and he jabs at a photocopy with a fat finger – "come from real far away. Two hundred miles away. And the guys who built this thing didn't even know about *the wheel*. Look at that," and he pokes the paper again, "forty-five tons. Each. If that's not energy, if that's not get up and go, I don't know what is."

He pushes himself away from the table and it rocks on its one wobbly leg. "Go wake up your brother," he says. "I've got to make a phone call. There's things I want to tell the both of you."

I go into the bedroom. John is awake, sitting up in bed. His eyes are wary. "What's going on?"

For a minute I don't know what to say, because I suddenly realize I don't know whose side I'm on. John wants things to be normal, like nothing is happening; and for a while I'd wanted that too. But things are changing. I'm not so scared anymore.

"Something big, John," I said. "Something really big. Just you wait and see. Come on."

I laugh, really loud, so I sound like Dad, pull him out of bed and he lands with a bump on the floor.

"What I want to know," Dad says, "is when they *forgot*." The three of us are walking fast towards Operation Dynamo, fast enough so that John and I sometimes have to trot to keep up. I can see the diggers moving at the end of the street.

"You build this tremendous thing, this great construction out of stones you had to go and get in the middle of winter – imagine that, boys, dragging those things with ropes over icy ground, with only a wolf-skin or something to keep out the cold – you had to convince people that this was an important enough thing to maybe risk your life for. So it had to be something they all believed in, right? And this wasn't done all at once. This went on for *thousands of years*. It was developed, it was improved; it was a big part of people's lives. It's hard for us to even imagine something like that, isn't it?"

It is. I try, and I really can't. I try and think of some cultural thing that's always been there and that's very important to me, but all I can think of is the Superbowl or the Major Leagues and I know it's not the same. Dad waves to the man in the biggest digger. The man gives him a kind of salute. Although it's early, a small crowd is gathering around the chain-link fence.

"Hi, folks," Dad calls out as we get close. "Lovely morning for working, ain't it?"

There is a little ripple of laughter. All these people have the same face as John: cautious, uncertain, frightened. It occurs to me that people don't like big things in their lives, and whatever else he may be, Dad sure is a big thing.

"Stay there a minute, boys, will you?" He plants us just inside the perimeter of the fence and jogs up to the digger. Over the noise, I can just hear him call the man Howard, but I can't hear much else, though I see him gesturing, and pointing at the plans. Dad slaps him on the back through the slid-open door, then jumps down off the cab and comes back to us.

"Now jump forward in time a little," he says to us, taking up where he left off. "And think of – well, think of a father and his two sons taking a walk around Salisbury Plain, in England, and coming up to this big thing. They walk around it, they go inside, it's a nice Sunday morning just like this one. And one of the sons turns to his dad and says, 'Dad? What is this big thing?' And all Dad can do is scratch his head and say, 'You know something, son? *I just don't know.*' "

John looks up at Dad, looks over the diggers, looks back at Dad. All the time Dad's been talking he's been glancing at the crumpling papers Dad still has clutched in his hand. He takes a deep breath. "But what's that got to do with all this?" he asks. There is a desperate edge to his voice; this is the question he's been wanting to ask for so long, and maybe it was me who made him feel that he couldn't.

"It's a powerful place," Dad says. He's talking like he hasn't heard John, but John is looking up at him eagerly, waiting for answers. "I've never been there, and I'd sure like to go. But I know one thing: that power like that is important, and pretty hard to find these days. There's a little of it in McCulloch's bridge, and maybe some in the Empire State Building or the Statue of Liberty. But I think we need some right here. And that," he says, "is exactly what we're going to get. And this time we'll make sure no one forgets. That's your job, kid." And then he looks right at John, and it's almost like a spark flies off him and lands on my brother, like it landed on me. Dad is electric.

John is smiling, the first real grin I've seen on his face for a while. "Wow, Dad," he says.

"You bet your life Wow," Dad says as he puts his arms around us. "A Wow and a half."

I can hear the crowd getting bigger, chattering and whispering behind us, as the diggers with their ferocious clanking heads begin to bite into the earth, throwing up clouds of dust that make the bright day hazy and blurred.

The digging takes a couple of days. Dad is running around all over the place, pointing and shouting and giving directions, measuring the big square holes that now pocket the ground with a bright yellow tape measure he keeps clipped to his old leather belt. In the afternoon of that first Sunday, Billy and Mike turn up, with their whole families, and so do a lot of other kids from school, and crowds of people we don't even know. News spreads fast in a place like this, and Dad is giving a great show. He's a cross between a construction site foreman and a talk-show emcee. Even Billy's dad is impressed. At one point he hands me a twenty and tells me to run to the 7–11 and bring back bottles of soda and plastic cups for everyone, and bags of pretzels too. When I go in, Zack Kowalski, who runs the place, is so eager to hear what's going on that he even gives me a lift in his car back to the field, turning his sign to "Closed" and locking the door.

And *The Republic* sends a reporter. She comes on Monday morning (John and I don't even think of going to school, and we know that Dad isn't going to make us), a girl with a ponytail and a baseball cap who doesn't look that much older than me. She has a pencil tucked behind one ear, a lined notepad, and also one of those itty-bitty tape recorders in the top pocket of her shirt. The ear with the pencil has a gold hoop in it, right up near the top. She doesn't have any trouble finding Dad; when she arrives he's right in the middle of things, directing traffic and grinning.

"Mr Snow! Mr Snow!" She waves the pad at him. Her voice is straining above the rumbling of the diggers. "I'm Lauren Armstrong, from *The Republic*! Can we talk a minute?"

Dad looks over at her, looks her up and down, and she wiggles her notepad at him. He walks over to her, his gait rolling and slow, his thumbs hooked into his pockets. I am standing by the chain-link, watching all this out of the corner of my eye. John is riding in a digger, hanging onto the controls with the driver's hands around his own. He's having a great time, and I'm glad.

"They didn't make reporters like you in my day," Dad says. He puts out his hand for her to shake, which she does, but I think she's also blushing. I look away. Dad is starting to give her his lecture about the first man who forgot, about power, almost the same stuff he said to us, so I don't have to listen.

For the first time in a while I think about Mom the way I did when she first left, a way that almost isn't like thinking at all because it doesn't seem to happen in my head; it happens in my stomach and chest and the fronts of my thighs. It makes me want to draw all these parts together and curl up on the ground, I miss her so much. I feel awful and I wonder if this is how John feels all the time and I hope that it isn't. I turn around and put my face against the warm chain-link so I can face out towards where the desert is.

This is how I am when Lauren Armstrong comes up to me.

"Hi," she says. "Greg? Greg Snow?"

I turn around because I don't know if Dad is watching me or not, and if I don't turn, and Dad sees, he'll yell at me for being rude. "That's me."

"No school, huh?" And she winks at me. I don't know what to say.

"I think some things are more important than school. I think this is. Your dad says you've been real helpful."

"He did? I don't know. I took some phone calls and stuff." I want Lauren Armstrong to leave me alone.

"Does your mom — I mean, is she — " Lauren Armstrong, Cub Reporter, knows she's stepped into some kind of puddle. She is embarrassed and trying not to be.

"Mom left a while ago. It's just the three of us now. There's my brother John, see? On the digger." I point.

Lauren Armstrong is quiet for a minute, like she is putting all the things she knows on file cards in her head and then laying them out and arranging them: Dad, Operation Dynamo, me and John, Mom-who-left-a-while-ago. Then she says, very brisk and cheerful, "This is really something, you know. Big news for the paper. They're sending a photographer. And you know what? I think with pictures, this may just go national."

She's looking off at the diggers as she says this, and smiling a little, and I have a feeling she thinks this may be her big break. Maybe it will be. But right now I'm not really interested in Lauren Armstrong, and I don't listen too hard to what she says.

"Well listen, Greg," she says, "thanks. It's been great. Exciting. I hope it all goes well. I might see you later. Okay? Good luck with everything." She puts out her hand and I shake it and say it's okay, no problem, anytime. She has a nice smile. She's pretty, in fact. And I think she means what she says about it being exciting out here, because it *is*, and I start to remember what I felt when Dad showed me his plans. Lauren Armstrong doesn't think my dad is crazy, and I start to like her just for that. I've never felt so many things all at once before in my life, and I decide that this is what Operation Dynamo is all about: that this is the power Dad is talking about, being released into the dusty air and infecting all of us, the men in the diggers, John, Lauren Armstrong.

Who's walking away now, taking off her baseball cap and running a hand through her hair. It's starting to heat up. Once she's outside the lot, she turns and waves, to my dad or to me I can't tell, but I wave back anyhow.

The cars come in a parade on Wednesday morning. Some of them can't be driven and so they have to be towed, but the tow trucks follow the line of exhausted, wheezing automobiles that limps through the centre of town towards Dad's lot, now pitted with craters and marked with little flags, the gap in the chain-link widened to admit cranes and winches and even a cement truck, its barrel-body rolling and rumbling like distant thunder. People come out of their houses and stores to see them go by, and Dad has had no trouble at all recruiting all the drivers he needs. And he lets me drive the one in front, the first car we bought – the beat-up Pontiac – because he knows we're going to go real slow and I'll never have to take it out of second gear. People are clapping and waving, and when we pass the 7–11 Zack Kowalski comes running out with his arms full of bags of potato chips and boxes of Ring-Dings, and he throws them in the back seat through the open window along with a load of those two-quart bottles of Coke and Sprite. He bangs the hood of the car and shouts "Good Luck!" and I can hear somebody yell out, "Go for it, Snow, you crazy bastard!" and I can tell they mean it in a nice way, though that's a funny thing to say.

When we get there I pull the Pontiac into the lot and Dad gets out. He guides the next three cars in line inside the fence, and then he stops the rest with his palms flat like a traffic warden's, shouting, "Okay, okay, hold it right there, fellas, that'll do fine for now. Just climb out and leave the keys in 'em. Pete – " he turns to Pete Charlap, our next door neighbour, who was pretty nasty about the whole thing at first (he used to leave mean little notes under the wipers of all the old cars and sign them "Anonymous" although we all knew perfectly well it was him), but who's come around like anything in the last week or so – he turns to Mr Charlap and says, "Pete, if you don't mind, would you just run on down to the tow trucks and tell 'em to bring those babies up here by the front? Then we can hook 'em right up to the winches."

"Sure thing, Steve," Mr Charlap says, and jogs off, the creases in his slacks jumping up and down as he goes. He runs Zappers, the small appliance store, which is shut today, like a lot of other things.

It's an amazing thing to watch. The cranes and winches start up their engines, and wait while Dad gets back into the Pontiac and drives it carefully into the centre of the circle, craning his neck out the window to make sure he avoids the deep pits that have been dug all around. He parks it carefully – after all this, parking a car is just the same – and then gets out and, raising his hand high with a kind of flourish, drops the keys into one of the big pits at the centre of the lot. "Okay, fellas," he calls. "Action! Let's get us some cement!"

And so the cement truck trundles over slowly, carefully, until it can't get any closer. Then the guy driving and his partner climb out and extend the big funnel at the back of the truck so the lip is over the hole. All Dad has to do is turn a lever when they nod to him and a slow flood of cement comes belching out of the belly of the truck and begins to slop into the ground.

John comes up behind me. He was riding in one of the tow trucks. For a guy who likes to ride in things (speedboats, tractors, he doesn't care), he's had a good few days. "Let's go see," he says, and we walk into the compound and stand at the edge of the hole across from Dad. The rattling cement truck makes the air around it throb.

Dad throws the lever back up when the hole is about a third full.

"Right," Dad shouts, so loud we both jump. "First car! Winch her up!"

The car has been hooked onto the winch by its back fender, which pulls away from the car a little as the cord begins to tighten. Dad and I had a big discussion the night before about whether the cars should go in nose down or nose up. He couldn't make up his mind.

"I think it's important for the flow of energy," he'd said. "We'd better get it right."

"But if the cars aren't running, they don't have any energy in themselves, do they? So can't you just flip a coin or something?"

Dad had looked worried. "I don't know," he said. "I'm just not sure."

John looked up from his meatloaf. "What about the exhausts, Dad?" he said. "Those are at the back of the car, and so is the gas tank. If you had the exhausts sticking up in the air, it would be like the energy from the car shooting up into the sky."

Dad nodded slowly. He knew John was scared of Operation Dynamo, but he never was one for comforting people. He didn't believe, like Mom did, that everything would be all right. He thought you had to make it all right. I guess he thought that John would come round in the end; and he had.

"Good thinking, kiddo," he said. "That's a very good thought. I'll bear that one in mind. Yes, that just might do nicely." And so all the cars were to go in nose down.

The winches lift them up in the air where they dangle, shining in the sun and swaying gently from side to side. When the nose of the first car hits the cement in the hole, it makes a squelching sound, like feet in wet rubber boots, and the steel rope starts to slacken as the car sinks into the wet cement. The back half of the car sticks straight up out of the ground.

Everyone leaning against the fence cheers when they see the car sink in solid, and Dad looks happier than I've ever seen him. "One down," he shouts. "Twenty-four to go!" And they cheer again. It's like a big party. When school gets out, all the kids – the ones who hadn't been out with us all morning anyway – come out, and Dad lets them drop pennies into the wet cement and the winch drivers let the littler ones sit on their laps. Nobody seems to mind that they're going to have this strange construction at the bottom of town: and by the end of the day it's looking pretty weird because the cars which will be the "lintels" have been hauled up on top of the others, with Dad underneath welding them onto the nose-downers in showers of sparks that look just like fireworks in the dusk.

It is at this point that I finally come to see what Dad means about energy. You can practically smell it in the air, blowing around like smoke. It's hard to tell where it comes from; part of me thinks it comes from Dad, or from all the happy people, but part of me likes to think it really is pouring out of the rusted and bent exhaust pipes which poke out of the ground like cosmic chimneys.

And that's how Operation Dynamo happened. It's still there, and has become a kind of local tourist attraction, though people don't exactly go out of their way to see it. Buf if they're passing through, they will. And Dad goes down a few evenings a week, after work – he didn't have any trouble getting his job back – and he'll sit inside, leaning on the Pontiac, and smoke a cigar. I know he does this because I followed him once; but I think he likes to be alone there.

He's put up a sign, carefully stencilled on white board, hooked to the chain-link fencing, which says OPERATION DYNAMO at the top and then all our three names beneath that in smaller letters. Below that there's a diagram of the place, like a horseshoe set inside a circle, with a painted compass showing you where north is. North is out towards the desert.

That's it. I was surprised, because I thought the whole point of the sign would be to tell people why we built it, so they wouldn't forget, like Dad said. But he said that the thing that he learned in building Operation Dynamo, the secret, was that the reason for it was inbuilt – like a car with an automatic choke, he said. All you had to do was look. And if you looked hard enough, he said, you'd find your own reasons too, not just his – and that was why people still went to Stonehenge, and why people walked over London Bridge and were happy without ever knowing who Robert McCulloch was. In the end, you can't ever know how anything started: real immortality, he said, is when things change and stay the same all at the same time. That's the biggest energy of all.

Still, I like to make sure the sign stays clean and that the paint doesn't chip. If Mom comes back, I don't want her to have any trouble reading our names.

kathy page

my beautiful wife

So all this, here, is the beginning of spring: the snow has melted; it is a yellow-grey day, and faintly raining. Gulls tear the still air with their screams, wheel between the concrete blocks, settle on the chimneys and on the mud-green balconies and their empty flower troughs. And now for the first time in many months the tape has been peeled off, the catches oiled, the double-glazed panes pulled in: the windows are flung open and cleaned. Siiri Nistsoo shakes her rug from her balcony. My neighbours pause at the doorways to the staircases and talk. Perhaps they seem to stand straighter than last week; certainly the courtyard paths have reappeared now that the snow is gone and children play on the red climbing-frame by the stand of birch trees; they spatter themselves with mud and the last of the slush as they rush from the bottom of the slide to the steps at the back. Two of my neighbours' wives, both hatless for the first time this year and wearing the self-same purple anorak from Lauduhama, watch over them with half an eye, while Ralf Jarlik, once an engineer, now a member of the parliament, crosses from 134 House to empty his rubbish bucket into the skips that stand in the middle of the courtyard. He's wearing a good coat these days. A scrawny Alsatian sniffs at the mud. The gulls caw and wheel, caw and wheel. Television aerials stretch from the flat roofs, quiver, point in the direction of news: there is more of it now, and more reliable.

Soon, Liia said this morning, we will be able to wear our summer clothes. All these small changes are important.

For example, because it is the weekend, Liia makes proper coffee, from beans, which last year were unavailable. The quality could still be better, but even so we savour its complex bitterness as our eyes rove through the window – out, always out. The place would look less anonymous, I think, if the windows and balconies of each block were painted a different colour. I tell Liia I might suggest it: little improvements are happening all the time. But really they should blow the whole district up and start again. If it could be afforded.

At least, says Liia (she always tries to make things bearable), there are trees within sight of the windows, on one side. But the kitchen is too small, as the English say, to swing a cat in. It always has been so, but I find it seems even smaller now. The sink on its brackets, not level, a row of the green swirled tiles behind it. The folding table, the round-topped plywood stools pushed under it, the two shelves: everyone has them. The cooker, once white enamel, its lid that no longer folds down, its leak that no one could ever fix. How sick of it I am. We are lucky to have no children and so three other rooms – a study each and a bedroom which we also use as a lounge. We need all that space for our books.

Yesterday, my wife Liia said to me: "Tell me, Toomis, why is it that I can never ever find a book in this collection of ours?" She stood at the threshold between our two studies. Her white gold hair was just brushed and bristled with electricity. She wears it cut simply, straight, at shoulder length with a fringe. She has scarcely aged in fifteen years. Her voice, I thought, was teasing.

"I don't know, my love, my little berry," I told her, "but what is it you want? I will find it for you." The library system is perfectly workable. Chronology is the most important factor, but here and there I think an author deserves to have all his works next to each other, however long he lived. And then again sometimes a volume on the history of France makes connections with one from Political Theory or English Literature and so I might put the two of them together. Then, of course, I put those I use most nearest to my desk, which can only be sensible. I have explained this before, but she will not agree.

"You are just like a man," she said. Of course I am! But that, she said, is not what she means. She went back into her own study. She is a translator, I am an historian (though I have worked mainly as a language teacher and currently am of necessity in a clerical role): perhaps that explains this disagreement over the library system.

And then mischief entered me. Just like a man, I thought. What a statement! I went from shelf to shelf, pulling out books. The yellow books and then the red and the blue, the white spines and the brown. It took an hour or so, extracting them from their correct places, deciding where to draw the line between orange and red, and which colours to put next to each other. I dusted them and ranked them, by hue, on a single shelf. It cheered me up, as physical work can, so I started to whistle, and the sound of that brought her in.

"What's this?" she said.

"Is this a woman's system then?" I asked. "Will this suit you?" and I found myself laughing like a schoolboy, uncontrollable; I did not understand why I was doing it. I am not a frivolous person, I thought, even as I continued to laugh and she stared gravely at me. Eventually, she smiled and only then I stopped. Oh, she said, but how long did it take you to do this, my love? Do we have so much time to spare? It was a joke, I told her, only that. But somehow it was not the truth.

There are cars now, parked in a neat row at the edge of

the green. All sorts of people have them. What use is a car, Liia says. Books are more important. A car can only take you half as far as the petrol you can pay for lasts, and then you have to come back; but books are infinite journeys and each one can be taken many times. We two, she smiles, are old travellers, *n'est-ce pas?*

I was her teacher once, and she the cleverest student I ever had. And I was married to someone else, but I left, because not to would have been unbearable. In books, we renewed our passion, secretly at first, then frankly. We met other worlds and then returned to each other. Much of the past twenty years Liia and I have spent reading.

Back then, what we read rarely had consequences. The ideas could not grow. They came from elsewhere, like seeds blown on the wind, and depended on freedom's climate to grow: that was why we loved them so. I realize now that when I imagined the revolution, before it happened, I thought of it in terms of what we would be able to read. I thought of reading works by people who were only reputations to me, magic names, pregnant with many possibilities, of finding books I had hunted for in vain; they would fall into my hands like ripe plums. I dreamed of owning my own copy of an important text, being able to write pencilled notes on the page. I imagined gifts of books between me and my wife and the conversations we would have about them; I thought of books in our own language as well as foreign ones. That was what excited me about freedom. Since it has happened, I see of course that it means other things as well. Instead, even. Perhaps the thing is that before we had only books? In any case, I cannot read today.

The spring disturbs me. It is a time of longing. Paths cross and recross the courtyard, leading to other blocks like this and other courtyards and eventually to the woods, where the March bells will soon be out, then the crocuses and daffodils. We will go there as soon as the mud has dried. Oh, summer ... At this point, how we all long for it, for the trees, the myriad rustlings and the light through leaves, for the long days, the feeling of sun on our skins, the other pleasure of shade. Picnics. I would like to have a car.

That is the future still. Now, the rain begins to fall more heavily. One day in this country, I often say, we will learn to make drains, which currently exist only in the dictionary. One day, Liia said to me yesterday, we will learn how to talk to each other in different ways. Which way? How different?

In the afternoon, I take the trolleybus to the market. My wife used to do this but some time back she said that she goes three times in the week and why should it not be shared? And I said that I am both working and studying at night school and so have less time, but, she said, who makes you do so? So I go to please her. At the entrance a row of people stand with puppies huddled in their coats or sleeping in straw shopping bags, all newness, shining fur, half human faces, clean paws. Even a mongrel is beautiful at birth.

I go past the tools and vacuum parts, the military paraphernalia which only tourists buy. On through the new clothes, stall after stall, garments I don't even recognize, colours I don't have names for. Past the imported groceries tied to the shelves with string, the fat over-wintered carrots in their dirt, the new potatoes, the churns of milk, the apples in piles. There are bananas everywhere now, but still too expensive for regular use. I buy sausage, bottled peas, bread and a chicken. Old women stash their money away in broken purses, kept among the cuts of meat. There is never enough change. A plastic bag costs thirty cents. It takes longer than you might think. All these things, the quantities, the choices, it is tiring somehow.

When I get back, there is a small pile of books on the rug in the centre of my room. The door to her study is ajar. What is this? I call. Those: they are the books written by women, she calls back. I am sure that she is wrong, and look for myself, but I only find two more.

But what do you mean by it? I ask, standing at the threshold of her room. She pauses in her typing but doesn't turn her head. A good book is a good book, I say, surely, whoever has written it? I'm not sure, she says, it's just that I never thought to do it before. Simply to count. She laughs. She looks at me then and I can't name the expression. Somewhere between shy and amazed.

Something must have made you think of it, I say. This is the twentieth century and she is no longer translating just the classics, but contemporary works also. Yes, she says, I wonder: would I ever have thought of it on my own? She is talking to herself. For a second, I feel invisible.

Currently, at the office, I am compiling biographies of our politicians. There is to be a brochure, issued to everyone in the country, detailing their professions, family status, beliefs as well as a symbol for the party they stand for and a photograph. And at night, I read about economics and make summaries – this is for my Diploma in International Relations: it is no use being only an historian. Neither is it much use, in my opinion, having a government of poets for ever. Besides, they stop writing and soon we will have no literature!

We need a new kind of politician, I tell Liia over supper. She has forgotten to take off her reading glasses and they steam up in the heat of the soup. The ingredients are much better now. We can savour what we eat, make it last with talk as they do in Europe, in novels. Yes, I say, we need a new kind of man, one who has an overview, and has not served under previous conditions of course, because old habits – not so much of thought but of behaviour – die hard. I study her as I speak.

My wife is a very elegant woman. The cloth we have here is not of the best quality, but she wears the things she has made as if they were couture. She is slender, her hair the colour of winter sunlight, her skin, though it suffers a little at this time of year, is smooth as the finest paper. Her grey-green eyes call to mind the sea, the flecks of gold are sun on the waves: she is beautiful, there is no other word; no one like her. Myself, I am not handsome and I am older, ordinary. I have a potato face, but she has told me often that she loves it.

Visitors say that they find us inexpressive, and this may be a result of the long years when to preserve one's self was to conceal it. But we two read each other well enough and I see a tremor pass over Liia's face as I talk about government – the faintest of frowns, just for a second as she bends forward over her plate. I have not yet told my wife that I see myself as a statesman eventually, an ambassador perhaps. Of course, it may not be possible. But I think I am as qualified as anyone else, and am beginning to build up the connections. Only last week I drank a beer with the Minister for Foreign Affairs.

I'll do it then? I say, meaning the dishes, which I also do at weekends. Toomis, why *ask*? she says. Then I am angry. She and I have run through gunfire across the Town Hall Square, and hidden in a cellar until morning. We have suffered countless indignities and wiped them away from each other in the night with words and caresses. We have not gone through all that, become free, in order to argue over greasy dishes. I want to tell her this and other things, I want to talk of the future, of international relations, of the possibilities, the right way to proceed. But she is not there. She has slipped away and back to her damned books. I almost want to take her by the shoulders (but they are so very thin) and shake her and say –

But I am not sure what, and I plug the sink with the bit of rag and fill it. We are making our own washing up liquid now, faintly scented with something like lemons. The bottle is bright yellow plastic, with a picture of bubbles on it, though not so many come in reality. I search my mind for things I have read which might bear on the situation and I find nothing. Then I think that it is all over in five minutes and that if I can one day be an ambassador, to have gone to market and stood with my hands in greasy water on weekends will be neither here nor there. So long as I can take my place, I think, and this is a new feeling for me – I was before a medium and a repository for ideas, a memory, never a man of action. I realize that I am reading differently now: not all books interest me equally, as they once did. I examine them for their use, their application. I see that I have already bypassed who I was, even though I seem to be the same and even though my circumstances are lagging behind me.

She works late in her room. I get out the bed and arrange the quilts and pillows for later. I go to the window. Karel from downstairs stands stock-still while his half-breed dog careens about in the night, its breath smoking. On Monday, if the weather holds, the old women will be out with their twig brooms, clearing everything away, last year's rubbish, the weekend's dogshit. I see too that the old person in the torn coat is rummaging about in the bins again, pulling out the cardboard cartons and the bottles and putting them into separate carrier bags: another new thing. Lights burn behind the thin curtains. Most things are thin here and curtains are a good example, I have seen foreign ones in magazines, velvet drapes on heavy rails, but here they are scanty pieces of cloth or net which only gesture at concealment. I made our curtain hooks myself, bending them from wire. I am an intellectual and not a naturally practical man but circumstances compel. The flat opposite ours has a brand new white venetian blind, but that is unusual. Carpets too are thin, not like the ones you find in hotels, pileless, flat, and mostly clothes are thin as well, which surprises visitors. Coats are one exception: woollen, kapok-lined. Without such a coat, here you would die. Things, so many things.

I love my wife. I want her to come with me into our future. But the washing of dishes and the making of soup and the counting of books – trivia, surely – should not occupy too much of our time?

It is easier to talk in the dark. When finally she comes to bed I whisper my plans. She does not seem surprised – after all, she knows me well. You would enjoy the life, I say, would you not? You would make a fine ambassador's wife. We could live part of the year in a foreign city. We would be more at home in a cosmopolitan atmosphere, a city centre – an apartment with high ceilings, shutters, wooden floors, close to the cafés and shops. Perhaps a drier climate, milder winters. You could go on with your translations, of course, meet the writers and talk with them so as to get your words exactly right. Yes, she says, perhaps. You would like it, I tell her. The wallpaper would be on straight. The plumbing would be fixed. And neither of us would have to do the shopping and so on.

I love you, but you don't quite understand, she says. What? What is it I don't understand? What? We must learn to talk to each other differently now, she repeats.

Can some things not stay the same? It comes from outside, this, from something she is reading, but she will not tell me what. She says she is not ready to; it is difficult, she wants to be sure. She has always been careful that way.

I taught my wife English, in which she has since far surpassed me. I gave her personal tuition, because she was a gifted student. Also because I liked to look at her. I remember explaining the tenses, the future conditional, the future in the past – all those tenses we do not have in our own language; they are hard to translate. I remember watching her mind work while her lips waited for the right word to come; I remember the dim light of the classroom, the creaks from the stove as it cooled and the metal contracted. In winter her lips were cracked, in summer they glistened. She was still a child. Afterwards I went home to my first wife, and lay next to her, and my young son was in the cot beside us. I lay sleepless the night through: I knew that there was more to life than I had expected, and there could be no peace until I had it.

And now at the beginning of spring neither of us sleep. Our flat is near one of the few working lamps that stand like extra trees in the courtyard and pinkish light glazes the room. They have not yet installed individual switches and so the heating will be on until May; tonight it is too warm, we have thrown the covers off and lie, naked but not touching. The books we have read together, or separately and then told each other about, surround us. I am sometimes tired of books now, I whisper to my wife, I feel I have read enough for a lifetime. To say this feels like a confession.

Toomis, it is not the same for me – I am still looking, she says, lying on her back with her eyes open as if there were words on the ceiling for her to read – with her body open too, as if she read what was there with all of it, the soft skin of her belly, her tender nipples, the velvet between her thighs: all eye.

Tomorrow we will go to my mother in the country, eat lunch, help with anything she asks. We will bring bags of home-grown potatoes and apples home with us. We did this every Sunday before Liberation and during it too. We do it always. But at the same time things are changing in ways I cannot predict. I was never afraid before, just angry and waiting. But I am afraid now, as I lie beside my beautiful wife. Silently I ask: Is this fear also the beginning of spring?

buchi emecheta

a man needs many wives

from *The Joys of Motherhood*

Humans, being what we are, tend to forget the most unsavoury experiences of life, and Nnu Ego and her sons forgot all the suffering they had gone through when Nnaife was away.

The first important thing to attend to was the celebration at which they would give their new child a name. All the Ibuza people living in Yaba, Ebute Metta and in Lagos island itself were called to the feast. Palm wine flowed like the spring water from Ibuza streams. People sang and danced until they were tired of doing both. To cap it all, Nnaife brought plentiful supplies of the locally made alcohol called *ogogoro* which he discreetly poured into bottles labelled "Scotch Whisky". He assured Nnu Ego that he had seen the white men for whom he worked on the ship drinking this whisky. Nnu Ego had asked wide-eyed, "Why do they call our *ogogoro* illicit? Many of my father's friends were jailed just because they drank it."

Nnaife laughed, the bitter laugh of a man who had become very cynical, who now realized that in this world there is no pure person. A man who in those last months had discovered that he had been revering a false image and that under white skins, just as under black ones, all humans are the same. "If they allowed us to develop the production of our own gin, who would buy theirs?" he explained.

However, Nnu Ego's long stay in Lagos and her weekly worship at St Jude's Ibo church had taken their toll. She asked suspiciously, "But our own gin, is it pure like theirs?"

"Ours is even stronger and purer – more of the thing. I saw them drink it on the ships at Fernando Po."

So on the day his baby boy was named, Nnaife served his guests with lots and lots of *ogogoro* and his guests marvelled at the amount of money he was spending, for they thought they were drinking spirits which came all the way from Scotland. They did not think of doubting him, since most ship crew members brought all sorts of things home with them. Their masters, not able to buy these workers outright, made them work like slaves anyway, and allowed them to take all the useless goods which were no longer of any value to them. They were paid – paid slaves – but the amount was so ridiculously small that many a white Christian with a little conscience would wonder whether it was worth anybody's while to leave a wife and family and stay almost a year on a voyage. Yet Nnaife was delighted. He was even hopeful of another such voyage. But on the day of his child's naming ceremony he spent a great portion of the money he brought home. He and his family had been without for so long that the thought of saving a little was pushed into the background.

Nnu Ego, that thrifty woman, threw caution to the winds and really enjoyed herself this time. She bought four different kinds of outfit, all cotton from the U.A.C. store. One outfit was for the morning, another for the afternoon, when the child was given the name Adim, Adimabua meaning "now I am two". Nnaife was telling the world that now he had two sons, so he was two persons in one, a very important man. She had another outfit for the late afternoon, and a costly velveteen one for the evening. This was so beautiful that even those women who had been her helpers in time of want looked on enviously. But she did not care; she was enjoying herself. Not to be outdone, Oshia and his father changed their clothes as many times as Nnu Ego. It was one of the happiest days of her life.

A month after that, Oshia started to attend the local mission school, Yaba Methodist. This made him very proud, and he didn't tire of displaying his khaki uniform trimmed with pink braid. Nnu Ego sold off the spoils from her husband's ship over the next few months, and with this they were able to live comfortably.

Nnaife was developing a kind of dependence on his battered guitar. He would sing and twang on the old box, visiting one friend after another, and not thinking at all of looking for another job. "They promised to send for me," he said. "They said as soon as they were ready to sail again they would send for me."

Nnu Ego was beginning to realize something else. Since he had come back, Nnaife had suddenly assumed the role of the lord and master. He had now such confidence in himself that many a time he would not even bother to answer her questions. Going to Fernando Po had made him grow away from her. She did not know whether to approve of this change or to hate it. True, he had given her enough housekeeping money, and enough capital in the form of the things he brought from Fernando Po, but still she did not like men who stayed at home all day.

"Why don't you go to Ikoyi and ask those Europeans if they have other domestic work for you, so that when they are ready to sail you will go with them?"

"Look, woman, I have been working night and day non-stop for eleven months. Don't you think I deserve a little rest?"

"A little rest? Surely three months is a long time to rest? You can look for something while you are waiting for them."

If Nnu Ego went further than that he would either go

out for the rest of the day or resort to his new-found hobby, the twanging of Dr Meers's old guitar. She decided to let him be for a while. After all, they still had enough money to pay for the rent. She also made sure of another term's fees for Oshia. She was now able to have a modest permanent stall of her own, at the railway yard, instead of spreading her wares on the pavement outside the yard. Oshia was helping, too. After school, he would sit by his mother's stand in front of the house, selling cigarettes, paraffin, chopped wood, and clothes blue. His mother would let him off to go and play with his friends as soon as she had finished washing and clearing the day's cooking things from the kitchen.

On one such evening, she sat with her neighbours in front of the house by the electric pole which provided light for yards around the house. Adim, Oshia's little brother, was now four months old, and he was propped up with sand around him to support his back, so he would learn how to sit up straight. He kept flopping on the sand like a bundle of loosely tied rags, much to the amusement of all. Nnu Ego had her stand by her, with her wares displayed, and Iyawo Itsekiri had started selling pork meat in a glass showcase. Another woman from the next yard had a large tray full of bread, so in the evenings the front of the house at Adam Street looked like a little market.

The women were thus happily occupied when they heard the guitar-playing Nnaife coming home. This was a surprise because when he went out these days he would not return until very late, sometimes in the early hours of the morning.

"Look," Iyawo Itsekiri pointed out to Nnu Ego, who was trying to make sure she was not seeing things. "Look, your husband is early today. Is something wrong?"

"Maybe he has decided to make use of his home this evening, for a change. And look at the group of friends he has with him. Are they going to have a party or something? Even our old friend Ubani is with them. I haven't seem him for a long time." With this statement, Nnu Ego forgot her husband's inadequacies and rushed enthusiastically to welcome their friends. They were equally glad to see her. Nnaife didn't stop twanging his guitar throughout the happy exchanges. Nnu Ego showed off her children and Ubani remarked how tall Oshia was growing and told Nnu Ego that his wife Cordelia would be pleased to know that he had seen them all looking so well.

"Oh, so you didn't tell her you were coming here tonight?"

"Few men tell their women where they are going," Nnaife put in, trying to be funny.

"I did not tell Cordelia that I would be seeing you all because I met your husband by accident in Akinwunmi Street, having a nice evening with some of his friends, so we all decided to come here and see you."

There was a kind of constraint on the faces of their visitors, she thought, though Nnaife did not seem to notice anything, but she was becoming uneasy. None the less, she said airily, "Please come in, come inside. Oshia, you mind the stand. I shall not be long."

Nnu Ego noticed that only Ubani was making an effort to talk. The others, Nwakusor, Adigwe, and Ijeh, all men from Ibuza living around Yaba, looked solemn. Well, there was little she could do to alleviate their glumness, though she was going to try. She gave them some kolanut and brought out cigarettes and matches. Nnaife added his ever-present *ogogoro*, and soon the gathering resembled a party. After the prayers, Nwakusor gave a small tot of *ogogoro* to Nnaife, and another to his wife. When he urged them to drink it, Nnu Ego sensed that something was very wrong. These men were there to break bad news. All the same, like a good woman, she must do what she was told, she must not question her husband in front of his friends. Her thoughts went to her father, who was now ageing fast, and her heart pounded in fear. She started to shiver, but drank the home-made alcohol with a big gulp. She coughed a little, and this brought a smile to the faces of the men watching her. Nnu Ego was a good wife, happy with her lot.

Nwakusor cleared his throat, forcing furrows onto his otherwise smooth brow. He addressed Nnaife in the full manner, using his father's name Owulum. He reminded him that the day a man is born into a family, the responsibilities in that family are his. Some men were lucky in that they had an elder brother on whose shoulders the greater part of the responsibility lay. His listeners confirmed this by nodding in mute assent. It was an accepted fact.

"Now, you, Nnaife, until last week were one of those lucky men. But now, that big brother of yours is no more . . ."

Nnaife, who all this time had kept his old guitar on his knee, waiting for Nwakusor to finish his speech so that he could start one of the songs he had learned during his short stay at Fernando Po, threw the instrument on the cemented floor. The pathetic clang it made died with such an echo of emptiness that all eyes hypnotically followed its fall, and then returned to Nnaife, who let out one loud wail. Then there was silence. He stared at his friends with unseeing eyes. As Nnu Ego recovered from the shock of the loud guitar the news began to register. So that was it. Nnaife was now the head of his family.

"Oh, Nnaife, how are you going to cope? All those children, and all those wives." Here she stopped, as the truth hit her like a heavy blow. She almost staggered as it sank in. Nnaife's brother, the very man who had negotiated for her, had three wives even when she was still at home in Ibuza. Surely, surely people would not expect Nnaife to inherit them? She looked round her wildly, and was able to read from the masked faces of the men sitting around that they had thought of that and were here to help their friend and relative solve this knotty problem. For a time,

Nnu Ego forgot the kind man who had just died; all she was able to think about was her son who had just started school. Where would Nnaife get the money from? Oh, God ... She ran out, leaving her baby on the bed.

She ran into Mama Abby who with many others was wondering what the noise and crying was about. Nnu Ego blurted out the first thing that came into her head: "Nnaife may soon be having five more wives."

Seeing that her friends were in suspense, Nnu Ego went on to explain: "His brother has died and left behind several wives and God knows how many children."

"Oh, dear, are you bound to accept them all?" asked Mama Abby, who knew little of Ibo custom. "You have your own children to think of – surely people know that Nnaife is not in a steady job?"

"Maybe he'll be asked to come home and mind the farm," said one of the curious women.

They all started talking at the same time, this one telling Nnu Ego what to do, that one telling her what not to do. The voices jangled together, but Nnu Ego thanked the women and went back inside to her menfolk. Her husband was being consoled by his friends, who had poured him another glass of *ogogoro*. Nnu Ego was asked to bring more cigarettes from her display stand, with a vague promise of repayment by someone. Many neighbours and friends came in, and they held a small wake for Nnaife's brother.

Ubani was the first to take his leave. But before he did so, he called Nnu Ego and Nnaife out into the yard, as their room was filled with people who had come to commiserate with the bereaved family and stayed for a glass of gin or whisky and a puff of tobacco. The air outside was fresh, and the sky was velvety black. Stars twinkled haphazardly against this inky background, and the moon was partly hidden. Ubani told them that he could fix Nnaife up at the railways as a labourer cutting the grass that kept sprouting along the railway lines. Unless he wanted to go back to Ibuza, Ubani suggested he come the very next day.

Nnaife thanked him sincerely. No, he said, he would not go to Ibuza. He had been out of farming practice for so long that he would rather risk it here in Lagos. At home there would be no end to the demands his family would make on him. He had more chance of living longer if he didn't go into what looked like a family turmoil. Of course he would be sending money to the Owulum wives, and would see that their sons kept small farmings going. But he would help them more by being here in Lagos. He would definitely go with Ubani the next day to take up the job if they would accept him.

Ubani assured him that they would; he himself now cooked for the head manager of the whole Nigerian Railway Department and his work was permanent. He was employed by the Railway Department and not the manager himself, so that whenever he decided to leave he would simply be transferred to a new master. Ubani laughed bitterly. "I talk like an old slave these days, grateful to be given a living at all."

"Are we not all slaves to the white men, in a way?" asked Nnu Ego in a strained voice. "If they permit us to eat, then we will eat. If they say we will not, then where will we get the food? Ubani, you are a lucky man and I am glad for you. The money may be small, and the work slave labour, but at least your wife's mind is at rest knowing that at the end of the month she gets some money to feed her children and you. What more does a woman want?"

"I shall see you tomorrow, my friend. Mind how you go with these Hausa soldiers parading the streets."

Nnaife was given a job as a grass-cutter at the railway compound. They gave him a good cutlass, and he would wear tattered clothes while he cut grass all day, come sunshine or rain. The work was tiring, and he did not much like it, especially when he saw many of his own people making their various ways into the workshop every morning. However, like Ubani, he was working for the Department and not for a particular white man, and he intended using that as his basis for getting into the workshop.

One thing was sure: he gained the respect and even the fear of his wife Nnu Ego. He could even now afford to beat her up, if she went beyond the limits he could stand. He gave her a little house-keeping money which bought a bag of garri for the month and some yams; she would have to make up the rest from her trading profits. On top of that, he paid the school fees for Oshia, who was growing fast and was his mother's pride and joy. Adaku, the new wife of his dead brother, would be coming to join them in Lagos, and after some time the oldest wife Adankwo, who was still nursing a four-month-old baby, might come too. Ego-Obi, the middle wife, went back to her people after the death of Nnaife's brother Owulum. The Owulum family said that she was an arrogant person, and she for her part claimed that she was so badly treated by them when her husband died that she decided she would rather stay with her own people. In any case, she was not missed; first, she had no child, and secondly she was very abusive. Adaku, on the other hand, had a daughter, she was better-looking than Ego-Obi, and she was very ambitious, as Nnu Ego was soon to discover. She made sure she was inherited by Nnaife.

Nnu Ego could not believe her eyes when she came from market one afternoon to see this young woman sitting by their doorstep, with a four-year-old girl sleeping on her knees. To Nnu Ego's eyes, she was enviably attractive, young looking, and comfortably plump with the kind of roundness that really suited a woman. This woman radiated peace and satisfaction, a satisfaction that was obviously having a healthy influence on her equally well-rounded child. She was dark, this woman, shiny black, and not too tall. Her hair was plaited in the latest fashion, and when she smiled and introduced herself as "your new wife" the humility seemed a bit inconsistent. Nnu Ego felt that she should be bowing to this perfect creature – she who had once been acclaimed the most beautiful woman ever seen. What had happened to her? Why had she become so haggard, so rough, so worn, when this one looked like a pool that had still to be disturbed? Jealousy, fear and anger seized Nnu Ego in turns. She hated this type of woman, who would flatter a man, depend on him, need him. Yes, Nnaife would like that. He had instinctively disliked her own independence, though he had gradually been forced to accept her. But now there was this new threat.

"Don't worry, senior wife, I will take the market things in for you. You go and sit and look after the babies. Just show me where the cooking place is, and I will get your food ready for you."

Nnu Ego stared at her. She had so lost contact with her people that the voice of this person addressing her as "senior wife" made her feel not only old but completely out of touch, as if she was an outcast. She resented it. It was one thing to be thus addressed in Ibuza, where people gained a great deal by seniority; here, in Lagos, though the same belief still held, it was to a different degree. She was used to being the sole woman of this house, used to having Nnaife all to herself, planning with him what to do with the little money he earned, even though he had become slightly evasive since he went to Fernando Po – a result of long isolation, she had thought. But now, this new menace . . .

What was she to do? It had been all right when this was just a prospect. Not hearing anything definite from home, she had begun to tell herself that maybe the senior Owulum's wives had decided against coming. For she had sent messages to Ibuza to let Nnaife's people know that things were difficult in Lagos, that Lagos was a place where you could get nothing free, that Nnaife's job was not very secure, that she had to subsidize their living with her meagre profits.

She could imagine this creature hearing all about it and laughing to herself, saying, "If it is so bad, why is she there? Does she not want me to come?" Yes, it was true, Nnu Ego had not wanted her to come. What else did Nnaife want? She had borne him two sons, and after she had nursed Adim there would be nothing to hold her back from having as many children as they wanted. She knew this kind of woman: an ambitious woman who was already thinking that now she was in Lagos she would eat fried food.

Nnu Ego knew that her father could not help her. He would say to her, "Listen, daughter, I have seven wives of my own. I married three of them, four I inherited on the deaths of relatives. Your mother was only a mistress who refused to marry me. So why do you want to stand in your husband's way? Please don't disgrace the name of the family again. What greater honour is there for a woman than to be a mother, and now you are a mother – not of daughters who will marry and go, but of good-looking healthy sons, and they are the first sons of your husband and you are his first and senior wife. Why do you wish to behave like a woman brought up in a poor household?" And all this for a husband she had not wanted in the beginning! A husband to whom she had closed her eyes when he came to her that first night, a husband who until recently had little confidence in himself, who a few months ago was heavy and round-bellied from inactivity. Now he was losing weight because of working hard in the open like other men did in Ibuza, Nnaife looked younger than his age, while she Nnu Ego was looking and feeling very old after the birth of only three children. The whole arrangement was so unjust.

She tried desperately to control her feelings, to put on a pleasant face, to be the sophisticated Ibuza wife and welcome another woman into her home; but she could not. She hated this thing called the European way; these people called Christians taught that a man must marry only one wife. Now here was Nnaife with not just two but planning to have maybe three or four in the not so distant future. Yet she knew the reply he would give her to justify his departure from monogamy. He would say: "I don't work for Dr Meers anymore. I work as a grass-cutter for the Nigerian Railway Department, and they employ many Moslems and even pagans." He had only been a good Christian so long as his livelihood with Dr Meers depended on it. It was precisely that work, when they had seen each other every day and all day, that had made her so dependent on Nnaife. She had been in Lagos now for more than seven years, and one could not change the habits of so many years in two minutes, humiliating as it was to know that this woman fresh from Ibuza was watching her closely, reading all the struggles and deliberations going on in her mind. Adaku, however, was able to disguise any disgust she felt by wearing a faint smile which neither developed into a full smile nor degenerated into a frown.

Like someone suddenly awakened from a deep sleep, Nnu Ego rushed past her and, standing by their door with the key poised, said hoarsely, "Come on in, and bring your child with you."

Adaku, tired from her long journey, bit on her lower lip so hard that it almost bled. Without saying a word, she carried the sleeping child into the dark room, then went back to the verandah to bring in her things and, as expected of her, Nnu Ego's groceries. She had prepared herself for a reluctant welcome something like this; and what alternative did she have? After mourning nine whole months for their husband, she had had enough of Ibuza, at least for a while. People had warned her that Nnu Ego would be a difficult person to live with; yet either she accepted Nnaife or spent the rest of her life struggling to make ends meet. People at home had seen her off to Lagos with all their blessing, but this daughter of Agbadi so resented her. Nnu Ego was lucky there was no Ibuza man or woman to witness this kind of un-Ibo-like conduct; many people would not have believed it. Adaku did not care, though; all she wanted was a home for her daughter and her future children. She did not want more than one home, as some women did who married outside the families of their dead husbands. No, it was worth some humiliation to have and keep one's children together in the same family. For her own children's sake she was going to ignore this jealous cat. Who knows, she told herself, Nnaife might even like her. She only had to wait and see.

Nnaife was delighted at his good fortune. Beaming like a child presented with a new toy, he showed Adaku, as his new wife, round the yard. He pointed out this and that to her, and he bought some palm wine to toast her safe arrival. He took her daughter as his, and vowed to his dead brother that he would look after his family as his own. He called Oshia and introduced the little girl Dumbi to him as his sister. Oshia, who suspected that his mother did not like this new sister and her mother, asked:

"When will they go back to where they came from, Father?"

Nnaife reprimanded him, calling him a selfish boy and saying that if he was not careful he would grow into a selfish man whom no one would help when he was in difficulty. Nnaife put the fear of the Devil into Oshia by telling him a story which he said happened on the ship, of a white man who died alone, because he was minding his own business.

Nnu Ego, who was busy dishing out the soup while this tirade was going on, knew that half the story was not true. She felt that Nnaife was being ridiculous and, rather like a little boy himself, was trying to show off his worldly knowledge to his new wife. Nnu Ego was the more annoyed because the latter was making such encouraging sounds, as if Nnaife was recounting a successful trip to the moon.

"For God's sake, Nnaife, was there anything that did not happen on that ship you sailed in so long ago?" She expected the others to laugh, but her son Oshia was so taken in by his father's stories that he strongly disapproved of his mother's interruption and protested indignantly:

"But it is true, Mother!"

"Some strange things do happen on those ships that sail on the big seas, and the men do see peculiar sights. This is well known even in Ibuza," Adaku put in, uninvited.

Nnu Ego stopped in her movements. She knew that if she did not take care she would place herself in a challenging position, in which she and Adaku would be fighting for Nnaife's favour. Strange how in less than five hours Nnaife had become a rare commodity. She ignored Adaku's remark as unanswerable but snapped at her son:

"What type of a son are you, replying to your own mother like that? A good son should respect his mother always; in a place like this, sons belong to both parents, not just the father!"

Nnaife simply laughed and told Oshia not to talk like that to his mother again, adding with a touch of irony, "Sons are very often mother's sons."

Again in came that cool, low voice, which Nnu Ego had been trying all day to accept as part of their life, at the same time as telling herself that the owner of the voice did not belong, or that, if she did, her belonging was only going to be a temporary affair – but Adaku, the owner of that disturbing voice, seemed determined to belong, right from the first:

"In Ibuza sons help their father more than they ever help their mother. A mother's joy is only in the name. She worries over them, looks after them when they are small; but in the actual help on the farm, the upholding of the family name, all belong to the father . . ."

Adaku's explanation was cut short by Nnu Ego who brought in the steaming soup she had been dishing out behind the curtain. She sniffed with derision and said as she placed a bowl on Nnaife's table: "Why don't you tell your brother's wife that we are in Lagos, not in Ibuza, and that you have no farm for Oshia in the railway compound where you cut grass?"

They ate their food in silence, Nnu Ego, Adaku and the two children Oshia and Dumbi eating from the same bowl of pounded yam and soup. Nnu Ego's mind was not on the food and she was acting mechanically. She was afraid that her hold on Nnaife's household was in question. She took every opportunity to remind herself that she was the mother of the sons of the family. Even when it came to sharing the piece of meat for the two children, one of the duties of the woman of the house, she pointed out to Dumbi that she must respect Oshia, as he was the heir and the future owner of the family. Their few possessions – the four-poster iron bed which Nnaife had bought from his journey to Fernando Po and the large wall mirrors – were things of immense value to Nnu Ego, and if her son never grew up to be a farmer, she wanted to make sure that whatever there was should be his. She knew again that she was being ridiculous because no one challenged her; it was a known fact. However, she felt compelled to state the obvious as a way of relieving her inner turmoil.

After eating, Nnaife looked at her reflectively and said: "The food is very nice; thank you, my senior wife and mother of my sons."

It was Nnu Ego's turn to be surprised. Her husband had never thanked her for her cooking before, to say nothing of reminding her of being the mother of his two boys. What was happening to them all?

Nnaife was still studying her from his chair; the other members of the family were eating sitting on the floor.

"You see, my brother's death must bring changes to us all. I am now the head, and you are the head's wife. And as with all head wives in Ibuza, there are things it would be derogatory for you to talk about or even notice, otherwise you will encourage people to snigger and cause rumours to fly about you. No one wanted my brother's death. And do you think, knowing him as you did, that he was the sort of man to let you and Oshia beg if anything had happened to me?"

Nnu Ego could think of nothing apposite to say. She was a trifle disconcerted. To try and be philosophical like Nnaife might tempt her to ascribe profundity to the ordinary. None the less, she was intrinsically grateful to him for making what must have been a tremendous effort.

She was determined to attack with patience what she knew was going to be a great test to her. She was not only the mother of her boys, but the spiritual and the natural mother of this household, so she must start acting like one. It took her a while to realize that she was stacking the plates used for their evening meal and taking them out in the kitchen to wash.

"I should be doing that," Adaku cooed behind her.

Nnu Ego controlled her breath and held tight her shaking hands. Then she spoke in a voice that even surprised her: "But, daughter, you need to know your husband. You go to him, I'm sure he has many tales to tell you."

Adaku laughed, the first real laughter she had let herself indulge in since arriving that morning. It was a very eloquent sound, telling Nnu Ego that they were going to be sisters in this business of sharing a husband. She went into the kitchen still laughing as Mama Abby came in.

"Your new wife is a nice woman. Laughing with so much confidence and happiness on the day of her arrival."

"A happy senior wife makes a happy household," Nnu Ego snapped. She suspected that her unhappiness at Adaku's presence was by now common knowledge and she was not going to encourage it further. After all, Mama Abby had never had to live as a senior wife before, to say nothing of welcoming a younger wife into her family. To prevent her saying anything further, Nnu Ego added: "I must go and see to our guests."

She hurried in and, to take her mind off herself, busied

herself entertaining people who came throughout the evening to see the new wife. Nnu Ego fought back tears as she prepared her own bed for Nnaife and Adaku. It was a good thing she was determined to play the role of the mature senior wife; she was not going to give herself any heartache when the time came for Adaku to sleep on that bed. She must stuff her ears with cloth and make sure she also stuffed her nipple into the mouth of her young son Adim, when they all lay down to sleep.

Far before the last guest left, Nnaife was already telling Oshia to go to bed because it was getting late.

"But we usually stay up longer than this, Father."

"Don't argue with your father. Go and spread your mat and sleep; you too, our new daughter Dumbi."

The neighbours who had come to welcome the new wife took the hint and left. Did Nnaife have to make himself so obvious? Nnu Ego asked herself. One would have thought Adaku would be going away after tonight.

"Try to sleep, too, senior wife," he said to her, and now Nnu Ego was sure he was laughing at her. He could hardly wait for her to settle down before he pulled Adaku into their only bed.

It was a good thing she had prepared herself, because Adaku turned out to be one of those shameless modern women whom Nnu Ego did not like. What did she think she was doing? Did she think Nnaife was her lover and not her husband, to show her enjoyment so? She tried to block her ears, yet could still hear Adaku's exaggerated carrying on. Nnu Ego tossed in agony and anger all night, going through in her imagination what was taking place in the curtained bed. Not that she had to do much imagining, because even when she tried to ignore what was going on, Adaku would not let her. She giggled, she squeaked, she cried and she laughed in turn, until Nnu Ego was quite convinced that it was all for her benefit. At one point Nnu Ego sat bolt upright looking at the shadows of Nnaife and

Adaku. No, she did not have to imagine what was going on; Adaku made sure she knew.

When Nnu Ego could stand it no longer, she shouted at Oshia who surprisingly was sleeping through it all: "Oshia, stop snoring!"

There was silence from the bed, and then a burst of laughter. Nnu Ego could have bitten her tongue off; what hurt her most was hearing Nnaife remark:

"My senior wife cannot go to sleep. You must learn to accept your pleasures quietly, my new wife Adaku. Your senior wife is like a white lady: she does not want noise."

Nnu Ego bit her teeth into her baby's night clothes to prevent herself from screaming.

melissa murray

on the wall

Hand in hand Mary and Maeve Seagrove walked down the steps to the basement flat at 28 Hall Road. The leaves of the dark hedge were filmed in dust, a soapy dust that had burst unevenly all down the passageway. Water gushed hot and loud from the drainpipe to the open drain.

"Great," said Mary and kicked the door. "Another bloody palace."

"Let's go in," said Maeve. "Let's see first."

"What do you need to see? Have you no imagination? We'd be better off sleeping on the Embankment, or under the Westway. Jesus Christ, can you smell that drain?" She put the key in the lock and gave it a vicious wringing turn.

The air that greeted them was musty and damp. There was furniture everywhere, a herd of wooden and woebegone creatures who'd lumbered into the flat and had died there blocking all the windows.

"The windows are very dirty," said Maeve.

"And what about these curtains?" asked Mary, holding a handful of material. "Tell me honestly, what colour do you think these curtains are?"

"Purple," said Maeve. "Let's explore properly."

They wandered separately from room to room, calling out comments to one another. Finally they sat down at either end of a draped sofa in the living-room. Mary rolled a cigarette and lit it, the signal for serious conversation.

"You first," said Mary.

"Well, there is a bit of a garden, sort of, and a shed."

"A convenient place for every cat in the country to come and piss in. Great."

"The rooms are a good size."

"Good for what? A good size for what?"

"I don't know. Parties I suppose."

"You don't like parties."

"You do," said Maeve.

Mary got up and began moving restlessly round the room. "Somebody's died in here, I bet you. You can feel it. Some poor old lady. Of bloody hypothermia." She shivered.

"We could paint it. We could paint it with lots of bright colours. It wouldn't look the same."

"Anything to get out of that squat, eh?" said Mary kindly.

"They don't like me."

"Ah now."

"You know they don't."

Mary bent down and kissed her on the forehead. "It's not personal, you know."

Maeve shrugged and looked away. "Maybe it'd look better if we took off these filthy old dust sheets." Cautiously she lifted the corner of one that covered a colossal armchair, then dropped the sheet back. "I have never seen such an ugly object in my life," she said triumphantly.

Down the road at The Winchester their prospective landlord was breaking the filter off a Silk Cut cigarette. If he noticed them coming in, he gave no sign. Mary sat down sideways in the chair, she always used her profile when nervous.

"It's a kip," she began.

The man pursed his lips thoughtfully.

"And you're asking too much." There was a clatter and the key with its cardboard ticket lay between them.

"It's your choice," he said agreeably, not picking up the key.

Maeve was looking at the bronze, brown and clear liquids that dazzled in bottles behind the bar. She loved the way the glass pushed up the silver nozzle and made the liquid pour. The barman caught her eye in the mirror and winked at her. She looked away.

"You must think I'm drunk or daft," snorted Mary.

The landlord was rolling his cigarette clockwise, very gently between his forefinger and thumb. His fingers were the same colour as his signet ring. "As I said, it's entirely up to you Mrs . . ." He hesitated the barest moment.

"I'm not married."

Maeve watched the man's other hand lift up from the table and tug at the long lobe of an ear. He was smiling.

"It does need a lick of paint," he admitted, and finally lit his cigarette. "I tell you what, my dear, how would it be if I let you off a week's rent, no let's make it two. Two weeks rent-free."

"Month," said Maeve.

"Two weeks," said their landlord calmly. "You'll both have a drink with me I hope, to settle the business."

"I'll want a proper rent book."

"Ask and you shall receive. Gin and tonic do you, and an orange juice for the little lady?"

"I'll have a Pepsi Cola," said Maeve, "and my mother drinks whisky."

Clearing out their things from the squat was a slow resentful procedure. Steve's new girlfriend trailed after to make sure they didn't accidentally walk off with anything that wasn't theirs. Maeve sat on the stairs, listening to the arguments, the most bitter over a red mixing bowl, Mary claiming it was definitely hers, the girlfriend that it was Steve's. Maeve could have told them it really belonged to Janice. She didn't because she knew it would do no good.

"We should tell Grandma we moved," said Maeve.

"Damn right we should."

"We should," insisted Maeve.

"And we'll have to fix up a nice school for you, of course," Mary said in her far-away voice. "I'll bet there are lots of really nice schools just round the corner."

Maeve said nothing, there was a limit to pushing Mary. She wouldn't mention Grandma again.

"What in the name of God will we do with all this junk?" Mary looked despairingly on the massed ranks of oak and mahogany. She paused. "We'll have to drag whatever we can into the garden and set fire to it there."

"Won't it kill the grass?"

Streams of dust rose from the discarded sheets, flakes of newspaper scattered over the undistinguished carpet. Chairs with burst bottoms, cracked lampshades, gritty mats and a mouse-eaten mattress were the first things to go. Slowly they walked out with a solemn old chest of drawers, a table, a box of books, until the pile was halfway between the height of Mary and Maeve.

"Have a last check round," Mary called as Maeve ran back into the flat.

In the shed Mary found a rusty can half-filled with something that smelt like petrol. She splashed it all over the heap, pouring it in great satisfying glugs into the heart of the mattress. "It's going to burn, Christ, it's going to burn," she hummed excitedly. "Come on Maeve, where are you?"

"I'm here," said a clear voice.

"You can't be here because I'm here and I can't see you at all."

"Don't be silly, I'm in the lounge."

"The lounge, the lounge," sighed Mary. "Now where would an innocent child pick up an expression like lounge?"

Maeve was flushed with the effort of trying to tug something from behind the sofa. Her nose wrinkled up at the smell on Mary's hands. "It's trapped," she said.

"What is it?" said Mary, and untangled a carved corner from the material at the back of the sofa. "A picture, is it?"

It wasn't a picture, it was a mottled and ugly-looking mirror set squarely in an over-ornamented piece of walnut. Mary wiped it with the sleeve of her work shirt but only a dingy sheen broke over the glass surface and their faces were poorly reflected in the discoloured depths. A set of hooks had been screwed in the bottom of the frame.

"What are these for, I wonder?" asked Mary. "For hats or for hanging mice?"

"I don't know."

"We'll have to get a cat, you know." Mary leant the mirror against the body of the sofa. "It's got more freckles than both of us put together. Okay, I'll lift it out and we can start the bonfire."

"Don't let's," pleaded Maeve. "Don't let's burn it."

"It's not bad luck to burn mirrors, only to break them."

"Look." Maeve pointed out a half-clean patch on the wallpaper in front of them. "That's where it comes from. Besides, there isn't any other mirror anywhere, I've looked."

"It'll be too high up for you."

"I'll stand on the sofa then."

Maeve took Mary's hand and they went out into the garden.

The fire flashed noisily into life the moment Mary set a match to it. The flames seemed higher than the house and the heat haze made the sky pucker and wilt. It was too large a fire for such a small place, smoke choked them and Maeve was very nearly frightened. It was difficult to see anything, even each other, just glimpses between the fume of yellow smoke and the colourless twists of flame. But when the fire burnt back eventually, half the heap of rubbish was still there, thoroughly changed and blackened. It hadn't been so powerful after all. Mary kicked a lump of wood and a weary puff of grey dust and smoke rose up.

"We'd better go to the Soc, then," she said. "Before it closes. Come on and wash your face."

In the waiting-room they shifted slowly from chair to chair. The first time Maeve had played musical chairs was at a party, she disliked parties and she disliked this place. There were newspapers here and there, limp from use and with all the crosswords completed. A small child in a red furry all-in-one suit counted cigarette butts under his mother's chair. His nose was running, there was a thin crust of matter on his upper lip.

"Seagrove cubicle seventeen," came an exhausted voice through the microphone.

The woman behind the counter was thirty years old, her face was brown and divided up inch by inch by the green wire embedded in the glass. Mary was talking.

"It's a change of address, that's all, no change in circumstances. I haven't married, had more kids, got a job."

"I'd be grateful if you could just fill in the forms, that's all I want you to do," said the woman. She was wearing a pink sari and a pink cardigan. Maeve couldn't decide which pink was the wrong pink but one of them was.

"I'm telling you now," said Mary, ignoring the last remark, "none of your bloody delaying tactics – I want my money and I want it by Thursday."

"Your address is secure? There's no one sharing with you?" The woman sounded tired and polite.

"Why don't you send someone round to check," sneered Mary.

"You will get a visitor in due course." The woman blinked very slowly. Maeve copied her and saw the whole world crushed into one black line. She doesn't like Mary, Maeve realized. "And you will have your giro on your doormat on Thursday."

The giro was there on Thursday but not on the doormat. They hadn't a doormat. Some of the money went on food, some on paint. On the way back from the supermarket Mary phoned Sally and told her to come round that afternoon to begin painting. They both agreed that Sally was very trying but she was also very obliging.

"We won't bother stripping the walls," Mary began when they were all assembled. "We'll just slap the paint up as it is."

"Did I tell you what Mark and I did last week," Sally said, her eyes wide open.

"I'll go and play in the garden," said Maeve, and went out.

She walked round the unburnt bonfire and over to the shed. The heat had raised some very interesting blisters on the door, they were like scabs or skinny milk. Maeve ran her finger, then her tongue along one of them. She liked them for the same reason she liked cracked mud and dead motorcars.

"Hello," she whispered to the door.

Steadily she chipped and picked little green half-moons of paint off the wood. It would take time to free this door, perhaps months. She would clear a small square every day, saving the hinges until last. The wood underneath was splintery and too wet to be brown or any other colour. It always delighted her to watch something change, to be the one to make it change. When she'd finished maybe the door wouldn't open into the shed at all. She longed always to find the opening, the passageway into that other world. She was thinking this and balancing a wrinkled strip of paint on the back of her hand, not allowing the wind to blow it away.

"Look at your runners," said Mary when she came in. Maeve looked at them. "Take the bloody things off. Sally's made us a nice vegetable stew." Sally popped her head round the kitchen door, still smiling. "So eat it."

"I like your cooking best," said Maeve loyally.

"Creep," said Mary, and Maeve blushed.

Sally came in carrying two slopping bowls of stew, one for Maeve at the table and one she left on a chair near where Mary was lying stretched out on the sofa, flicking an extinct cigarette against the side of an ashtray.

"Well, what do you think of the wall Mary painted?" asked Sally, bringing in her own bowl.

"She thinks it's bloody marvellous, don't you?" said Mary, rotating her left foot, then her right foot, ignoring the stew. "What a life, what a total . . ."

"Don't," said Sally.

Maeve was moving the uncooked carrots in a neat ring round the rim of her bowl, five slices so far. The beans were hard as well. "I'm going out tonight," said Mary, "I'm going out and getting totally legless. Okay?"

In the bathroom Mary sat on the side of the bath watching Maeve brush her teeth. "You're too young to be left without a babysitter. Supposing you wake up and you're frightened. Do you remember where The Winchester is even?"

Maeve inclined her head, her mouth full of foaming spittle.

Mary stroked her hair. "You look tired, you'll sleep well. It'll be weeks before this dump is liveable in."

"I hoovered your bedroom and mine, you know," said Maeve. "Twice."

"Mother's little helper," said Mary and grimaced, then laughed.

The bedroom was small and quiet. The crack of light from the doorway fanned out over the floor. She could see flying bits of grey in the high corners. They moved, just a little. Mary and Sally were in the corridor, one voice quick and impatient, the other smudged.

"Goodnight," they called out and the front door slammed behind them.

She lay without breathing to the count of fifty but nobody came back. To be on the safe side she recounted all the numbers before deciding it was all right to slide out and explore. The flat was very cold so she put on the Mickey Mouse slippers that Mary had bought her for Christmas.

The light switch in the hall was hidden behind a branching pole of clothes but Maeve found it and turned the light out.

Immediately the lino in the hallway was darker and longer, it even looked wet. In the lounge the new wall glowed white and smelt of paraffin. It was pleasant to stick and unstick her fingers on that fresh surface. She was in a box of shadows that flickered with the branches of outside trees and the bars across the windows. The light here didn't come from the sun or from a switch, it was a natural quality that all objects left in peace radiated. It was everywhere, it was indiscriminate and even her slippers, if she had glanced at them, would have seemed, would have been, transformed.

She glided round the room, touching old satin and hardwood, everything was colder than cold. She danced a little and sang under her breath to show that she was here and ready. Now she must do something, she must find some way to push herself past the last bit of familiarity and over the bearable edge. That was the hardest thing and only rarely had she approached the brink of that moment when the whole world changed. She lifted her arms at angles from her body and fixed one foot to the floor while the other pushed against the carpet. She began to whirl. Hair spun round her, nonsense syllables spilled breathlessly out of her mouth, and still she went faster. The windows went by so quick they were disappearing and faster still she beat her foot against the floor. It was a race now but the sickness was winning, coming up to her throat, and soon she could not contain it. Then she was lying in the lap of the sofa, dizzy, panting like a dog for air. She had failed, she felt hot and stiff with shame and the room wore a sarcastic expression on its face. She ran back to bed.

Next morning Mary asked, "How am I supposed to eat

toast without butter or margarine or something to spread?" She stabbed the empty tub with her knife.

"I could go to the shops," said Maeve from the bathroom.

"No point unless you can shoplift," replied Mary. "I should have got some yesterday while we still had money." She paused. "I could teach you to lift stuff, I suppose, but you're bound to get caught. You've that sort of face. Like mine. They'd put you in care and call me an unfit mother. I'm not an unfit mother, just unfit. Isn't that right?"

Maeve came into the living-room. "Are we broke so soon?"

"Have some tea," advised Mary, "and I saved you a banana."

Maeve had sat down in her chair before she noticed anything unusual. Quickly she hid her nose under the rim of her mug and, so disguised, could stare without seeming to at the carpet. What was there? Long, semi-shining lines, not silver but possessing last night's midnight uncoloured light. It could be a sign, it could be a message traced out for her alone to see.

"What do you want to do today?" asked Mary, "because I'm not doing any more bloody housework."

"I don't mind."

Mary got up, teapot in hand, and walked over to the kitchen. It was clear that whatever was on the carpet was invisible to Mary. Her feet made no impression on it. Maeve's lungs hardened with all the air that was in them but she knew better than to shout with excitement. Here was a secret she must not share.

In the afternoon Maeve cleaned the bathroom while Mary worked on the cooker. It helped Mary if Maeve did things, it encouraged her. It was important to get the place clean and comfortable because Mary, who was restless, might want to stay then. Maeve watched the water swirl round and round the plughole for as long as the tap was turned on. In the centre was a hole the size of the round O her finger and thumb made when joined together.

Just as she was crossing the threshold of the living-room, her cleaner and cloth in hand, she caught sight of the mirror. Then, immediately, she knew the place where her creatures hid during the daylight hours. What else possessed that exact shade of translucence when not covered and camouflaged with a mirage of reflections? It was a disguise so magical, so variable that no hint was given of what lay hidden inside. Almost without thinking she climbed up the sofa arm to stare down into its depths. If she was quick maybe she would see the effervescent astonishing ... but Maeve was only looking at Maeve. She dared the reflection to blink before she did.

Mary laughed. "Look how you've grown, you're taller than me." She turned Maeve's hands between her own and blew on them with her warm breath. "Christ, you're cold. This flat's an icebox."

"How's the cooker?" asked Maeve. "Did you get it clean?"

"I'm not cut out to be a housewife." Mary moved over to the table and her tobacco pouch. "You can't really like this place, you know."

"I love it," said Maeve.

"Why?" asked Mary. "Wouldn't you rather be at Grandma's with all that lovely central heating, lovely dinners and lovely – "

"No."

That night and the next Maeve slept on and on through dreams until daylight and woke up furious with herself for having missed them in the night. In the bathroom her gums bled and she could see that her hair was greasy. She was tired now and sitting on the sofa she stared almost listlessly at the long wavering silver lines on the carpet.

"Guess what's for breakfast," called out Mary. "It's pancakes, pancakes and more pancakes. With maple syrup and cream."

"Great."

Mary entered, a plate in either hand, she was happy. "We got another giro today." She blew a kiss in the direction of Notting Hill DHSS.

"But – "

"That was only an emergency payment, but this is our real one. Have you ever known them that quick? Isn't it great? Eat this while it's hot."

That afternoon Mary went up to the market but Maeve said she didn't want to go. First she went out to the shed and picked another few square inches of paint from the shed door, but that was too easy. The burnt bed springs she had snapped before, and nothing else was interesting. In the end she went to the sofa and climbed up. There was a kind of excitement in her stomach but the crossing and uncrossing of her eyes produced no effect. Mary would certainly go out this evening and there was more chance of them appearing if she was alone in the flat.

At ten o'clock she was tucked up and lying there drifting in and out of sleep like a ship at anchor. Then gradually out of the creaking quiet of the flat a sound of the soft splashing and lapping of liquids began to come clear. It was only after a while that she realized she was hearing the sound of them sliding through the skin of the mirror and onto the floor next door. Each individual arrived with a curious musical echo, more audible than anything ordinary could be. Her skin began to tingle and her fingers to drum in rhythm with the sound. It wasn't the weight of the blankets or the warmth of the bed that held her there but a sudden sense of how different they might be. For the first time she was afraid. Perhaps these creatures didn't like strangers, and they might find her very strange indeed. Violently she pressed one ear against the pillow and wished they lived in another house.

The week began to go past. On Friday the landlord called round for his rent and offered to take Mary down for a drink in The Winchester if she fancied. She said she wasn't in the mood and nobody sat down during his visit. A few of Mary's friends had found out where she was living and began to call round.

There'd be parties soon, all-night affairs and people would sleep in the living-room if they were too tired to go home. That would keep the beautiful creatures shut away behind the mirror. Maeve wasn't sure whether to be glad or sorry about that.

"You'll have to go to school soon," said Mary.

"I don't want to."

"We all have to do things we don't want to do. I'll get into trouble if you don't."

"Why?"

"Don't be stupid, Maeve." Mary picked up a book that someone had left behind and yawned just the way she did when Sally bored her. "You know the score."

"You don't. Why should I, if you don't."

Mary smiled and began reading her book as though everything had been agreed and settled. There was nothing Maeve knew to say or to do, she sat and tapped her foot against the table leg. She thought of going to her room, or going to the shed door to pick at the paint but somehow couldn't leave the room. There was nothing on the mirror but a blank expanse of whitened wallpaper.

The doorbell rang. Mary threw the book across the room and got up. "Who in hell is that?" she asked and went to answer it.

The book had landed on an armchair. Maeve picked it up to pretend that she was absorbed in reading.

"Well," came Mary's exclaiming voice through the doorway, "well, will you guess who it is?"

A tall man with a packed brown briefcase stood in the doorway, his sheepskin jacket swinging open. Clearly he was not a friend, from the way he looked round the room and back to Maeve.

"It's Mr Baker from the DHSS. Give the gentleman a big smile, won't you?"

Maeve gave him a look, not hostile, as he wasn't a school inspector. Without wasting any time he sat down and surreptitiously patted his nose with his gloves before taking them off. "Let's keep this brief, shall we?"

"Don't mind us, we've nothing else to do." Mary moved all the things that were on the table and crammed them down the end furthest away from Mr Baker. He took out a file without comment.

"So, Mrs Seagrove – "

"I'm not married," said Mary triumphantly.

"I'm sorry."

"I'm not."

"No I meant . . ." he regained control, "and this I take it is your daughter?"

"I'm Maeve."

"She's home from school with a cold," announced Mary. Maeve sniffed. "Go and get a handkerchief."

She got two squares of toilet tissue and waited until she was back in the room before blowing her nose. It was obvious that Mr Baker wanted to blow his nose as well but was not in a position to ask for a tissue. Every now and again he would lift his glove as if absently and touch the tip of his nose with it.

"So you live alone then, you live alone apart from Maeve here." He tapped the biro against the file.

"Why don't you search the place?" suggested Mary.

"I'd be obliged if you could just answer me in a civil fashion."

Maeve could see that the muscles on his face were flat and tight already.

"And I'd appreciate being treated in one," said Mary.

"There are regulations concerning cohabiting." Mary

raised an eyebrow in mock surprise. He continued, "As I am sure you are aware. As I hope you are also aware, it is an offence to give false information when submitting a claim to the Department."

"There's just us living here."

"Thank you." He cleared his neck from his collar and wrote something down.

"Would you like a cup of tea?" asked Mary.

"No, thank you."

"You don't mind if I smoke, do you?" said Mary anxiously. "They're only very small cigarettes." She showed him one rolled up like a matchstick.

"I don't myself," he said, and made a gesture permitting her to light up.

She did and suddenly smiled at him. "Christ, I bet that coat's lovely and warm."

"It's very shabby, I'm afraid, now if we could – "

"But warm, doesn't it look warm, Maeve? Come here, Maeve." Mary lifted one of Maeve's hands and waved it at Mr Baker. "Her hands are like blocks of ice. The sheets she sleeps in are damp with cold. Is it any wonder she has bronchitis? The old lady who lived here before us died of bloody hypothermia, did you know that?"

"There is, calculated in your overall entitlement, a specific allowance for both heat and light."

"It's not enough."

"You can make a special needs application but frankly – "

"There's fungus in the kitchen. One wall is completely covered in it. Come and see for yourself. Isn't there any regulations about cohabiting with fungus?" High on adrenalin, Mary gripped the table and dared Mr Baker to avert his gaze. He continued to regard her with a look of settled weariness.

"I'm sure you realize Ms Seagrove – " he didn't seem to mind when she interrupted him again.

"And what about this?" She was on her feet and pointing down. "What do you suppose that is on the carpet?"

There was total silence, absolute zero in the room. Maeve's mouth was dry and in her chest was a thumping like someone methodically beating down a door. She kept her eyes fixed on the round bumps of her knees but she could see and feel Mary rushing across the room and over to the sofa.

"Look," commanded Mary. Lockjawed Mr Baker and mesmerized Maeve in synchronization turned their heads and saw Mary straining with all of her strength to pull the sofa onto its back.

Its stubby little legs were helplessly exposed, but there was something else to see. There, underneath, clinging to the open-weave canvas Maeve saw curled-up scraps of pinkish grey flesh. They were soft like tongues, curled like thumbs, and all of them pulsed, pulsed to some slow nearly extinct rhythm.

The adults were talking. "Well – ?"

"As I've said – "

"As you've said."

"You don't appreciate – "

"Appreciate what? Appreciate having slugs in my living-room?"

Maeve didn't move, she was standing still but not too near them, her eyes fixed and her lips loosely working. She watched the blunt-branched movement of their heads and knew to an exactitude how cool and sticky they would be to the touch. She would not touch them. She knew of what kind and quality they were. Who knew how many more were hidden away in the open hole of the mirror above their heads?

The man had disappeared, there was only Mary in the room, silent at first, but then talking, exulted, reliving her repartee. Lack of success always enlivened her. She was recalling other caustic remarks and cunning stories of the past that had nevertheless led nowhere. She was even trying to turn the sofa back on its right side, but without the fury she lacked the strength. She was cursing now.

"Why don't you help me? What are you staring at? Give us a hand. What are you staring at?" Mary shouted.

"Nothing," said Maeve.

sylvia brownrigg
....
leaving home

I *Wine Lake: New Hampshire*

Then there was the day of the picnic.

We had packed herbs and cheeses, crusty French bread, and probably a little pâté for my mother, since her tongue has a taste for liver and the other inward organs. To fend off the salt, there were oranges; wrapped in a towel, cool Perrier. Just one knife, so we'd have to share, but luckily we'd brought separate novels. The sky was a bruised yellow, suffering the dark zigzags of a few planes and gulls, but the air was hot and dry. It wasn't the weather for mosquitoes.

What she read my mother would pass on to me, though it took me years to read it. What I read she would manage to pick up, some time when I was off walking or climbing, or talking to the friends I made while we were out. By the time I came back her finger would be a chapter into it, her eyes eating up my story. "It looks interesting," she'd say, if I rebuked her with my look. "Can I read it when you're done?"

It was an early afternoon there by the lake, and our two fleshes, more exposed than usual, stared at each other like the drawn faces of boxers, sweating under the nerve of the lights, taut and twitching hotly. We sat on separate colourful towels and pretended not to notice that each of us was secretly sizing up the other on her crucial points: body weight, agility, confidence in the eyes. To break the rhythm we were building my mother raised herself to standing. Her feet effectively blocked out two of the brightest fruits on her towel, the cherry and I think the pineapple.

"You should have some pâté," she offered kindly. "It's delicious." She inhaled deep, taking in the sound of the idle beach chatter, the oily smell of a distant barbecue, and the hard sand that tickled the tiny hairs of her nose, causing her to shake her head a few times like a baffled dog. "I'm going into the lake," she told me. "For a swim."

While she was gone I breathed more slowly and ate the oranges. I wasn't hungry, but I hungered for sensation: the savory touch of the juice on my chin, the tart sweetness of the pulp on my tongue. I watched the spiral of the peel fall away from my fingers, and tore the small globes into neat half-moons. Some of them I buried in the sand with my toes so my mother wouldn't see the waste.

When I looked up I saw her face, bobbing in the little sea of red. The wine was still today and looked ripe for swimming, but no boats were out in it, or children. The swimmers all seemed to be women, like my mother, who had left their daughters out in the sun to air. As for the daughters, we lay in separate strips on the yellow sand, not talking to each other just now, each lapping up our independence. The good women had left us to our contemplations.

My mother waved to me as I watched her, with the big enthusiasm of her brighter moments. Even from where I sat I could see that her eyes were glittering.

"You should come in!" she shouted to me. "The wine is lovely!"

But I pickle easily, so I stayed out. I'm not really suited to the summer, I've always said, the heat and wine of it: inside I pickle, outside I flake. Already in the sun I was dried out like a piece of salt fish, and turning pink. But even that was better than succumbing to the soft swallow of Wine Lake, which left me dizzy, turning in circles with my weak dog-paddle, unable to make my way to shore.

"No thanks!" I shouted back, waving an orange in her direction. "But you stay out there as long as you like!" I watched with satisfaction as her head sank under the surface another time.

When I closed my eyes to erase the sun I found it easier to remember who I was and who I would be. You can't be sure at sixteen who will take you, but I nursed my will that afternoon and made a few predictions about my future. I'd be loved by many, once I started, though I wouldn't love them all in return. My long spine would shiver at their touch. Boundaries would be overstepped, and dues duly paid, but we'd go somewhere – *somewhere* – where other voices would be silenced and our passion could be raucous. Already, in the dark, I'd written blasphemies which detailed these adventures. In the light I newly drove, my appetite whetted by the smell of escape. Me and the other daughters on the beach, I thought, as I looked at them – all waiting our various turns for the first seduction. I sighed in the sun when I thought of it. I wanted my turn to happen soon.

By the time I opened my eyes again my mother was making her way back out of the lake, shaking her arms and laughing, spitting a little at the taste in her mouth. She was all hilarity at first, some great joke I'd missed while I closed my eyes. I stiffened when I saw her.

There was something odd about my mother as she waded back towards me through the shallows of the wine. Her walk was unsteady. I tried to tell whether it was just my suspicious eye that saw her crooked and unable to keep a level head, but as she grew larger and larger I knew the wobbling was real. She simply wasn't keeping balance.

"Honey?" she called to me in a quavery voice, from the edge of the lake. The laughter was suddenly gone. The sounds of the others left my ears and soon it was just her voice and my breathing that swirled the air. "Honey, can you help me? I seem to have done something to my foot."

When I stood up on my towel the blackness fell before my eyes and I teetered, myself, for one long minute. I blinked twice or three times and finally saw her again, closer to me now and clearly limping. My heart went ragged in my ribcage.

"What did you do? What happened?" We moved towards each other movie-slow, our arms outstretched. Her eyes were a little bleary, and they registered pain.

"I must have cut my foot on a piece of glass," she said faintly. "The mud is so soft there, you know, in the lake, and I felt it oozing up between my toes. It must have been in there – a piece of glass – and cut my foot."

Sure enough, a slice of her foot was candy red, brighter than the soft purple of her skin from the swim. I clasped her arms and steadied her, told her to keep her foot off the sand if she could, and waited for the wisdom of first aid to dawn on me.

"Wash it," she said to me through closed eyes. "Can you wash it, sweetie?" Most of her weight was leaning against me, as she offered up her foot for me to hold.

"With what?" I turned my head to look for a pipeline. Hundreds of yards off were the communal bathrooms, over whose cool cement ran the water from the showers. "We'll never make it up there," I said gloomily. "It'll take us all day."

My mother swayed a little towards the picnic basket. "Perrier," she said with a slight slur, though with authority. "We do have *Perrier*."

"Perrier?" We had two bottles, it was true – sheltered in the towel. Still, I was doubtful. "Do you think it will work?"

"Perrier will work. Of course. You know how pure it is."

"It may be pure," I admitted. "But what will we have to drink when the Perrier's gone?"

"Do you want to see my foot inflamed instead? Is that it?"

"No, I don't. I just wondered – "

"You want to cripple me, after all?"

Her eyes flew open to reveal the bloodshot whites, so I knew just where she'd been and how she felt about it: all the way down and back up, her look said, and it hadn't been an easy trip. She stared at me now, as if noticing me for the first time in weeks, and she wasn't the least bit pleased with what she saw. I looked a little weak, a little spent – a little guilty, I'm certain. Her eyes thinned to a glare as they landed on my breasts. They had swollen during my fantasies of before.

"You've crippled me already with your ways, you know," she said to me, with the coldness of the lake's dark bottom. Still, she had to be cautious with what she said; I was holding her foot between my palms.

"What do you mean?" I asked in a steady voice, holding firm her sole.

"You've crippled me already with your ways," she repeated, but she looked down as she said it, so I couldn't tell if she was crying over my betrayal, or over the salty, drying pain in the arch of her foot. Without pausing to ask her, I reached with my right hand for the cheerful French green bottle, and opened it. Then I tilted it down and watched it carefully, as it spilled its fuzzy white liquid over the sharp half-smile of the bloody wound.

II *Alaska (as I imagine it)*

Have you ever gutted a fish? Black eyes shocked and staring, mouth open in protest, toothless usually, and bald, like the older men waiting by the bus stop or laboring to post a letter in the blue mouth of those boxes on the street. You can pull the strings out as if you were reeling in the line, that efficiently, if you get the right beginning, if you place your fingers under the throat just so. They're clean creatures, their flesh is waiting for you. Off with their heads (or a good incision, at least, deep, in the neck), then one straight line down the belly and they're yours. You flip open the two halves and find the spine, that delicate comb, waiting for you like the pearl glistening in the prismed brine of an oyster. Take that out and, pink-white, the fish is ready for your fingers, for the boiling water, or for the foil you've carefully prepared to rest it on before you slide it under the flames.

It was that way with my mother, later. A hand on my shoulder, the words I'd never heard before or even imagined. She knew where the opening was, and pulled. I imagined myself a fish in Alaska, swimming in a trough of other dead things, shunted from salt water home to greasy black nets to the crowded, bleak compartments that made our common grave – the great dark canneries on the shore. I lost my sense of motion or balance once I was outside the waves; I felt the landscape shifting and the air becoming thick with voices. That was when I waited for the hands – at some point there are hands that reach you there, muscular hands, brown hands they've shipped in for the summer just to do this job – to find out what my fate would finally be. Would the gutting be neat and dignified, the work of a professional, or would I be left with some red mark, some blood or heart, that someone had missed by accident?

Outside there, outside the cannery, I imagined the stretches of snow there must be. White on white on white, no words or sound to worry over. Only shadow and nightfall made their mark on the snow and if you were bodiless and airborne, as I would have been afterwards, you left no footprints of your own that anyone could follow. There was the suggestion of a peace beyond words in this place of coldness and absolution, where everything was present and indistinguishable, and voices were far too small to be noticed. It was heaven or hell, this whiteness, depending on what it was you had left behind. I found it heaven.

Her words spoken, the judgment delivered, my mother took her hand from my shoulder. That one time, and always. After that there was nothing left of her touch but something dry and feathery, noxious, like the grey scale-flakes left on your hands after the gutting.

III *Mount Everybody, Arizona*

It took me a good deal of time to get to the top of the mountain. (There was a range.) I wanted to have adventures along the way.

There was a full-hipped woman who smoked like a man and spoke with a drawl, and she became my chief adventure. Together we ate up miles of country and yards of poorly cooked meat, each of us daring the other a little deeper in to an excursion that slowly took us from the flat-landed east all the way up to greatness. So far we had passed through places of moist heat and rashes, hot grits and craw-daddies, country clubs and huge saloons. We were headed west. We stayed with just-discovered relatives or gullible acquaintances, who kindly gave us a taste of their homes and forestalled any awkwardness by putting us together – one room, twin beds. This suited us. The age we were, it wasn't quite clear whether we were girls or women. In that situation we learned you're better off girls, because more doors open for you and they open more innocently.

To date we had only misadventured once. The Sleeping Giant Inn was a place we found one night in a dark corner of an unfamiliar state when we were nearly gasless on a midnight forest road. Not knowing the ghosts or mores of the region, we pulled over to the inn and pounded on the proprietor's door until he finally, begrudgingly, gave us a room. "No showers till morning. Checkout by noon."

The room smelled sour and rang tinnily with our neighbours' cries, but we set up shop on the rancid covers and soon kicked up a little fuss of our own. By the time we were sated and almost sleeping, the owls in the woods had picked up our calls, throwing them back to us as hollow recordings of our passion. It was spooky. We both had nightmares; I bled on the sheets. Not till morning did the light reveal the place we'd taken for safe harbour as a shamble of peeled paint and skinny dogs flickered by the shade of a confederate flag flying from the porch. A place where the man, white-red-faced, who'd taken our money the night before, told us to our faces the Sleeping Giant's policy: No coloured guests allowed. And no queers, either. We left him, wondering if he knew.

But here we were now, afternoon a few days later, ripe for the big one. We were at its feet at last: the western mountain everybody climbs, to reach the attraction everybody wants to see. The place we all get a postcard from, sooner or later – of a long string of mules on the narrow trail or a shot of the stomach-tightening depths of the great canyon, or of the astonishing richness of the sky canned into reproduction blue. This woman and I were making our way to the top of the spectacle, where when you look down you can see all the way into the heart of the planet.

It was hot, and the driving was slow. The car smelled of sex, sweat and cigarettes; looked like two people playing a game about escape. Books and empty cans swam around the back, clothes tumbled out of backpacks and plastic sacks. A sleeping bag uncoiled in the heat. Cherry bubble gum melted over her western romance from which she sometimes read me racy passages. The novel I was reading I'd hidden carefully beneath the cooler.

My sunglasses kept slipping down my nose as I drove. My back was tired. There was nothing to do but read bumper stickers on endless campers, the litany of so many travel prayers: One Day At A Time; God Bless this RV; Honk If You Love Jesus; I ♥ my MTV.

"We should have something on our car," my girlfriend said, sliding deeper into her wet seat and staring out at the heatwaves. "Like 'We are Everywhere', or 'So Many Women, So Little Time'."

"My car, you mean."

She reached for a cigarette. "Sorry. *Your* car. *Your* trip."

"*Our* trip." I took it from her freshly lit, and dragged. "Our trip to someplace famous overcrowded with tourists."

"Pass 'em," she advised. "And don't worry. The view will make it all worthwhile."

As if she'd been there, and knew what to expect. She didn't. Neither of us did. Neither of us even really knew why we were together, except that we had a driving hunger for each other and after eleven days cooped up in a hatchback we didn't yet hate each other's guts. This must mean something flowed between us. Besides, we enjoyed the attention of puzzled stares, the half-hostility provoked in people who didn't get it right away. "Wait – they're *both* girls!" they said, with shock and a little blood-lust. We laughed: we weren't innocent, exactly, but we weren't guilty, either, the way you get to be after a while. My girlfriend and I felt we deserved this mountain and this road, and so when she said "Pass 'em," I stepped on it, slaloming around tour buses and trailers on the skinny freeway as we made our way up to meet the sun at the top, or a head-on collision, whichever one came first. The air thinned, and our spirits flew. "We're high!" my girlfriend giggled, and we were. "What a way to get your small town problems in perspective!"

Finally we arrived.

The parking lot swarmed with people, but this didn't take away from our very private triumph as we disembarked, stretched our legs, stamped our feet in the dusty littered lot. Children were screaming and demanding bathrooms, but we could hardly hear their voices.

The two of us stepped out and over to the path to see the sight – from the parking lot it wasn't a hundred feet. What we saw shocked us. There is nothing like seeing such an opening in the earth to prove just how tall and deep people's travels can be: the air and light prove how high you've come, while the very smallness of the blue thread river proves how low it is possible to go. The canyon there delivers line by line a ragged history of earth and color, ice and fire, rock and sand: generation after generation of quakes and faults and shifts and growths. The sky, hovering and sprawling over the spectacle with pride, has never seemed bigger or wiser than it does then.

But what happened, finally, when we had this chance to smell the air and look down and up and all around us? The sky, which had been kind till then, quickly darkened, and black clouds ballooned overhead. The other people chattered and tisked and ran for cover. We didn't want to leave now, though – we had a dare on. Sure, the clouds threatened rain, but here we were at the top of the mountain, after all that effort. How could we turn back now? I took my girlfriend for a moment and kissed her lips. It was a question. The savvy woman opened her mouth a little wider and we touched tongues, once. Then she pulled away. "Let's keep going," was her answer. "I'm not afraid of any storm." We separated and continued climbing.

The rain came raucously down from the open heaven. As the path grew steeper and the sky even darker, my heart started knocking hard and loud in my ears. We were alone now in this magnificence – the others had completely scattered – and for once I think I felt exposed. If it was thunder coming, as it seemed, wouldn't we be at risk for lightning? I pulled her back so we could rest a minute on the ledges of a pair of rocks at one sharp corner of the path. I suddenly felt quite tired.

It was there that the truth crackled down to us at the end of the first long arm of lightning. The sky had grown dramatic, the noises louder – howls and growling like I had never heard. Though my girlfriend seemed oblivious, my heart kept pounding as I began to realize that the storm we'd found was something personal. It was the wrath of my mother coming down upon our heads. "It's her," I told my girlfriend nervously. "It's my Mom."

With the clouds so thick the view was shortly all but gone. Our skins were bumpy with the cold and our hair clung wetly to our heads. We held each other's slippery hands, to make sure we didn't lose each other. My girlfriend looked worried, now, and impatient. She hadn't bargained for this. She hadn't wanted it.

"She'll get over it," I shrugged apologetically, as the sky snapped and sizzled all around us. I half believed it. "It will just take some time."

"How much time?" she asked. "How long?"

But just then the thunder turned to language, and my mother was on the line directly, leaving me no doubt about what she thought. I recognized the tone at once: wine-sloppy and blunt, not holding anything back. It had been a while since I'd heard her this bad.

"I see you, there," she started in. "Of course I see you. Did you think you'd hide?"

"I'm not hiding." I tried to stay calm. "I'm out here in the open. Wide open."

"Yes, to my shame. Where people can see you, and make remarks."

I turned to my girlfriend now, but she looked away. She didn't want me to catch her eye. "Are you sure you're all right, Mom?" I stalled. "You sound a little – you know – "

"Am I all right? Am *I* all right?"

"I just wondered."

"It's you that's not right. It's *you* that's got this sickness."

My heart got wormy as her voice continued in my ear. I would have said something, but what can you say to that?

"I'll tell you what I think. I think it's foul. I can't imagine anything fouler."

"It's not – "

"And how do you suppose it is for the mother – to have a daughter be what you are? Shall I tell you? Shall I say?" This was the real point. The one she'd been working towards. "It's worse than going blind. It's worse than cancer. And it's much, *much* worse than having maybe one too many every now and then."

The rain careened down my back and shoulders, and though I still held her hand, I could hardly feel my girlfriend any more, with all the pressure of the water. My skin, gone white with shock, had started to flake off from me into the crevices of the lichened stone.

"You know what this means?" The rain was lessening; she was growing tired. The voice that had been my mother's gathered its years of instruction, its years of comfort and enthusiasm, and packed them up in a small bag to take away with it after the outburst. "I cannot think of you as my daughter any more." Goodbye, she might have added, but she didn't.

Well, my heart was gone by now; my skin was falling off in chunks. It would be a while before I would be fit for making love again. I looked over at her, my full-hipped woman, to see if she'd stay till then, till I was ready. But she stared distastefully at her nails, and wouldn't let on what she was thinking.

"My mother sometimes says things she doesn't mean," I ventured, wanting to believe it. My girlfriend was silent.

The rain rained; the air was thick with whispers and the smell of salt. I didn't mind the water so much now, since, after all, it soothed and cleansed. Like an ocean, it had the capacity to swallow grief.

I decided just to sit there, waiting until the rain slowed

down. The thunder had quieted, and eventually the view would clear. When it was over I'd collect my skin from round about me and make my soft-footed way back down the slope.

carla toney

mrs benton's dildo

It was twilight when I reached the Heath. Crickets chirrupped in the undergrowth. Bats swooped down from the tree tops, chased moths in zig-zag paths against the darkening sky. At the men's pond I could make out shadows, the glow of cigarettes like beacons in the night. I crawled into a clump of shrubs and crouched close to the ground. I took my dildo from my Harrods bag, threaded the belt around my waist, reached back for the rubber strap and snapped it under my crotch. I heard the click of a cigarette lighter, men's voices like a low hum in the dark. In the distance, the crack of breaking branches. A fern tickled my ankles. I smelled the sweetness of rotting leaves and earth.

The fantasy started three years after Julian, our youngest boy, was born. I'm not really a night person, so on evenings when Jeremy was out, I tucked Julian in under his Pooh Bear duvet and switched on his thatched-roof cottage nightlight that we bought from a Crafte Fayre in Cornwall on holiday last year. I read Laura *Clare's Secret Ambition* about a girl whose mother wants her to be an actress, when all she wants is to be a vet when she grows up. I kissed Laura good night. I checked Martin's spelling on his Industrial Revolution history project and laid out his school uniform.

I boiled a pan of milk and stirred in Ovaltine. Jeremy says if I'm not careful I'll get fat, so I only drink Ovaltine on nights when Jeremy's out.

I fished the latest Jackie Collins from its hiding place in the bottom of my drawer and curled into bed with two Scottish shortbread fingers and the mug that Laura gave me for my thirty-seventh birthday that says, "World's Greatest Mum", alone.

Up till then we'd lived quite normal lives. When Martin was five and began school, I had Laura; when Laura was five, I gave birth to Julian. Jeremy insisted that we space the children so that each child had maximum attention. Jeremy says if it wasn't for him I'd be surrounded by a menagerie of animals and children, and I expect he's right. I'd probably have had half a dozen children helter-skelter, with everything from goats and chickens in the garden to mice, guinea pigs and rabbits in the house.

Jeremy isn't averse to a little mild sexual improvisation. He was happy to oblige when I asked if I could ride him for a change. He even got excited when I asked him to mount me from the rear. Unfortunately, he reached orgasm as he entered, so it wasn't particularly satisfactory. Jeremy does try to be considerate, so after that, we went back to missionary where Jeremy could manage fifteen minutes at a stretch.

But how could I tell Jeremy I wanted to fuck him? Jeremy and I have been married eighteen years. We have three children. I'm his wife.

So how could I tell him? And more important, when? When I served his three-minute free-range egg on organic toast for breakfast? When I squeezed his morning orange juice? When I handed him his briefcase as he gave me a goodbye peck on the cheek?

"Oh, by the way, Jeremy, I'd like to fuck you with a dildo."

As Jeremy brushed his teeth with his Braun Oral B plaque

remover for two minutes before bedtime, should I have announced, "Darling, come here, I have a little surprise for you this evening"?

Should I have just snapped the waistband of his 100 per cent cotton thermal pyjamas, pinioned him to the floor and shoved it into him?

Jeremy is not the type of man who responds well to surprises. Also, he's six-foot-two and I'm only five-foot-one.

Jeremy qualified for the bar just after his twenty-second birthday. He went into practice in his father's firm, Mather, Benton and Livingston. We married, and while we didn't have a honeymoon, his father gave us a four bedroom Tudor house, situated on five acres, just outside of Guildford.

Three years after Julian was born, I began having fantasies. During the day when I did the shopping or fixed Martha, our daily, a cup of tea, when I took paper, tins and glass to the recycling depot, I was fine. Even evenings when Jeremy was in, I didn't have trouble. But the three nights a week he attended Conservative Party meetings, the fantasies returned with a vengeance. Jeremy lay, legs splayed, on the floor, murmuring over and over again, "Fuck me, Felicity. Please, Felicity, fuck me." It was quite ridiculous really, Jeremy has never used the f-word in his life, but Felicity is my name and for the first thirteen years of our marriage, before Jeremy became involved with the Conservative Party and decided to run for Guildford Council, he used to wrap his arms around me and call me his little bit of happiness.

Great Expectations was set back from the street. An iron gate barred the door. I pressed the buzzer.

"Yes?"

"Great Expectations, please," I said.

A young man, blond hair, golden tan, sat behind the counter, surrounded by rubber body suits and books. For an instant it looked like a macabre cross between a deep sea diving shop full of scuba gear and W.H. Smith's. A giant arrow pointed towards a small back room. I went down the steps. Riding crops stood in an umbrella stand. Cat o' nine tails poked out of a wooden barrel. On the wall hung hand cuffs, gags, nipple clamps and penis rings. Steel braces to lock the legs in place. Iron masks that looked like they'd been used in a medieval torture chamber. Condoms in rainbow colours lined the shelves, some with tiger's heads, some shaped like dragons, some that looked like nothing I'd ever seen on earth.

And dildos! I could hardly believe the selection. A two foot, flesh-pink double-headed number designed for lesbians. A DIY that you strapped on, that went in instead of out. And a giant phallus that looked like it belonged to an elephant, black rubber protruding from a thick black rubber belt with buckles and gold studs.

Where to hide it was the next real problem. It wouldn't do to hide it in the house. The thing was not only gigantic, but with buckles it jangled when I walked. I finally hid it in the tool shed behind the fish pond. Jeremy only ever went into the shed on warm evenings in the summer when he rolled out the barbecue, piled on lighter cubes and coals and barbecued texturized vegetable protein steaks while I prepared French bread and tossed green salad in the house.

On Friday I baked wholemeal bread and organic oat-flake biscuits for the children to snack on after school. I prepared a nut roast for the evening, all they would need to do was pop it in the microwave while I was out.

It was one thing to fantasize fucking my husband, but it was quite a different matter to walk into a gay men's pub. I hovered on the pavement outside Heaven's Gate on Earls Court Road. Men clad in leather, gold studs in their ears, rings the size of knuckle-dusters on their fingers, entered in ones and twos and threes.

I took a deep breath. Now or never. Move.

I pushed the door that said Public Bar and swaggered through. I stomped up to the bar, growled, "A pint of Guinness," and slammed down a ten pound note. I swigged my Guinness and peered around the room.

"Sift the flour and mix in the sugar before you add the melted butter and eggs."

"Do you use crushed almonds or walnuts? Orange peel or grated lemon rind?"

Half a dozen men dressed like avengers from the middle ages, were swapping biscuit recipes.

The toilet was so packed it made the Central Line during rush hour look spacious. In my black leather jacket and biker's boots, they thought I was just another leather queen. I couldn't use the urinal so found sanctuary in a cubicle. There were no hearts and flowers like in every ladies' toilet I've ever been in, no political graffiti, no "A man without a woman is like a bicycle without a fish", no initials encircled by hearts, no "Roger loves Andrew", no "Jerry loves Ken". Scratched in the paint were testicles and pricks, from miniatures to a monolith that covered the whole of one wall. "Wanna fuck?" was followed by a phone number. "For the best blow job in your life, Nigel 368–4019".

I'd rehearsed it a hundred times in the bathroom at home in the dark. I slipped a rubber over the giant black phallus, thick as rhinoceros hide. I greased the thing with KY jelly and crept out of the shrubs to troll the Heath when a shadow very nearly knocked me down.

Hair, he felt like a gorilla. Big, he was twice my size.

"Top or bottom?" he whispered.

I hissed back, "I'm top."

A cat on heat, he pressed towards me. "Sweet Jesus, you got a giant cock!"

He kept moaning and moaning and just when I thought

he was about to come I heard a whistle six inches from my ear and a searchlight went on.

"There's two in the bushes here!" A hand grabbed the back of my jacket and dragged me out from the shrubs.

"Two here!" Another voice shouted. "Jesus, there's three here! I think they're stuck!"

Police crawled over the Heath, some in plain clothes, some in uniform, some you couldn't tell from the men in the bushes. There must have been a hundred.

In the wagon, I heard one of them laugh, "This clown's got a dildo. He couldn't even get it up."

We lined up around the room. The sergeant called us one by one.

"Name?" He barked the question.

"Benton," I replied. "Mrs Jeremy Benton."

Jeremy says he's going to file for divorce first thing in the morning. "How could you ruin me like this? How could you do it? How could you? You used to be a good convent girl! Now I don't even know you!" Jeremy's face was frozen, his voice dry ice.

What could I say? How could I explain it? Jeremy was not in any mood to listen.

Stuck in this cell with four white walls and the ceiling closing in, I wonder whether I'll ever get out again.

"Cheer up, little lady," my gorilla from the Heath scratches his name, Pete, and his phone number on a scrap of paper. "You got more balls than the men I know. Looks like your husband has buggered off. My mate'll be here in a couple of hours. You want him to post your bail? You want to doss at my place tonight?"

joanna rosenthall

taking flight

She found the maggot on one of the kitchen tops. She picked a crumpled piece of paper out of the bin, smoothed it, then folded it deftly, halfway to making an aeroplane. She used the pointed end to prod the creature to see if it was alive. It was. It had segments and it seemed to expand and retract. Very slightly. It didn't move anywhere. It was like a worm but thick and short, about one centimetre and no head. At one end there was a little black knob that looked like it was defecating. A thick, dirty pinkish skin sac full of something. God knows what. She rummaged around in the bin for another piece of paper. She used one piece to push it onto the other, then balancing carefully she opened the door and threw it outside into the garden. It wasn't a caterpillar. She had never seen anything like it.

That evening she heard Sydney's footsteps outside the front door before he had put his key in the lock. She looked up from the ironing and said nothing. He loped up the hall and shuddered out of his jacket. He was so tall and thin, he had never lost that adolescent stooping and looseness. The jacket which he threw over the bannister knob missed and fell on the floor. He ignored it. He had probably noticed but he never did anything twice. As he plodded up the stairs the kitchen ceiling responded with subterranean shudders. Unconsciously Doreen looked upwards as he must have been entering the bedroom to take off his overalls. He would be putting on his khaki shorts with at least six conspicuous pockets standing off his body like pouches.

When he came into the kitchen he grunted. The noise was directed quite firmly at her.

"Good day at work?" Her voice sounded light and thin.

He grunted again. "I mended cars." As if she didn't know. There was little to say. His work was in one of the railway arches behind St Pancras station. He mended exhaust pipes. He drove the car a couple of yards onto a plinth, then he pressed a lever and loved it for a moment as it rose above his head, suspended in the air, revealing the underbelly. Then he had to get to work. The best moment was over. Usually it was straightforward, a missing bolt here, or a hole there, a section to replace. It wasn't much. The most complicated jobs never took more than a couple of hours. I look up cars' backsides, he would say at the pub, which always got a laugh.

"Did you speak to Janie's school?" He asked the question with the certainty that she would have done. He wanted confirmation. Doreen never forgot things. She always did what she said she would do. Her face went a deep red and her eyes were hot. She blinked and swallowed. A little bubble of air was stuck in her throat. For a moment she was about to do a small burp but it turned into a sickly gurgle like a choke. They had been together for twenty-seven years but she didn't want to cry.

"No," her voice was small.

"Why?" he bellowed, his bottom lip flapping. She flinched again, willing her face to return to its normal colour. She put the iron upright on the metal stand and folded her arms across herself. She stared straight ahead for a minute or two and eventually the colour dropped down, back into her neck. She felt it redistributing itself around her body.

"I found this thing on the kitchen top. It looked like a maggot only it was very big. It was like a huge maggot."

She was looking down whilst she took up the iron again and started swiping at one of his shirt collars. She should scrub them. The machine made them look clean but it never got the real dirt off.

A low dismissive noise came from the back of Sydney's throat. What could he do about it?

"Well, I wondered where it was from. It came from nowhere," her voice rose in pitch in spite of her efforts at control. Sydney raised his eyes and his mouth tightened into a curious little oval shape. He was sitting at the table waiting for his food.

"What's to eat?" the question was short and hard.

"Hamburgers," as she spoke her movements quickened as if she had suddenly realized she was in a hurry. She switched off the iron at the wall, and bent low to peer under the grill at the same time as striking a match. She didn't finish one task before she was well on her way to the next one. The sink, then back to the cooker, washing, putting away and arranging, as well as checking the food and cooking the vegetables. The table had already been set. One place. A knife, a fork and a spoon, the three lonely sides of one square.

"How do you think a thing like that got into the kitchen?" She walked over to the table with a plate packed with food. Then she returned to the sink and ran the tap to get a really cold glass of water, just as he liked it.

"God knows." He was eating. His back was bent slightly and his neck craned forward as if he was bringing his mouth down to the food rather than the other way around. His fork was upturned and he used it like a spoon, never leaving his mouth empty. He chewed and chewed.

"Food good?" she was hovering near the sink, every so often lifting a raw carrot to her mouth and crunching on it. Her hand wandered towards the switch on the wall. The iron was still plugged in. Was it worth flicking it on? She might get another shirt done before he needed pudding.

"Not bad."

She remembered then that Barbara had brought a bag of apples round from her garden. They were sitting in the corner waiting to be turned into apple pies. She picked the bag up. She took it out to the dustbin. The whole lot went because that's where that damned maggoty thing must have crawled from. Why in hell's name had she not thought of that before? She felt a leaping of excitement. Her body was straighter when she came back inside.

"Sydney," she said, her voice warm with relief, "it's almost hot out there. It's creepy. November and you still don't need a coat. No wonder the insects are thriving. There's no cold to kill them off. They're all bigger this year too. I've never seen a maggot as big as this one was."

"Yeah. I know what you mean." He chewed his food fast, and his whole chin moved like it was on a loose screw, but when they were eating together he always finished after her. She thought of the food inside his mouth moving round and round in a revolting wet lump but not much happening to it. She didn't want to watch him eat, but she sat down anyway, encouraged by his agreeing with her.

"Why didn't you ring the bloody school?" A little bit of thick white saliva was stuck in the corner of his mouth like wet glue. It stretched when his mouth opened.

"The maggots put me off. I've heard there's an overrun of rats on this estate, even though it's new. Someone at the corner was saying it's a problem all over London. They don't get killed with the poison any more. First rats, now maggots. I don't know what will be next." Her elbow was on the table with her forehead resting heavily on her hand as she spoke. Her eyes gazed with no focus at the brilliant white shiny tabletop. When she looked up the room was filled wherever she looked with square grey ghostly shapes.

"She'll end up bloody pregnant. It'll all be your fault. All you had to do was make a phone call. You had the whole day." There was a pause whilst his face was working. His forehead knotted with thoughts and anger. Then there was another burst. "Well that's that. That's her life ruined. And she's only fifteen. In a year or two . . ." he had made his point. He sat back after the exertion of speaking and feeling, and picked his teeth with an expertly folded bit of cardboard from the lid of his cigarette packet. His face was still scrunched with thoughts.

She was standing now, statuesque, holding his dinner plate raised and uncomfortably in front of her.

"Pregnant?" she said softly as if in a dream.

"Yes," he sniped. "She's just like all the rest of them. Just because she's a slow learner as they like to call it, it doesn't mean a bloody thing."

Janie. Her slim girlish body, the gentle curve of her hips which Doreen had noticed when the child was in the bath, or drying herself afterwards, the towel falling to one side. Her questions, her stories, her inner thoughts all coming out joined onto each other with no warning. A joyful but remorseless trickle that in the end had begun to drive her mad.

She moved over to the sink, pulling on the rubber gloves and washing the few dishes under the half-turned hot tap. Janie . . . Janie who had been with them all her life, had come from them, was gone. Janie was at boarding school. This autumn she had gone. Gone now. Gone. She turned off the tap and absent-mindedly pulled the tea towel from its hook and dried the one plate, the knife and fork, the grill pan and the saucepan. They were all put away, like spirits who have no place here.

He was looking for a beer in the fridge. There weren't any. He slammed the door shut and the milk bottles chinked together. She hoped they hadn't sloshed over, the thought of more wiping up made her feel sick.

"Janie's not like all the rest," it hurt her to use his words. "Can't you be more sympathetic? Everyone makes mistakes." She wanted to say, even you, but she knew that her truthfulness hurt him too much and his retaliation could last for weeks.

"Yeah, but that's the kind you ought to pay for. It's someone else's life you're talking about." He seemed to have got the idea that Janie was already pregnant. The next thing is she wouldn't be fit to be in his house . . . Doreen could already hear him saying it.

They had both of them agreed when the social worker had suggested boarding school. After the words were out Doreen had looked at him shiftily sideways and caught his eye. She had also noticed the furry cardboard orange file on the coffee table and the visitor's heavy shoes and thick tights. The social worker looked about twenty-five. Maybe she was twenty-seven. No wedding ring. She had a long face, a big nose and an impressive fashionable haircut. She had even entered the house hesitantly, aware that she might not be welcome. They could have kept Janie at home, but the inevitable had happened. Their darling girl had changed. Neither of them had wanted this unfathomable outsider to know that it didn't even need a discussion. It was the only thing they had agreed about for a very long time.

After his food she followed as he walked heavily down the passage. She knew his shape so well but couldn't stop herself scrutinizing the familiar lines. His thighs were enlarged and hard and his calves fell away to nothing, almost girlish. He slumped onto the settee, the whole length of him stretched out, his great brown boat-like woolly slippers pointing upwards hoisted onto what would have been the armrest.

"She's not pregnant. She's only sent us a letter with a sex poem in it. Kids do that kind of thing. She's not even ready for sex yet, it's all talk. She sent it to us. That's what's odd. She's always wanted us to know everything . . ." but her voice trailed into a thin monotony. Sydney was sampling each channel in turn before choosing. Even when he had chosen, every so often out of the blue he would flick the buttons in turn. He did it secretively and there were many times when she was thrown into confusion about the programme she thought she was watching.

She went back to the kitchen to finish the ironing. It was so strange the way Sydney seemed to have forgotten that all these things had happened to them. The first pregnancy was so unexpected. The child, if it had grown, would be an adult now, maybe even with children of its own. But they hadn't been married so they hadn't let it grow. A friend had lent them the money and they'd got rid of it. At the time there hadn't been much of a question which seemed strange now that she knew that babies are the most precious thing. She had felt sick though. Not just in the mornings. She had felt sick the whole time. She had cried too and wondered whether to tell her mother. Sydney had been irritated with her. That was as much of a shock as the rest of it because it had never happened before. That baby came to mind quite a bit as if some of it had got lodged in her for life. But then look at what happened after. They were punished for it. Neither of them had doubted that nor had they discussed it. There were no more babies. For thirteen years each month ended with the same disappointment. Then of course there was a baby. It was Janie. That was such a shock. Something went wrong at the birth and in the same year her mother had died. There were no more babies after that. She was sure that she owed a debt to someone and it could never be paid off.

The next morning she found two more maggots on the kitchen surface. She made a V-shape with two postcards, coaxing them into the apex. She dropped them into a bucket and threw the cards away. She poured boiling water from the kettle into the bucket on top of them. Boiling water but there was no noise or movement. They didn't respond. They didn't look alive or dead. Just the same as they had been. A streak of feeling pierced her lower abdomen at the thought that they were immune, unkillable. She eased the feeling away by telling herself that they were dead now, it was just that they didn't move much.

She put the plug in the sink and turned on the cold tap, pouring a good capful of bleach into the water. Then using the dilution she cleaned the surfaces, the cupboards inside and out, even the floor. After she had finished she wrung out the cloth, hung up the yellow gloves on the drainer and sighed a big puff of air. She took off her cardigan. Really she had not needed a vest on a day like this. The air was whispering with warmth.

She peered into the bucket. They were still there. She had half expected them to have grown legs and climbed out of the bucket, like she sometimes thought there might be snakes breeding in the London sewers, waiting in the S-bend to uncoil out of the toilet. But the maggots hadn't grown legs. They were the same size. They were like two small grey lumps. She could still see the segments across their bodies and the little black bits at the ends. It couldn't be shit because the two of them were identical. She put the bucket with the two creatures' bodies and the water outside the back door.

About an hour later she was upstairs in the bedroom sitting in front of the dressing table mirror, when she realized that the two maggots this morning had been on exactly the same spot on the kitchen surface as the maggot she had found yesterday. She didn't finish rubbing in the rouge on her cheeks. She hurried downstairs. Her heart was beating fast. They couldn't possibly have come in with the apples. There must be a nest of them somewhere in the kitchen. They were in the house, a whole seething mass of huge, pinky-grey maggots. She moved the breadbin. Nothing. She looked inside all the cupboards in the kitchen, carefully and quickly moving crockery and pans out of their homes and then back before moving on to the next one. Nothing.

Where the last cupboard met the wall there was a tiny space. She couldn't look inside it because there was no room to position her face, it was too close to the wall. They must be in there. She dragged a chair over and hitched her skirt up, buckling it over her hips. It flashed through her mind that if middle-aged women fall and break bones, they can take months, maybe even years, to mend. Was it worth it for the sake of a bloody maggot? Probably not even for a nest of bloody maggots.

The chair wasn't a great deal of help. She had to climb up onto the kitchen top. Her stockinged feet had no grip. She was holding onto a rim around the top edge of the cupboards. It would be awful if the strain pulled it away from the wall. She looked down at the floor and then round the whole kitchen. She had not seen it from this point before. Her head was touching the ceiling, so she craned her neck slightly and peered down the gap from above. She was surprised to discover only one indifferent cobweb which was misshapen and uninhabited. Nothing to be seen.

Getting down was awkward. She had to stick her bottom right out whilst her foot made tentative lunges, looking for the chair. Once down, she swivelled round, still searching. She looked at the window. The frames were new, no cracks, no little spaces. She unfurled the blind right to the bottom, stood on the chair again and stretched from her ankle to her wrist to reach and run her cloth right across the top, along the whole length of it. It was a big window. All the time she kept looking up to the ceiling as if the white expanse of unbroken plaster would reveal something. There was nothing. One thing was clear, the two lots of maggots landing up on exactly the same spot on the kitchen surface was sheer coincidence. That must be the end of it.

She unlocked the back door decisively. She looked into the bucket and grasping the handle she tipped the contents down the outside drain. She did it slowly so that the water did not splash her shoes. It was neurotic to keep them. She squeezed some washing up liquid and poured more boiling water into the bucket and again left it outside. It could sit like that for a while. Getting clean. No sense in keeping the corpses. That was the end of them. It was hard to imagine that there would be any more. Winter really must be coming on now. The whole of London would be cleansed.

She stood there looking at the two apple trees in the small patch of garden. The gardens in this stretch used to be a huge orchard and market garden. That was why whenever she did a bit of digging she would find clumps of broken glass in each spadeful. There had been a glorious Victorian greenhouse, wrought iron, very grand. Bombed during the Second World War. She was thinking of the men and women who had tended the trees, cleaned the greenhouse, collected the fruit. Now it was this clean-lined estate, all modern and cardboardy. She had never thought Sydney and her would get a place like this. Why them? Although the rent was always on time. But so must a million other people's. It was probably because of Janie. Her eyes narrowed with the thought. She hated the way people felt sorry for them and tried to make up for it. Perhaps she should get the bleach out again and go over the kitchen tops.

She had her hair done the following day. It was lucky they could fit her in without an appointment. Quite an extravagance. She didn't do it every week, although it was tempting. It made her feel clean and good.

When she got home she found two more maggots on the kitchen top. They were in the same spot as the others. She cried. Horrible panicky crying. Someone was doing this to her. They couldn't fly in. There was nowhere for them to fall from. She checked the ceiling again and again. Always bland and white. Sydney? Could he be tormenting her like this? He did seem to have turned against her so much, especially recently since Janie had gone to the school. He had agreed to send her too. She hadn't made the decision alone. If anything it was more him than her. Was it the right thing? Janie needed them so much. Of course she always had. That was one of the things which didn't change as she grew. But then that had been its own problem. She had started to be difficult, shouting at them and not doing as she was told. She had grown breasts and started periods. Everything went bad after that. Sydney had done a lot of shouting. More than was right. Doreen had a picture of herself from that time with her arms out, palms down smoothing imaginary demons out of the air in circular sweeps so that they would do no harm. Exhausting. They had both known it couldn't go on, the three of them for ever. Sydney solved it in the end. Janie had been taunting him and laughing. It was obvious to Doreen that something would happen because he had gone quiet like an underwater swimmer scooping in more breath than is natural. When it burst out it was an inhuman sound that made her leap to her feet and run to stand between them. His arm came down anyway, he had already given it the instruction. Because her head was there instead of Janie's he had reined in the violence although his fist did still punch her quite firmly on the crown of her head. Afterwards she had wanted to laugh because he had sounded like a pig breaking wind.

Sydney could be a bastard but would he plan a thing like the maggots? He would know that something like this could drive her over the edge. Especially now. It was right that Janie had gone but it did leave an awful gap.

She kept old margarine cartons at the back of the cupboard. They were stacked one inside the other. She took one out, it smelt faintly of rancid oil and tiny bits of grit and dust were stuck on the inside of it. She washed it, then used the lid to lever the creatures inside. Each one had the little black nodule at the end. They curled and recoiled as she touched them. They were so fattish and firm, but she imagined them full of awful goo, thick greedy fluid, no bones or tissue.

She put the lid on the carton and surrounded the container with an elastic band. She wound it round twice and put it on the window-sill, behind a plant. Someone might know what they were. She would ask someone.

After that she started to look around the kitchen again, re-searching every inch of wall and cupboard. There was something different about it this time. She didn't stop. She just kept on looking and looking.

A thin squeal came from her when she noticed two long thin black insect legs coming out of the base of the light fitment. There were hideous creatures living in the roof cavity! They were trying to get out. There must be so many of them multiplying. A heaving mass of . . . of what? What sort of creatures were they? They were squeezing their way out of this crack where the light was screwed onto the ceiling. It was barely visible it was so small. The shade round the light had obscured it. Her head was expanding. What could she do?

She stood for a few minutes breathing deeply. That's the thing to do when panic comes on. She walked slowly to the cupboard under the stairs and got the steps that Sydney had used. She put on an old pair of rubber gloves and rummaged round in one of the drawers for a screwdriver. There was a very small one. It looked like a child's toy. She ran upstairs to the bathroom and pulled on an old stained plastic shower cap, otherwise something might fly out and get stuck in her hair.

She allowed herself no hesitation as she climbed up the steps. Her eyes fixed on the gap. The legs were reaching then bending as if they were trying to find something, the movements very deliberate and slow. The screws were stiff. Very stiff. Perhaps she should ask Sydney to do it when he came home, but she didn't stop straining at the screw, willing it to turn. It would be better to manage it herself. He would be so reluctant and blame her.

The small cylinder of plastic which held the light in place

came loose. There were bits of dried paint stuck to it. She eased it away very slowly, wanting to scream, to lose control and run. She tried to peer over the top before it was far enough away from the ceiling to let in any light. Something large and grotesque might fling itself at her and . . . She could see. The cavity in the ceiling was jammed full of dead wasps. Bloody great wasps. She had never seen such big ones. They had all died together. No. They weren't all dead. She jerked her hand, wanting to let go of the fitment which was stemming the tide . . . She would have been showered with wasps . . . Now she looked there were quite a lot of them slowly moving their legs. They would stop, as if dead, and then move again. They had all been desperately seeking an exit. The crack was too small to let more than a spindly leg through. No chance. Translated into human terms it made her feel sick. There had been some sort of a hell hole going on in the kitchen ceiling.

She hung an opened plastic bag from her thumb and deftly lowered the fitment. Each shell hard body cracked on the bottom of the bag, until there were so many that they tumbled in soundlessly. There were a lot more up there stacked behind the opening. She would leave them. She tied a knot with the bag handles very tightly. There was a lot of trapped air in the bag. It looked like a big white balloon. She took it out to the dustbin and felt squeamish when she was replacing the light. Now that she knew what was up there she didn't want her hands so near. She was looking forward to telling Sydney. She had been so brave.

Upstairs in the bathroom she put the plug in the sink. She turned the hot tap on fast, and then ran the cold one too, but slower. She bent over carefully, so that the ends of her hair got wet first, then the rest. Using a plastic mug, she scooped beakerfuls of hot water all over her head. It was very nearly scalding. As hot as she could bear. When she'd washed and rinsed it she wrapped a towel turban-like round her head, and the whole of her scalp was tingling.

She sat on the edge of the bath for a good ten minutes. She felt dizzy. It dawned on her slowly that she'd only just had her hair done that day. What a waste. What a waste.

When Sydney got home she told him. He said, "What? You took the light fitting off without turning off at the mains? You could have bloody killed yourself." She hadn't considered that. Invading monsters had seemed more important at the time.

"We must have a wasps' nest up there," she said, "at least one. Now I know what they mean when they say London's overrun with them." Sydney shrugged.

"What's for tea?" he sounded tired.

The next day she went shopping with a lightness in her step. There was nothing left to worry about. They had a wasps' nest, that was all it was. Maybe two. The maggots must have fallen out of the light fitting. They were wasp larvae. Without a doubt. Except they were so big. Each larva much bigger than a wasp itself. But then the wasps were unusually large as well. Of course it was still worrying because it was November and they should all be dead and gone by now. There shouldn't be larvae about to hatch in early winter. But that wasn't her problem. The authorities would have to deal with that. The whole of London was being affected. Once you've done something to change the weather it might be too big a thing to change back.

She was walking fast, not even noticing the heavy shopping bag. When she got home she felt clear and light. She turned her key in the lock. The kitchen door was shut. She put the bag down. The handles were cutting into her hand where her wedding ring was. She opened the door.

Strangely enough the noise was a warm welcoming one and it took a moment for her to feel afraid. There was a low-pitched encompassing hum. It wrapped itself around her, getting inside her throat and down her back, muffling her senses. The shafts of light sent by a watery sun through the kitchen window were speckled and moving. Small shapes filled the air. The kitchen was teeming with full-bodied wasps. At her realization, the steady hum seemed to rise, deafeningly soft, they were erupting from the roof into the kitchen. They had escaped. There was a way out and they'd found it.

She dropped her key and ran. She didn't close the front door, she just ran and ran. Finally she stopped. Panting, she turned around. She had to bend over and rest her hands on her thighs for a while before she caught her breath. When she looked up again she needed to squint. Up the street, near the house, she fancied that she could see a thin stream, like smoke from a chimney, a thin stream which billowed and shook with the shock of finding fresh air. It was like a small cloud, too thin and far away to be black. More like a shadow. It quivered for a moment as if it might collapse and fall. There must have been some regrouping. She watched quite startled as it appeared to fly away with some realization of its freedom.

She turned then, facing nowhere. She was walking down the road soundlessly on rubber shoes. She heard nothing because of the silence. Then she noticed another woman alongside her, heels clacking on the pavement. Their feet touched down at the same time, but there was no race. It was as if they might be going somewhere together.

deborah moggach

making hay

I worked, the next day. Well, what else could I do – book one of those round-the-world cruises? Throw a party?

Mind you, I'm not ruling those out. There's months to go, they told me, and I won't be ruling anything out. But I'm telling you about that particular day, the day after I'd heard, when the sun was blazing through the windscreen, heating me up. It was a perfect June morning; you don't get many mornings like those. The sky was the colour of that bird's egg – I've forgotten what sort, but it was like a pure blue dome above me. Bloody beautiful.

I sat in the coach, waiting for my passengers. Though the door was open, there was this glassed-in silence around me. I was double-parked on Haverstock Hill; behind me, cars hooted and queued, then revved up as they drove past. What's the fuss? I thought. What's the bloody fuss?

At the delicatessen, this little Pakistani bloke was pulling out the awning, just like he must always do; just like this was a normal morning. A woman dragged her squatting dog away from a lamp-post. I thought: let him. Let the bugger relieve himself.

The trees threw dappled shadows on the pavement. I told myself I must notice this; why hadn't I had the time before? People were crossing the road as if it was important where they had to go. There was a man with a briefcase who danced back, with a hop and skip, when a car drove past. He shouted some words that echoed, far away. I watched him mouthing them.

Everything seemed sharp as crystal, that morning. Yet I felt sealed-off, as if I was in this aquarium and the whole city was coming alive outside my glass walls – people going to their offices, answering phones, painting yellow lines in the road. I suppose it was because the news was just beginning to sink in.

It's unexpected, little things you think of when you're in my position. Sitting there in the sun, I thought irritably that it had to be some little creep in a white coat, a complete stranger, who'd told me. I couldn't even remember his name. But he was half my age, and he had acne.

Then I watched some blossom float down from a tree planted outside the cinema and I thought: I don't even know the name of that tree. This made me depressed. I made a resolution to find out, and then I thought: what the hell.

I hadn't told Doriza. That's my wife. I hadn't told her all the night before; I hadn't said I'd been to the hospital. She's Hungarian, you see. Highly-strung.

Eight-thirty. People were wandering towards the coach. More were coming out of Belsize Park tube station, in ones and twos. They were all women – I'd been warned about that – and some of them had pushchairs with babies in them.

"Is this the coach?" one of them asked.

"Oh no," I said. "It's a Morris Minor in disguise."

"You know what I mean." With a half-smile, she swung herself on board. Other women climbed in, unstrapping their babies. You can always tell a middle-class bunch of passengers because they get on the coach without waiting for somebody to tell them what to do.

I climbed out and went round the back to load the pushchairs into the boot. I'd already lost some weight but you wouldn't have believed it to look at me. "All British beef," Wally had said at the depot the week before, punching me in the ribs. Well, he didn't know, did he? Nobody did, except that bloke with the skin problem.

In the back window they'd already sellotaped up a placard saying CND, and another one saying WOMEN AGAINST THE BOMB. Most of them were loading their stuff themselves. They looked muscular; they were dressed like garage mechanics. I glanced wistfully at a girl passing by, wearing a floaty summer dress. But she was going to work, and disappeared into the underground.

"You've a nice day for it," I said to one of them. I jerked my head at the blue sky. "Not a cloud."

She looked up, frowning. "Not yet."

"I heard the weather forecast. Set fair."

"I'm not talking about the weather forecast."

Blimey, I thought. We've got one here.

I usually like it, once I'm out on the open road. Foot down, radio playing, steaming along the fast lane at 75 m.p.h. That's the best thing about this job – the independence. They've usually all gone to sleep by this time . . . It's just you and a dreaming coachload, heads nodding, and that wide motorway with the fan blasting cool air into your face and a few dawdlers to flash at. It made a change from home, what with all the little jobs that needed doing – fixing the guttering, decorating the kitchen; well, I wouldn't be doing them now.

It made a change. Doriza likes the heating full up. She says she feels the chill in her bones; it must be her coming from Eastern Europe, and what her family went through in the war. But it makes the house so stuffy; it makes the rooms feel so small. And her leaning across the table asking me don't I like her goulash; is that why I'm not finishing it? And her needing me to hear her complaints about the neighbours; she's always squabbling with them. And why had I forgotten our wedding anniversary; did it mean I don't love her any more? Her voice, it's like the wrong tune on the piano played over and over.

It's the speed and the solitude I enjoy. But that day it didn't feel like solitude, it felt like loneliness. I told myself it was all those women, forty-five of them, and what chap wouldn't feel separate?

Someone behind me lit a cigarette. I turned round and wagged my finger at the notice, underneath the cartoons and my St Christopher, which said NO SMOKING.

"But *you* are," she said, pointing to my smouldering fag.

"I'm different."

"You're different because you're driving?" She shrugged – I saw her in the mirror – and grimaced at her companion. "That's not fair."

"You're right about that." I drew on the cigarette. That morning I needed it.

I thought: all these years I've been a forty-a-day man; all these years I've been trying to give it up. I looked up at the vast blue sky ahead of me. Somebody up there had a sense of humour.

'*All things bright and beautiful, all creatures great and small . . .*"

A few of the women were singing in high reedy voices. I remembered the hymn from when I was a lad; I thought, how nice they're teaching it to the kids. But then I realized they'd altered the words.

Instead of "*The Lord God made them all*", they were singing "*And we destroyed them all*".

I looked in the mirror. Through the perspex roof, lurid orange light bathed their faces and the bowed, sleeping heads of their children.

"Jesus Christ," I said to myself.

It didn't sound like an oath; it sounded like a conversation-opener. I turned up the volume on the radio.

*

I'd been warned about the traffic jams but this rally lark was even bigger than I'd expected. I'd turned off the M4 near Newbury, and the lanes were choked with traffic and people tramping along on foot – men, women and children – and DIVERSION signs. The air-conditioning had broken down and the coach was sweltering. My shirt stuck to me, it felt like I was wrapped in cling-film. But nobody seemed to be complaining. Behind me the women pressed their noses to the window and exclaimed about the turn-out. The hedges were grey and dusty from the traffic. Beyond them, in a lush green field, black-and-white cows were munching, unconcerned. I thought: nice to be a cow.

The coach park was a large field. I sat while they filed out. I was tired; nowadays even driving tired me. Now there was a word for my exhaustion, it seemed worse. Trapped in my seat, I felt that echoing, glassed-in sensation again ... that everything was happening a long way off, and separate. Yet crystal-sharp, as if I'd never seen a line of coaches before, or the deeper-green clumps of thistles amongst the worn grass. I realized, too, that I hadn't listened to what the women said, or stored up their daft conversation as jokes for Wally. A bunch of dungareed peace women – what a subject! He would have enjoyed that. Why hadn't I bothered to take it in? I felt panicky.

They trudged off across the field, looking purposeful. I opened the boot; the mothers took out the pushchairs. Then I leaned against the coach. Over the far side of the field there was a coffee stall. A crowd of drivers stood there; they looked as small as insects and shimmered in the heat. I knew I should go over and join them, for my own sake. I'm a sociable bloke, you see, and if I started behaving out of character I'd give myself the creeps.

I stayed, leaning against the coach, my eyes closed. I heard the murmur of the crowd, way beyond the field, and the muffled booming of a loudspeaker. It seemed to come from another year. My passengers had all gone. I told myself I was reassured by the smell of warm metal and the diesel fumes from another coach that was just parking in front of me. Trouble was, nothing smelt familiar. Or rather, it felt only too familiar but it was out of reach. It was like the first day at school, when you're closed off in a classroom and you hear the familiar noises in the street outside but you can't get at them. Like that, but worse.

I was thinking about Doriza, and how I'd have to tell her. Sooner or later, I'd have to. "Why don't you finish it up?" she'd been asking me recently. "You don't like my cooking?" Our kitchen seemed so cramped with her in it, fussing me. I suppose most marriages aren't as happy as people hoped, if we're being truthful about it. (I was telling myself the truth that day, for the first time. You would too, in my position. The truth, it rears up and stares you in the face.) Fifteen years ago, when we first met, we had this fiery relationship. I'd met her at Paddington station and she'd been what they'd call voluptuous. Wally would say big tits but it was more than that, she seemed soft and scented and foreign. Mysterious. But mystery's the first thing to wear off, isn't it?

If we'd had children it would have been different. She's always seemed so dissatisfied. She's always asking me if I love her. If I get up to go to the toilet she asks me where I'm going. If I'm reading the paper she asks me to read it out loud. Sometimes I feel my head's going to burst. Don't get me wrong, I'm still fond of her. We're probably no worse than most people. Maybe if we'd had kids we'd have had more in common.

Dolly (I call her that), *Dolly, I've got something to tell you . . . Know how I've been feeling not quite the ticket? . . .*

A skeleton climbed out of the coach opposite me. Well, it was somebody wearing a skeleton suit. He or she loped off down the field, amongst the crowds of people.

I closed my eyes; the sun beat down on my face. I

imagined Doriza smothering me in her arms – she's a big woman – and soaking me with her tears. I imagined us having to be loving to each other, all the time. After this, we'd never be able to lose our tempers. I imagined the house hushed, and hotter, and closing in around me. I thought of Wally and Dave, my partners, shutting up when I came into the depot office ... shuffling their feet and stopping their jokes.

I went to lock up the coach. There was somebody still sitting in it.

"Hello," I said. "We've arrived."

"I know. I felt queer. Ill." She paused. "It must be the sun." She was sitting in an aisle seat, near the front. "I felt awful on the motorway," she said. "I thought I was going to be sick."

"On my new velour? You wouldn't dare."

She looked pale, but then she was one of those redheads, with that white skin. Nearer to, I could see she was covered with freckles. Her hair was bushy; in the orange light it was like a halo around her face.

"Yes, you do look peaky," I said.

"Great. Thanks."

"Sorry."

"I'm not marching. I'd probably faint and let everybody down. I'll just stay in the coach."

She didn't. She climbed through a fence with me; we walked across two fields until we came to a little triangular meadow where they'd been cutting hay. Woods closed it in on two sides; there were bales stacked up all over the place. We sat against a pile of them. Above us there were larks singing – well, I think they were larks – and the occasional clackety-clack of a police helicopter.

She was young enough to be my daughter. You should've seen her hands; they were so small, with faint bluish veins at the wrists.

"I feel better," she said. "I'm a bit anaemic, that's why."

We sat there for quite a while, in silence. She seemed to think it was perfectly natural, just to sit there with her coach driver. I didn't mind. I didn't mind anything, that day. It all seemed unlikely. I'm not in the habit of sitting in fields.

She closed her eyes. Most women feel they have to talk all the time, but she didn't seem afraid of the gaps.

For the first time since I'd heard the news I felt peaceful. I suppose it was the countryside, and the fact that she didn't ask any questions. She was a stranger, and I didn't have to tell her anything. Just because of that, I felt she was the only person I could tell.

Before I could speak, she opened her rucksack.

"Want a sandwich?"

"I've got some in the coach."

"Have one of mine." She passed me a doorstep of brown bread, packed with cheese and pickle and cucumber, and started wolfing down hers. For such a frail girl she had quite an appetite.

She paused, with crumbs on her lips. "You don't want any more?"

I gave her back the other half. "You finish it."

"Why?"

"I'm not that hungry."

"You'll waste away."

I looked at her sharply.

"Only joking," she said, prodding my solid chest. That decided me not to tell her.

She ate in silence, tearing at the crust. It did me good to watch her. Finally she swallowed the last mouthful.

"Got any kids?" she asked.

I shook my head. "Nope."

"All those kids in the coach, they made me feel so sad."

"Why?"

She paused. "Actually, I suppose they just thought it was a day out in the country." She was silent, staring at her toes. She'd kicked off her plimsolls.

"I'd have liked to have kids," I said.

She swung round and stared at me. "Would you?"

"Yes," I said, realizing just how much. "Why not?"

She gestured at the field, then up at the blue sky. "What, bring them into this world?"

"Looks beautiful to me."

She made an impatient sound, and turned away. What was the matter with her? A young girl like her, who'd eaten her sandwiches with such relish, greedy as a child, she shouldn't be talking like this. I looked at her horrible baggy khaki trousers, and her T-shirt the colour of mud. A lovely-looking girl like her ought to be wearing something bright . . . a mini dress. Something pretty, that would do her justice. I imagined her legs, under the trousers. Her ankles were as slender as a bird's.

She turned back. "What's your name?"

"Frank."

"Listen, Frank, don't you understand?" She stopped and sighed. "Oh, I wish I'd gone on the march."

"What's your name?"

"Tessa."

"Tessa . . ." I mulled over the name, fitting it to her. Then I grinned. "I know why you didn't. So you could sit here with me."

She frowned. "What?"

"Only joking. Don't mind me." I paused. "I mean it – you've made me feel a lot better."

"I couldn't have."

"No, honest."

She flung back her head. "It wouldn't have done any good anyway."

"But I just said – it has."

"I mean going on the march. Just a bunch of people."

"Well, you've done *me* good. One person."

She squinted at me, the sun in her face. "But what the hell are you and me? What can either of us do?"

She had a small, flat, hard voice. I wondered how she'd sound when she was laughing. She ought to be laughing – a beautiful girl like her, on a beautiful day like this. And she shouldn't be wearing those depressing clothes.

I wondered how her hair would feel – soft or wiry. I imagined picking wild flowers and putting them into her hair. She'd probably slap my face. Anyway, the hay was cut and there was only stubble left.

Beyond the woods, a helicopter clattered. Suddenly she turned and grabbed me. Before I could do anything, she pulled me towards her.

"Frank, I'm frightened."

"It's only a chopper."

She pressed her face into my chest. She repeated in a low voice: "I'm frightened."

I put my arms around her. She felt even more frail than she looked. I held her against me, feeling her sharp shoulder-blades and the knobs of her backbone. I pressed her bushy hair against my chest, bending my head and smelling her. She smelt of soap, and warm skin. She smelt young.

I said: "Not as frightened as me, love."

We clutched each other, rocking. The hay bales bumped our sides. Far away I heard the hooting of cars in the endless traffic jams, and the sound of a tannoy.

Then she disentangled herself, and in one violent movement she pulled her T-shirt over her head. She bent over to unbutton her trousers. For a mad moment I thought she was going to sunbathe. Then she swung round, tossing back her mass of hair.

"Come on." Her voice was flat.

"But – "

"You afraid? Who cares?" She gestured at the woods. "Life's too short."

"But – " I started again, and stopped. To be honest, this sort of thing doesn't happen to me that often. Like, never. But wasn't she going to smile or something?

She moved her face towards mine. I looked at her white, freckled skin and her dry lips. She searched my face, seriously. Then we kissed. I hadn't kissed anybody for a long time. She started unbuttoning my shirt and I tried to help her, with my clumsy hands, but before we'd finished she pulled me down on top of her, and wrapped her bare legs around me, holding me fast.

Greedily she wanted more. She gripped me; there was something impersonal and determined about the way she did it. She kissed me, her tongue pushing into my mouth; she ran her lips down my neck, but when I drew back to speak she twisted her head away and just pulled me towards her again. Once she bit my shoulder, hard.

At last she lay back, panting. Her skin was shiny with sweat. She was very thin; her breasts were so small they were barely there – just soft, pale nipples and a freckled chest. I wanted to hold her in my arms, but she was lying absolutely still, gazing up at the sky. She hadn't smiled, once.

There was a silence. Then she said: "Make hay while the sun shines."

"What about 'Make love while the sun shines'?" I said, trying to be friendly.

"Love?" She turned, and squinted at me. Then she said, in that flat voice: "I'd call it despair."

I parked the coach outside Belsize Park tube. There was this golden evening light across the parade of shops. Above the delicatessen the awning was still out; it seemed unbelievable that the shops had been open all this time, and that it had only been one day.

I missed her. By the time I'd opened the boot, she'd got out of the coach. When I straightened up and turned, I saw her disappearing into the tube; she was hitching the rucksack over her back.

I drove home from the depot and sat in the car outside our front gate. I knew what I was going to say; the words had been rolling round my head since the night before.

Dolly, I've got something to tell you. I'm not just off-colour . . . (How could I put it?) *As a matter of fact, I've got leukaemia.*

I've got leukaemia and I'll spend the rest of my days, short though they are, here in this overheated house with you, pretending we've always been happy. I'll have to behave like a saint because nobody, you or Wally or anyone, will let me behave like a jerk.

Life's too short. That's what she'd said.

Doriza was in the lounge, eating marzipan fancies. I paused at the door, and opened my mouth.

Then the words came out.

"Dolly, I've got something to tell you." I walked in and stopped in front of the gas fire. The words were different than I'd meant. "Today I met this girl, this bird . . ."

Suddenly I felt airy inside, and lighter. The words came out in a rush.

"See, we went into this hayfield . . ."

Dolly stopped munching and stared at me.

I watched her expression change.

glyn brown

the real thing

A summer night, on the cusp of autumn. Old Compton Street is the usual parade of performers – men, some women, the occasional dog – of every sexual inclination, flirting, acting up and dressing to be noticed. From an open window, Carmen Miranda trills a confidence – "ay-ay, ay-ay, ay-ay like you veee-rry much . . ." Alfresco at the Café Nero a girl, perhaps late twenties, with the build and features of a model, bedecked with African jewellery and new age pendants, reclines in a Giacometti-style wire chair. Beside her sits a jaded-looking boy, perhaps late teens. Spying someone struggling through the tumult, the girl shades her eyes as if strong sun beats down. Her expression remains neutral.

As her friend, diminutive, ashen, skirt flapping, and laden with bulging bag, furled umbrella and plastic carrier, lurches within earshot, the girl drawls a greeting. "Hello, kitten. You're a naughty kitten!" The boy glances over, turns away again, bored.

"What?"

"I've been here since six." Smooths a leather-clad leg. "And I'm cold and hungry."

"But we said seven. That's the time we arranged."

"Sure, but I called you at six to say I'd arrived. You told me you were coming."

The friend puts down a bag and lifts one foot a couple of inches off the ground, rotating it wearily. "I couldn't make it any sooner, short of an internal flight from Waterloo. Hey – what's *with* you?"

The model-type sighs. "Okay. All right. C'mere." Extending a lissom, attenuated arm, she lassoes the friend's neck and drags her forward, almost toppling the fragile table between them, for a loud kiss that nearly connects with skin. "Mwah. I forgive you." In the direction of the boy, who's gazing off, watching a pretty man have his hair cut in what looks like a glass-fronted disco: "She's always late."

The friend's jaw is set. "Lori," she grins, a kind of rictus.

Lori hurls a bale of hair back from her olive forehead. "This is Billy. He's waiting for his posse, aren't you?" Billy is, perhaps, deaf. "Have a good time, then." Catching up the strap of a tiny black silk purse and hoiking a slim case under her arm, Lori begins to activate her legs. She stands, unremarked by any man seated at the tables, but watched furtively by every woman. "*Vamos*, eh? *Bad* kitten."

Bad Kitten stomps off on her short legs. She has come to detest this "Kitten" business – once an endearment – but hasn't the heart to say so. Particularly now. After a string of busy, unavailable months, Lori had called, distraught, at midnight, incoherent, sobbing, saying she needed to talk.

"So tell me how you – " A police car, blue light twirling, siren like a cyclone, attacks the road briefly and vanishes. "How are you?"

"Exhausted, babe." Lori pulls distractedly at a strand of hair. "I've been at the Sanctuary – sauna, steam room, massage, it's very tiring, that place."

"Yeah, yeah, yeah."

"Then I had to get to the hairdressers. You don't know how I've rushed about all day. You've just been in the office, right? Sitting down. Huh?"

"Of course, I'd rather be sitting in the office. Ten-hour days on that ratty mag for the last month. I'm knackered."

Laughs feebly: it is, after all, the condition of work, should you have a job and want to keep it, in the nineties. Use it up, wear it out, like boots – that seems the employer's manifesto. "This is a madhouse. Jesus, my head's pounding. But the point is, are you okay?"

Lori isn't there – she has fallen behind, magnetized to a jewellery shop. When she catches up, bobbing along the pavement like a balloon, she offers, "What a sweet coat. You look like a little highwayman. Where d'you get it?"

Rather pleased. "Oxfam. It was . . ."

"Okay, here." Lori pulls up with a cartoon screech. "Here's where I want to go."

"Pronto's? It's seething."

"This is where I want to go." Lori shoulders into the tiny trattoria, a riot of noise and colour and crammed bodies. It looks to Bad Kitten's myopic gaze like a scene Bosch might have turned out on a down day, or an explosion in a high-class prosthetics factory, arms and legs shooting everywhere. "Hiya," trills Lori. "It's me."

"*Buona sera.*" The grey-haired boss nods, turns, a glass shatters somewhere and there is laughter and applause. "For two? We don't have . . . you wait?"

Bad Kitten: "Bugger, can't we . . ."

Lori: "Sure, we'll stand right here."

With an impetuous shriek, "La Cucaracha" begins belting from the overhead speakers. A laden waiter trips on one of Bad Kitten's bags with a curse. The owner waves a tea-towel, "Downstairs, please. Two?"

"Uh-huh." Lori grabs her friend by the coat collar, almost lifts her feet off the ground. "C'mon, kitten. And mind my stuff. That's my portfolio."

In the café's bowels, at a table where the staircase and two gangways converge, a table like a meeting place on Euston station, Lori installs herself, throwing back a rein of hair that catches BK in the eye. "You don't look too happy here."

"Ah – oh, I guess it's a challenge. If I can just wedge my bags – "

A menu drops on BK's head. "*Signorinas*, ready to order?"

As Kitten scuffles for the fallen menu, Lori yawns, "I'll just have the *fettucine alla carbonara* and a green salad and a cup of tea and a fresh juice." She hands back her unopened menu. "And some mineral water, sparkling."

"And I'll, er – can I get an omelette?"

"What omelette you want?"

"What is there?"

A shout from two tables back, "Can we have that carafe of red wine, please?"

The waitress shifts her weight. "Tomato, mushroom, cheese, mix vegetable, plain."

"Cheese, please. Wonderful."

"To drink?"

"Yeah, orange. Would be great."

And the girls are alone together, in a way.

"When you said am I okay, you meant the call, and Jason, right?" Lori planes a dismissive wave. "He's out of my system now. Rotten creep."

"Well, great." Lori's ex, Jason, was a painter she'd run herself ragged to promote. Once he hit the big time, he found Lori wasn't high-profile enough for him. (Who could have a higher profile? BK had wondered, craning.)

"Yeah, well I went on a shoot to Dorset week before last, and I had a chance to sort my head out. I called him fifteen times, day before I left. On his mobile."

"That takes messages?"

"It stores them. Uses up the battery, too. It was really funny, because he broke down that night in some country lane and couldn't call for help. He rang me next morning, sounding really pissed off." Assumes irritated voice. " 'I'm stuck miles from nowhere and when I turn the phone on I have to listen to fifteen stupid messages from you and then it goes dead'." She smacks the tabletop with an exuberant palm. The water bottle leaps, jauntily pirouettes, and BK just saves it. Glancing up to take a bow, she's struck again by Lori's amazing eyes, each painted with a slim dark line. She looks like Nefertiti.

"And how about the shoot? What was that for?"

"Oh God, *Tatler* or *Harper's*. My agent fixed it."

"Right, like fur bikinis no one can afford? Oops – thanks." The food arrives, steaming bowls and saucers flying onto the table. Lori wields salt and pepper without compunction.

"Some people can't, I guess. It was one of my biggest jobs so far." In her mid-twenties Lori, a designer, had been asked to pose for a fashion paper she worked on. The modelling took off in a way that can happen to those who don't expect it. When BK thinks about this, which is less now, she sees Lori as an escapee of the rat race's downward pell-mell, caught up and saved as if by a mighty parachute unfurling. "I was in a daze, at the Bass Clef till two the night before, looked like shit."

"And the rest."

"No, I did. But when we got to Dorset I had, like, this fabulous time. The photographer was this really horny guy, about forty, married but wants to get out – "

"He told you this, did he?"

"Yeah, no, really, we stayed up drinking that night, he wanted to talk. He's a Buddhist, too."

"I bet he is." BK picks up a knife and cleans it slowly with a paper napkin. This is always the thing with Lori, she's thinking: she cries wolf, but there's always a man on the scene. It's often another wolf, but still, Lori has never known want, not really.

Feeling bitter and uncharitable, BK hunts for the well of sympathy inside herself, and taps it. Sure, it's exhausting, hearing Lori talk this way, a narrative of chasing and being chased, just like in the old days. And yes, as soon as an affair ends, there's another lined up – but usually it really is one more calamity waiting to happen. BK tries not to see something of herself reflected there. Not now, at least. Nope, not these days.

"Anyway, I could tell he was into me, but I don't know how I feel about him." Lori pauses briefly. "But what I meant to tell you, there was this Maori girl on the shoot, the other model, Merola. We went to see the ley lines together." She drags hair out of her mouth. "Really sweet, sexy, sussed, said she'd never waste her life in an office. She's on this world tour, a birthday present from her parents, she's been to India, Africa, all round Europe, she's so wild. It was her first modelling tryout, and she got the photographer to take extra shots of her. Needs to get some money."

"A girl like this needs money?"

"Believe it." Lori cackles, then hooks a dollop of spaghetti and sucks it up with a whoosh. "She's spent six thousand just on clothes on the trip, and she hasn't got the cash. Overdrew her parents' account. I told you, she's wild."

Wow, thinks BK, taciturn. Throwing around someone else's money on clothes. Sure ain't a thing just anyone can do.

Pushing aside her dish, Lori hoists the portfolio onto the table and opens it out like a large, exhausted bat. Photographs of herself, draped against a sinuous girl with black Rapunzel curls, come tumbling out. She selects one and proffers it. "This is us in the hotel room. She bought some snuff – Jesus, it went everywhere. She said, 'Aow, ah don't lake thet, meks you sneeze snot thet looks lake sheet.' Really funny."

Lori flicks, stops at another shot where the girl stands on a rocky promontory, arms raised like Christ without his crucifix, the sky forlorn behind her. The brown face is a study in self-absorption, or despair at the English weather.

Bad Kitten swallows down a large and tasteless chunk of egg and cheese. The omelette is not cooked through, and a yellowy-white skein dribbles onto her chin. Finding some grubby tissue in her waistcoat pocket, she dabs her lip. "She's pretty, I guess. What's that she's wearing?"

"Gaultier kaftan. She bought it in Milan. Beautiful, huh?"

Another picture of the girl, posing in silhouette. "Takes herself kind of seriously."

Lori nods, still concentrating on the matt print. "Yeah, most people who know her can't stand her. I like her, though. She's making herself this fantastic dress for my party." Lori beams at BK, who notices with horror that she has a piece of parsley spread-eagled on a tooth. "I meant to invite you. I'm having a party."

Realizing the hand holding her glass is shaking weirdly, BK rests it on the table. She remembers a scene, the two of them, years ago in the thick of their closeness, Lori storming, "I don't know why you haven't got a man. They're all mad. God, I'd marry you!" BK's initial reaction was disbelief – she has been out with many men who said just this, declared undying passion and changed their minds next day.

On an impulse she puts down her fork, wanting to clasp Lori's fingers, just as Lori says, "So how's David? Still walking all over you?"

At that moment a few of the lights dim and a birthday cake studded with a ridiculous number of candles wafts to a table at the back. There is screaming and an impromptu chorus of "Happy Birthday to you", followed by shouts of "Blow 'em out, blow 'em out! Wanna burn down the building?"

When the bulbs reestablish themselves, Lori is licking the last vestiges of saffron sauce from a finger. "Thank God I'm over Jason. I barely think about him. But it's like, he's so successful now. He's everywhere – TV, radio, interviews in every paper. And it's all this peace and love shit. He's on a complete fucking power trip. He thinks he's got to preach universal understanding and the Buddhist way, through his art. Crap. He said in one interview, I'm opening myself right up, I've told the world my innermost thoughts and feelings. So how come he didn't tell me?" She shakes her head. "All his litt-le tricks." Lori said "litt-le' in the way she always did, like a child, emphasizing the "t" sound. "This latest one, the blonde – he's introducing her to Buddhism, too. She's a bimbo, I've seen her. I *met* her. I was blind to what was going down, even though I was chanting eight hours a day. Want anything else?"

Bad Kitten's appetite is playing dead. Lori orders apricot crumble and custard, then lightly plays her spoon on the table to a dance beat. "I don't know how you cope without chanting," she muses. "You're so strong."

Having heard this many times before, Bad Kitten takes the opportunity to bend and riffle through her carrier bag. "Guess what I've got in . . ." she begins, when Lori clamps her wrist. "Don't turn round, but there's a guy behind you – he's gonna walk past us, with the cute bum – he really likes me. He's been watching me since we got here." She lowers her lashes as someone brushes past. BK puts a package into the heavily-ringed fingers. "Happy Birthday for Saturday. Seems like the week for 'em."

Still peering over her shoulder, Lori tears away the wrapping, in strips, like orange peel; inside it, two tiny stars of studs, with garnet fires in their centre. "God, how sweet . . ." She puts on the earrings immediately, removing the ones she's wearing. "Anyway, finally, we met at a baseball match. We went for a drink and I said, so I've heard you're seeing someone? I was very cool. He admitted it. Then we got drunk and had some spliff, and went back to his. And after we slept together, I asked him if he'd used anything when he went with her. Know what? He hadn't!"

Lori's dessert arrives, and BK watches her inhale the fruity fumes, then in a childlike, slapdash way begin to eat. Suddenly, she can't tell what the time is, or the month, or year. She's caught in a sense of *déjà vu*. They seem to keep going round and round like this, the same old circus, same rickety music, though now it's off-key, less charming. She puts a hand to her aching temple. What is the point of it? Why does anyone eat, or shop? The magazines BK herself works on, that make Lori so aware of her appearance. Why do people buy and read them? The same fashions, stories, pieces about the lives of the same stars, for ever and ever, without end.

"I went mad. I ranted and raved. It was healthy, though, I needed to get my anger out." Lori chews on, trawling her big spoon around the edge of the bowl to pick up all the deep-brown chunks of caramelized sugar. "In the end, he said, what's your problem? He told me – listen to this – he told me I'm mental."

With the perfect irony you only get in films or stories, the music changes to Nat King Cole's mellifluous "When I Fall In Love". The heat seems to be building. Bad Kitten undoes one or two shirt buttons. "I thought he said that about all his exes?"

"Exactly! According to him, Jane was mental, Lisa was mental, Nicky was mental. I said, Jason, doesn't it strike you as a bit *odd* that they were all perfectly normal before they met you and perfectly normal after? What was it they had in common at the other times? You, Jason. You."

With thumb and first finger, she makes a V-shape and pulls back her hair, letting it drop round her cheeks. "Do you like my hair? These two bits are supposed to hang in my face, but you have to keep pulling them forward." She stares at herself reflected in a glass partition, pulls the hair forward again.

Leaning across to an empty table, Kitten grabs a menu and fans herself. "You look great. It really suits you." The fluorescent blues and yellows of an Italian beach scene on the wall leap up, slipping scarily out of true, dancing their own sick tango.

"When it's him who's crazy. I sent him a Max Ernst quote – 'My heavenly husband has gone mad, but I have arms of thunder', from my book of sayings. Hey, babe, you okay?"

"Bit hot. I'll be fine when we get outside."

"Well, I want coffee first." Lori signals to the waitress. "And where's Dave tonight?"

Kitten shrugs, feeling her stomach lurch like a breached galleon, her spirits plunge like lost souls. She pulls out her dumb cop accent. "Duh – soich me."

Lifting a large, tapering hand, Lori rips varnish slivers off an unsuspecting nail. "Maybe he's cheating on you?"

"Uh . . ." Man the lifeboats. Mayday, Mayday. "I don't *think* he'd have time."

Lori lights a cigarette and looks around. "Well, that's what I thought . . ."

This café – the whole street, really – has during the last couple of years become a hang-out for the city's gay population, almost exclusively male. The waitresses, two elderly Italian sisters with greasy pinnies and hair cut into neat, iron-grey helmets, mother the boys, who take the opportunity to pour out their hearts, exchange gossip and show off their black patent jeans, their cashmere roll-necks. Alessandra, the elder sister, is currently engrossed in a discussion with two young lovers, one of whom keeps touching his white-blond crop neurotically and murmuring that, now, he isn't so sure. As Bad Kitten watches, Alessandra tenderly strokes the spiky fronds. Then she says something and the boy lets out a relieved, soprano peal of laughter. Beneath the bleach, he is pale, and very thin, and his lover reaches out and takes his hand.

Lori tips her ash and fiddles with an earring. There has been a long and leaden silence. "I really love these little stars, y'know. You always get me such fab pressies." Struggling for breath, BK nods, feeling her neck rick painfully. Because of her job, hunched over keyboards for hours, she's prone to creaking muscles, robotic head movements, once told Lori it was the cause of all her problems – "I have to stop it with these short jerks." Slowly stirring coffee, Lori says, "God, remember those early days, when we were so mad? You screaming round town in the backs of cabs, from one lover to another, with no knickers on? I still think about it."

Ah, when they met. Back then, working on some new teen mag, they had bonded as instantly as a dangerous adhesive, seeing something in each other they couldn't back away from. They had lunch together, swanning past the postboys to the lift, daffy but enigmatic. BK envied her friend's physique and beauty but had never been jealous or hated her for it – partly because she always saw them as a glamorous pair, and because Lori made her feel beautiful, telling her how gorgeous she was. Not a total lie, at the time – she just didn't make men's heads explode like tropical barometers when she entered the room.

Both were in relationships which later came loose at the joins, like badly made Airfix models, but they got over those together, a cure involving drunken nights in clubs, dancing on tables to hellish songs. "Christ," they'd later marvel, wide-eyed, "we did the Lambada to 'Lay Down, Maggie' . . ." That year, and for the next three or four, they'd sent each other bouquets on promotions, sold each other drugs (always preaching elaborate safety drills), picked each other up from abortion clinics, interrupted fellatio to take each other's calls at four a.m., giggled in changing rooms, read the tarot and i-ching and had endless analytical lunches, dropping pizza from gesticulating fingers, swapping sardonic stories of sex in playgrounds, sex in churches, sex on the Metropolitan line.

That was the version of her Lori had loved, the crazed twenty-eight-year-old in fishnets and Wonderbra who skipped through a succession of romantic traumas but still rose, bubbling and hopeful, to the top. It had been exciting but painful and, finally, exhausting. BK still can't work out whether she's glad it all happened – no, she's probably glad. But, five years later, she feels like the mother or aunt of her former self. The daily grind has taken its toll. Now, thinks Bad Kitten, I wear combat gear, the greens and browns of camouflage, to blend in and not stand out, and I catch buses to work. A week ago, she heard herself say, "My ambition is to live calmly," and was aghast, but it's true. It may be better, often feels worse, but she couldn't keep that other stuff up, wouldn't want to, and she sees Lori almost knows.

How long was it before the things they did started keeping them away from each other, instead of bringing them together? Lori got Buddhism – or it got her – and now her friends were other Buddhists. She talked a lot about being "centred". BK felt Lori no longer knew her and, more than that, didn't want to find out.

Lori draws heavily on her Silk Cut. "You realize what an inspiration you are? Like, when you lost that job last year – you coped on your own, didn't you, you never once called me sounding upset."

"You weren't in much. I left messages."

"But you never sounded too bad, so I knew I didn't have to ring you right back. You are *so* strong." Smiling in awed disbelief, Lori shakes her head. "Not like the little girls in my Buddhist group." That word again, "litt-le", that same way. "They're only about twenty-two, twenty-three. I have to be there for them all the time."

"You barely know them."

"That's it. But I'm still there when they need me."

Bad Kitten feels another wave of nausea, rising round her knees, round her hips. She's working too hard, she can't go out without feeling faint. Where is the toilet?

Lori sees her craning. "What? Who've you seen? You looking for something?"

"No. It's just . . ." Wipes cold sweat off her upper lip. "Something real. Just, y'know, some little thing that's real. Oh, God." She makes a peace sign, goes cross-eyed. "Gee, *man*. What an idiot statement."

"No, I know what you mean." Lori stirs her coffee. "It can't be easy, temping. I hated it. But you'll get another proper job, you're good. Something else in journalism, or PR? I still have that advertorial you worked on about the soap that's kind to skin."

Bad Kitten mumbles, "It corrodes bath surfaces," but Lori's on a roll. "You should join the practice. Chant for what you want, and you get it. A job, a car, more money – whatever makes you happy. It works. Look at me."

Bad Kitten pushes back her chair and stands up. "Just be a minute."

In the smelly toilet, BK is sick. When she's finished, she wipes her mouth with tissue and leans her head on the clammy wall. Where *was* David tonight? As usual, he'd been evasive, and asking – "Where are you going? Who are you meeting?" – looked so desperate.

Did he love her? He said he did, occasionally. When he found time to call her. (Sometimes, when he'd ring, BK would say, "Who is this?" but he never laughed.) At their last meeting – for a couple of hours, a week ago, at a high-powered party – she had manoeuvred him into a corner, said in a low, urgent tone that she needed more. "I feel I know you less and less well as time goes by, instead of knowing you better. Can't we at least spend a day together, sometime?" They'd managed it in their previous, first, year, before his career had taken off. That first year, when BK had put her job on hold to concentrate on boosting his confidence. Had she created a monster? His brow furrowed. "Look, I can't think about this now – your timing is terrible. Jesus, you need constant attention." And he'd spun away again.

David had met Lori once, last year. He'd flattered helplessly but as soon as they left had joked that Lori was psycho, a dippy hippy chick. Relieved to have his attention back, BK had joined in, discussing her friend's dreamy idiocy. Now, it makes her sicker still to remember the things she said. Nevertheless, for months, David had probed for information about her exotic acquaintance.

Oh, come on, she chastises, you're overtired and paranoid. Standing up, she trickles cold water on her forehead, combs her hair, studies the pale girl in the mirror. You're so insecure, sister, she tells her. Get a grip. That's all you have to do.

Back at the table, Lori has paid the bill and, collecting their bags, they walk outside. Across the road, a corner building gutted by fire hangs onto its foundations like a carious tooth. A notice bangs loosely in the breeze: "Dangerous structure. No enterey." On a traffic island, a tramp with a saxophone is playing "Strangers In The Night". The air is still warm, and BK is wondering how they will part.

Crowds of shrieking teenagers pass, on their way to clubs in Charing Cross Road. Lori puts down her things to zip up her leather Alaïa jacket. She, too, seems at a loss. And then, taking BK by the elbow, she draws her into a stinking shop doorway.

"Look, I've gone on about myself again – "

"Damn right." The strength of BK's retort surprises even her.

"I know, and I didn't mean to. It's just that you seem so

centred these days, and I'm envious of your thing with David, that's," she smiles at herself, "why these stupid remarks come out. And, boy, can you be *quiet*, sometimes. It makes me gabble. What's ridiculous is, I still kind of want to impress you. And I wanted to give you this. I found it in my book of quotes." She hands BK a folded slip of paper. "Don't read it now, read it on the bus. It explains how I – look, I really want us to try and stay close."

And she bends – she really has to almost fold herself in half – and embraces Bad Kitten, kissing her cheek. "We should be happy. We're great, we deserve it."

They part at Goodge Street tube. As soon as Lori disappears, with her portfolio and long, thigh-booted legs, BK opens out the paper right there, as a light shower begins to rattle down. In Lori's almost dyslexic scribble, it says: "When things or people change, don't feel the carpet has been pulled from under your feet. Instead, learn to dance on shifting sands."

The 73 comes grinding, raggedly, along the road, and BK runs for it, remembering Lori's pulled and twisted hair, the bitten nails, and the time they both did the Lambada. "I'm dancing, we all are," she thinks. The bus turns the corner. "I'm trying."

joanna torrey

back rubs

I used to lie in bed, waiting for my father to come upstairs and give me a back rub. He did this almost every night, except when he had a meeting at church on Sundays.

My father gave the best back rubs. He pulled the sheet down around my waist and my nightgown up around my neck. With my head turned sideways, I could see myself in the long mirror on the outside of my closet door. I could see what was under the bed, sometimes a clump of dust, or a shoe turned over at a funny angle. I wouldn't do anything about rescuing what was under the bed right then, just remind myself to do it later. My arms were down at my sides, my palms curled upward.

He rubbed my back very lightly with the tips of his fingers so that I could hardly feel them. His hand went from the top of my neck, down to my waist where the sheets and blankets were bunched, then across from side to side and then down along my sides, but not underneath where my chest was pressed against the sheets. This was the map of my back he used. Right at that place along my sides where he stopped, it sometimes tickled more, but he didn't go past that place. I didn't want him to, but at the same time I held my breath when he got there. Tickling along my ribs was the best. Also, when he stroked around and around in circles that started out big and then got smaller and smaller until there was a tiny little spot right in the center of my back and his fingers were so light and barely there that my skin prickled. I was usually half asleep by then, and could feel the wetness under my face on the pillow where I'd drooled.

He always ended the back rub by counting the knobs of my spine, the vertebrae, he called them. He started at the top of my neck and counted down out loud, stopping at each one and rubbing it around and around in place for a second with the tip of his finger, so that I really felt the knob shape. He counted them, never missing one, until he reached the base of my spine. "How many?" I always asked.

"Just the right number," he answered. Then he pulled my nightgown down.

My mother's back rubs weren't very good and she didn't give them too often. I think she didn't want him being the only one who could do that. She would come in wearing her apron which she was always forgetting to take off after doing the dishes. She wouldn't bother pulling the sheet down or pushing my nightgown up, but would just put her hand underneath and rummage around. Hers were very fast and impatient; you could tell her mind was on other things. She'd whisk over my back really quickly with the hard pads of her fingers that were covered in tiny cracks from gardening and polishing the teapot and pressing down on the frets of her viola. It was like being tickled by a rough broom. I always wondered if they gave back rubs to each other. I tried to imagine my mother with her nightgown around her neck. I tried to imagine him counting her vertebrae. I wondered if he kissed her back afterwards.

The next thing I knew, the covers would be up around my neck and she was kissing my cheek goodnight.

*

He gets mad at me when I don't take my nightgown off, but I get cold. He never gets cold, even when he's naked. I tell him I'll take it off when we get going, when my blood gets going and I get warm, but he doesn't like waiting so long. When he starts giving me a back rub I'm all covered in goose-bumps and my skin feels papery and breakable. I'm lying under a bright pool of light from the lamp by the bed and I worry that my skin looks blue.

He starts rubbing my back. His back rubs are too hard. He scrunches my skin, bunching it up in fistfuls like he's washing clothes and then wringing them out. I don't know how to teach him. I feel my skin getting red under his twisting hands. Every once in a while he leans down and kisses my neck and then trails over and starts nuzzling my ear. I move my head slightly, away from his mouth and the heat of his breath. I know that he'll try to kiss my mouth next, sliding his tongue in from the side. I don't want him to. He knows I like back rubs to be separate. First a back rub, and then sex. He knows that, but he doesn't believe me. Back rubs turn him on. He won't believe me that for me they're something different. I turn my head away.

He straddles me, then lies down, covering my back with his chest. He keeps massaging my shoulders, bringing them up around my ears and down again in big circular motions, crouching low as though he's doing the breaststroke on my back. He starts riding me up and down, posting, up off the saddle and down again. I know he wants to fuck me this way.

His hands touch the sides of my breasts. I feel them flattened out and bulging to the sides a little, taut and swollen, painful, like they've been bitten by insects. He pats the sides of my breasts as though he's trying to open a cupboard, as though I'm going to lift myself up off the bed just to let his hands in there. I keep my chest and nose pressed against the bed. I don't want him there yet. I can't breathe. I turn sideways and am surprised to see the bare wall. I always expect to see a mirror, the white reflection of my face, shadowy shapes under the bed.

Still straddling me, he pushes off from my back like a springboard, then climbs off. He stands next to the bed. I turn my face to the sheet again, feel it smooth and cool on my face. I don't know what he's going to do next.

I want him to sit down next to me on the bed and start again, very slowly, breathing life back into me. I want the tips of his fingers to burn into my back. Right now, the room should be dark, with only a shaft of light coming through the door across the bed. My nightgown is as it should be, up around my neck, but he should be dressed and wearing a watch on his right wrist.

My two sisters and I are sitting in our "train formation", the three of us facing sideways on the sofa so that we are looking at each other's backs. We've pulled our clothes away from our shoulders and necks. I've unbuttoned the front of my shirt so that only the very bottom button is done up. This holds my shirt on at my hips, but allows it to drape off my shoulders and way down my back. My bra is undone, my breasts loose underneath the cups which have collapsed together in front.

I like to have the very bottom of my back massaged, below my waist, right where my buttocks begin, and this makes it easier for my sisters to reach. Our backs are all similar, straight and white with freckles on the shoulders. My sisters' backs always seem thin to me when I touch them, almost scrawny, and I wonder whether my back feels as insubstantial as theirs do under my hands.

We usually give back rubs within the first hours of a visit to my parents' house, or if we are visiting each other's homes. My older sister's husband seems to understand and smiles tolerantly at us as we gather our shirts up at our necks when he passes by, although he is ticklish and can't imagine how we enjoy it. My younger sister's boyfriend finds our behavior strange and perverted, an excuse not to have sex. He becomes jealous, banging pots in the kitchen until he storms out of the apartment. With this sister, we tend to give back rubs elsewhere, or when he is not there to comment.

In our train of three, one person always receives and does not give a back rub. After fifteen to twenty minutes, we reverse positions so that the non-participant is giving one, which means that one of us gets a back rub twice. We keep track of this in an informal way and make sure that the same person isn't favored each time.

We have never really discussed whether this is something unusual that we do. We are not, otherwise, a family that touches a great deal. In fact, small birdlike hugs of the shoulders and air kisses are the custom. I pull away from my father when we greet each other so that our bodies don't touch.

We are sitting in the living-room. The afternoon sun is wintry, slanting across the floor in panes of light onto three empty tea cups, a tray with a teapot, an empty plate that held cookies, and a small pitcher of milk.

I am at the back of the train today, the caboose. My younger sister sits at the front, the engine, her hands in her lap, idle. We give back rubs without oil, the slight dryness of our wintry skins shedding dust into the air. We don't speak. I stare into my older sister's back, feeling pity at the harsh red streaks I create, the tired slack of her shoulders as they droop down in relaxation, the constellations of freckles inelegantly dotting her shoulders. A sigh and another sigh. We communicate front to back.

As we begin the final circles, the light rubdown with the fingertips that signals a warning of the end, we hear footsteps on the stairs. Our fingers stop, just briefly, not quite frozen, but arrested in motion, and then continue in their light circles. There is the slightest adjustment of our draped open clothing, to close, not with hands and buttons, but with shrugs and shifting of our shoulders and upper arms, a token decency.

Our father stands in the doorway wearing his slippers, his hair upright from his nap.

We three sisters, the engine, the middle car and the caboose all look up. Our fingers don't stop. It is from him that we have learned our art.

"Hi, Daddy," we say. He is somewhat deaf now and doesn't seem to hear us. He looks at us and appears about to speak. He raises a hand toward us, his three grown daughters, our clothes in disarray. He half waves, then turns and walks away.

We continue the sad close of our ritual, the fingernails trailing up the sides, the feather-light circular movements around and around. We look behind our shoulders at each other, once, twice, slightly defensive, the very suggestion of guilt. We lift our fingertips and pause, then finish with a brisk brushing off, of sadness or grief, or the talc of our collective dander.

We straighten our clothes and button our shirts. My younger sister pours the last half inch of cold tea into her cup and takes a sip.

I know there is something trapped inside my back.

We are lying in bed having one of those awkward discussions about erogenous zones.

"My back," I say.

He's silent.

"Well, it is and it isn't," I say, embarrassed.

He turns me over and I feel him survey the wide flat bony field. He is lost without hills, points and valleys, the usual markers. He studies my back as though it is a chessboard. He plans his first move.

"Where?" he asks.

"Anywhere," I say. "The middle, up and down my spine." It is already hopeless.

His touch is tentative, as though I have asked him to blindfold, bind and beat me.

"Here?" he asks, a doctor prodding and palpating with his fingertips to find the exact spot for an injection.

"Fine," I say, giving up.

He lowers his mouth as though to a minefield and plants a small kiss in the exact bull's eye of my back, leaving his fingers there until his lips meet them.

His mouth stays, a soft and sucking leech.

I wait.

Bravely, his mouth roams and climbs the rocky face of my shoulder blade.

"Bite me," I command.

His mouth stops. I feel him opening his lips tentatively as though taking a bite of a strange new cheese. He bites down, softly.

"Harder," I say. "It doesn't hurt, you can bite me harder."

I feel an urgent chewing on my shoulder, and then coolness as the air hits the spit. He's given up.

"Thank you," I say.

I turn over and we continue, front to front.

I find his erogenous zones, standards, with ease.

The thing inside my back waits, trapped, under thick ice.

The room is soft and warm, dark as an incubator. She has left me, closing the door behind her without a sound as though the tiniest click might send me running. I take off my clothes quickly, piling them on a chair, and climb up onto the high narrow table. The mattress always astounds me, at once stern and hard, soft and yielding.

I lie on my stomach and fit my face into the padded brace at the head of the table that will carry the weight of my head for the next hour, funnel the rivers from my nose and mouth. I pull the top sheet up over my legs, leaving my back bare, and wait.

I don't turn around when she walks in. I hear only the sounds of her breathing, her palms rubbing, warming them, as she stands next to the table. The strokes on my back are long and fluid with scented oil. Her two hands slide up and down the cage of my ribs as though on runners, stronger and stronger. I imagine her palms, darkening to crimson with the heat.

On the fifth upward stroke, my tears start, as though squeezed from a cracked tube of paint.

The thing inside my back groans and awakens.

My breathing is clogged and muffled. I turn my head to the side and close my eyes. She pulls the sheet up over my back and tucks it under my shoulders. She rubs her hands up and down my back one last time over the sheet, and then stops, leaving both hands there for a moment. I pray for them to stay.

She tiptoes toward the door and shuts it silently behind her. I lie very still, my breathing shallow, reluctant to sit up, to climb off the table, to dress, to re-enter my life. For now, my back is as empty and clean as a new wooden box.

I didn't know it would be the last time.

It was soon after my twelfth birthday and I had begun to grow breasts, tiny swellings that barely pushed out my undershirt. I ignored them. Perhaps I knew that they would interfere.

After I'd said my prayers, my mother left the room and stood out in the hall talking to my father. In the middle of talking, she suddenly looked up into the darkened bedroom, saw me watching, and closed the door.

A minute later, my father opened the door and walked in and sat down on my bed. He sat down stiffly, right on the very edge. I could feel him almost falling off, as though he only planned to stay for a moment. I had already prepared myself, lowering the sheet to my waist and pulling my nightgown up around my neck, my skin gathering goosebumps.

Slowly, so lightly I could hardly feel it, he placed both hands, the very tips of his fingers, on my back, a pianist positioning for a performance. In the mirror, I could see them hanging down from his wrists.

His touch was so fleeting, his fingers hardly grazed my skin. He was tickling the air. I raised my back slightly, humping up, trying to make contact with his fingers. Perhaps he didn't realize. His hand pulled away when it met my back, up and down again, bounding. This was a new game. I didn't like it.

I shifted slightly, trying to urge his hand onto my sides, off the safe plateau of my back, but they stayed firmly on top.

Finally, he made a cross on my back, top to bottom, side to side, skimming my skin with one finger. I knew it was almost over. It had been so short this time.

He began the counting at the top of my spine, his touch finally firm again, rubbing each knob around and around. I turned away from the mirror and stretched out my neck so that my spine would be very straight, correct. He counted my vertebrae slowly, out loud.

I didn't want to ask the question. If I didn't ask, it wouldn't be over. I lay very still, my head buried in my pillow. He pulled my nightgown down and the sheet up around my ears. He leaned down and put his lips close to my ear. I could hear the dark gold whisper of his watch.

"How many?" he asked.

"I don't know," I mumbled into the pillow.

He sat for a minute or two and then he got up and left. He never came to my room again.

*

I dream about lifting my father's blue pajama top. His skin is so thin now that it wrinkles like white tissue paper. His shoulder blades jut out like the wings of a newborn bird.

Pouring rosemary oil into one palm, I rub my hands together hard to warm them until they glisten. I run my hands down the center of his back, top to bottom, side to side. An oily cross gleams in the half light. I trace circles round and around his back with my fingertips. His face is pressed into the pillow where I once struggled to breathe.

Beginning at the base of his neck, I move down the bony range of his spine, counting each knob, massaging it round and around until I reach the end, not missing one.

about the authors

Glyn Brown is a journalist who has written for such diverse publications as *i-D*, *Melody Maker*, *City Limits*, *Time Out*, the *Guardian*, *Independent* and *Literary Review*. She won the 1991 *Time Out* Short Story competition and has had fiction published in a number of anthologies.

Sylvia Brownrigg was born in Mountain View, California and grew up near there and in Oxford, England. Her fiction has appeared in various American journals; her non-fiction in the *Village Voice*, *New York Newsday* and the *Guardian* in London. She lives in London.

Idious Buguise is an anthropologist who lives in London and does fieldwork in West Africa. This is her second piece of fiction.

Margaret Elphinstone is the author of three novels: *The Incomer*, *A Sparrow's Flight* and *Islanders*, and a book of short stories, *An Apple from a Tree*. She lectures in English Studies at Strathclyde University, lives in Carrick and has two daughters.

Buchi Emecheta was born in Lagos, Nigeria, of Ibuza parentage. She has lived in London since 1962. She has written novels, plays, children's books and poetry. She is a Doctor of Letters, a fellow of London University and a well-known speaker and lecturer.

Susan Hill started writing when she was in her late teens and has since published twelve novels, twelve children's books and a number of works of non-fiction as well as radio plays. Her classic ghost story, *The Woman in Black*, has been a long-running stage success in which theatrical rights have been sold to fourteen countries. Her latest novel, *Mrs de Winter*, the sequel to *Rebecca*, was published in 1993. She lives in Oxford.

A.L. Kennedy was born in Dundee in 1965. She has spent several years working with an arts and disability charity in creative writing with special needs. She has published two collections of short stories, *Night Geometry and the Garscadden Trains* (1991), which won a Scottish Arts Council book award, Saltire Best First Book Award and a *Mail on Sunday*/John Llewellyn Rees Prize, and *Now That You're Back* (1994), which won a Scottish Arts Council book award. Her novel, *Looking for the Possible Dance* (1993), won a Scottish Arts Council book award and a Somerset Maugham prize. She was listed among the Granta/*Sunday Times* 20 Best Young British Novelists.

Deborah Moggach has written eleven novels and adapted several of them for television. She has also written film scripts and a stage play, *Double-Take*. She has published two collections of short stories, *Smile* and *Changing Babies* and other short stories have been broadcast on BBC Radio and appeared in anthologies.

Melissa Murray has written extensively for theatre, radio and television. Her awards include the Eric Gregory Award for poetry and the Verity Bargate Playwrights' Award. Her first book of short stories, *Changelings*, was published in 1987. She lives in Dublin.

Kathy Page's short stories have been widely anthologized as well as collected in *As In Music*. Her new collection is *Of Paradise and Elsewhere*. She has written for radio and television and published four novels, of which the most recent is *Frankie Styne and the Silver Man*.

Joanna Rosenthall has published a number of short stories. She lives in London with her husband and daughter, Esther.

Carla Toney was born in Los Angeles. She has worked in publishing for eight years and teaches Creative Writing at Hackney Community College. Her work has appeared in *Poetry Now*, *Dakini*, *Big Mouth*, *The Likes of Us* and *Come Together*.

Joanna Torrey's fiction has appeared in the anthologies *Lovers: Stories by Women* and *Love's Shadow*, and in *The Brooklyn Review*. She lives in Brooklyn, New York.

Janette Turner Hospital is an Australian who now divides her time between Australia and North America. She has published five novels and two collections of short stories, and won a number of literary awards. Her most recent novel, *The Last Magician* (1992), was shortlisted for Australia's Miles Franklin Award, Canada's Trillium Award and the Commonwealth Writers' Prize.

Erica Wagner was born in New York and lives in London. She works at *The Times*.